Sine Timore proudly presents

ON A WING AND A PRAYER

From The Case Files Of
Hannah Singer
Celestial Advocate

by Peter G

"On A Wing And A Prayer" copyright © 2011 by Peter G, all rights reserved. "Hannah Singer, Celestial Advocate" and all related characters and content are copyright © Peter G (2010). Unauthorized reproduction, in whole or in part, if prohibited (i.e. Fair Use is allowed).

All persons, places, and events depicted herein are entirely fictional. Any resemblance to actual persons, places, or events, living or dead, is entirely coincidental.

For absent friends and absent loves, and the day we will be together again, whether in this world, or the next.

From the case files of

Hannah Singer

Celestial Advocate

Altered Boy
7

Arc Enemies
31

Day Of Judgment
69

Devil May Care
87

Live To Serve You
117

Twist Of Fate
137

Bring 'Em Fast, Bring 'Em Young
153

Full Court Press
171

ALTERED BOY

It was another nice day in the Valley Of Death.

    Big. Surprise.

    There's no nightfall, no bad weather, if weather forecasters were needed, it would be the best job ever. Not that I would ever take it. Being a Celestial Advocate is rough, but I'm just not cut out for a simple, easy job. I don't have the right temperament for it. I'm a thinker. A fighter. A rebel. I'm angry. I'm confrontational. I'm defiant. Being a Celestial is pretty much the only job I'm qualified for up here.

    Because everything is sunny, bright, and happy, when real despair hits, it hits hard. Everyone notices. Here in the Archives of the Celestial Courts, there's angels all over the place. Some have specialized duties. For example, everyone knows about guardian angels. But there are others, like ministering angels. These specialize in comfort and helping those who are conflicted. The guardian angels protect, the ministering angels nurture. Interestingly, most but not all guardians are male, and most but not all ministers are female.

    The leader of the ministers is an angel named Shalmana. A great, compassionate spirit, she rarely ventures outside the Equilibrium, which is the place where souls are brought when they die and can't quite process or deal with what has happened to them. That's part of the reason no one is forced to petition for entry into Heaven. You face it when you are ready, and some people just aren't ready right away. Death is a bit of a surprise, after all. Especially when you get to the other side and find out things aren't quite the way you were taught back on Earth.

    I was out in one of the fields just outside the Archives. Clark Horvis, a really green Celestial, was teaching us to play a game called "bags" or "cornhole" or whatever. Apparently, even people in the Midwest where he lived didn't agree on a name. I was getting into it, too. It's a very sociable, casual game. "And the best part," Clark explained, "is you can play it without putting down your beer."

    I was holding a pint glass full of jasmine tea when he said that. "What a selling point."

    Clark was holding the biggest beer mug I'd ever seen. And I'm not talking casual, it was like someone cut a basketball in half and stuck a handle on it. Spirits can't get drunk, so the only reason to drink beer is the taste. And Clark really liked the taste, as his liver (if he still had one) would attest. "Hey, it's the only organized sport that's never been tainted by a steroids scandal."

    I rolled my eyes. "That's not true and you know it."

    It was then I heard a mild, "...uh...excused me...."

    I didn't need to look to know it was Shalmana. Her voice is quiet and tinkly. She's not timid, just quiet. She can be just as assertive as me when she needs to and yet she never loses that niceness. Where my robes were white with a blue tint and a blue overrobe, hers were pale yellow with a purple overrobe. I turned to look at her, but I couldn't smile at her. I felt the look of confusion on my face. "Shalmana? What brings you around?"

"Well, Hannah," she said, seeming a little quieter all of a sudden, "I wanted to ask you if you could please come to the Equilibrium. There's someone there who needs to meet you."

It didn't take me long to process what she was asking. Someone was there and freaking out that they'd be going to Hell. And for her to actually seek me out instead of asking a putto to locate me, this was really bad. Which also meant I was probably going to be handling the trial.

I became a Celestial specifically to help people facing long, nearly impossible odds, who were terrified that they were going to Hell. Sounded like this person needed Hannah Singer, and needed her bad. "Lead the way," I smiled, and we walked off to the Equilibrium.

As we walked, I started mining for information. "What can you tell me about who I'm meeting?"

"His name is Alex Sayles," she said. "Well, it was for a while. I've already requested his life scroll, and it will be waiting for you when we get to the Equilibrium."

"What made him change his name?"

"He changed his sex."

I didn't hide my bemusement. "That's it? A transsexual? I thought you were going to give me something hard!"

"He also committed suicide."

I had just finished chugging the rest of my jasmine tea. "Oh, I can bury that in the transsexuality. I'll have him on his way to Heaven before he knows it. Fairchild stands no chance on this one." Jeff Fairchild was the senior Church Advocate and he liked being the authority. As senior Celestial and senior grey, I was his most frequent opponent in the courts.

"I think it would do him a lot of good to hear that directly from you."

"You got it," I smiled.

Shalmana and I quickly made it to the Equilibrium. The context of it was startling. Unlike everywhere else in the Afterlife, the Equilibrium had no stark colors or dynamic presence. It was sedate, reassuring, and looked like it belonged to the realm of Earth instead of the Valley Of Death. It was supposed to be as relaxing and calming as possible. I've been here when I'm not stressed, and quickly felt like I was going to fall asleep. And spirits don't sleep. That's how well this place is done.

We got inside and she led the way. I tried to bob and weave and stay out of the way of all the angels moving about. One even snagged my empty pint glass before I knew it. Another came up and put a scroll in my hands. It had a tie around it. Most likely Alex's.

Rounding another corner, we stopped at an entry way covered by luxurious tapestry curtains. I looked at Shalmana, and she just nodded. I quickly untied the scroll and read through it. Alex didn't have anything to worry about. I rolled it up, tied it shut, and gave Shalmana a thumbs up. She smiled, nodded, and waved her hand, making one of the tapestry curtains lift.

I had to force myself to wait. My instinct was to just walk inside, but I figured Alex would be more receptive to Shalmana's soft touch than my assertiveness. The room was one of the smaller ones here. Still pretty large compared to, say, an Earth bedroom, but in relation to the other rooms at the Equilibrium, rather compact. The plush carpeting felt wonderful under my bare feet, and the scents, like a forest after a spring rain, filled my nose. Soft music, the kind angels sing, filled the air, and the earth tones felt reassuring. Curled up in the far corner of the room on a pile of pillows was Alex. His clothes, a fairly new T shirt and jeans, were fine, no cuts or tears or puncture wounds. Probably poisoned himself. No doubt about it, he was terrified.

We padded over to Alex and stood there. Shalmana cleared her throat. "Alex? Remember that person I told you about?"

Alex didn't open his eyes or make a sound. He just nodded as well as he could.

Shalmana's smile softened into one of infinite understanding. "Well, I brought her here. She wants to prove to you you have nothing to worry about. Please at least say hello to her."

Shalmana is good. Anyone else saying that would be ignored. But Shalmana's sweetness and kindness are a flower breaking a stone. Alex slowly opened his eyes and turned his head, but still didn't uncurl.

I flashed him my usual smile. "It's a pleasure to meet you, Alex. My name is Hannah Singer."

He was quiet for a moment. "You're a Celestial Advocate?"

"I'm THE Celestial Advocate," I told him. The bravado was for his benefit (that's my story, and I'm sticking with it). "I'm senior Celestial, senior grey, and the best the courts have ever seen."

"Isn't being prideful a sin?"

I pointed back and forth between me and Shalmana. "It's to make up for her. We balance each other out."

Alex smiled. It was a small smile, but still a smile. I simply plopped down on a pillow. Shalmana asked Alex, "Mind if we sit down with you?"

Alex noticed I had just done it and nodded. He started unfolding and sat up. He was still hunched over, but at least we knew we had his attention. Shalmana pulled over a couple of pillows and carefully lowered herself as I held up the life scroll and looked at it. "So, I'm here to prove to you that you're in the clear. Where should I start?"

Alex looked at me. "How can you be so sure?"

"How much do you know about the petitioning process?"

"...nothing."

"Okay, let me start by explaining how this works, then I'll tell you why you're golden. You start off by going to the clerks' office and file a petition. That officially makes you a Petitioner. You then go to Penance Hall. They review your life and what sins you have to atone for, and what sins you have to answer for. From there, the two sides of the Celestial Courts, the Church Advocates and the Celestial Advocates, review your petition. If neither side sees a problem, they sign it, 'No Contest,' and that's it. You're on your way to Heaven."

"It can't be that simple," he said. "I mean, you wouldn't have a job here if that was it."

"Top of the class," I told him with a smile. "If either side contests, it goes to trial. If one side filed, 'No Contest,' they become your defenders at trial. Your defender does everything they can to get your petition approved and get you into Heaven. Or, at least, keep the other side from getting their way."

"How likely is it that I'll get into Heaven?" he asked.

"Excellent," I told him. "Keep in mind, no one who deserves a Heavenly reward has ever been denied. They may have to do something else first, like guardian angel duty or something, but they have never lost it. Ever." I then opened the scroll and started reading. "What's more, you really have nothing in here that's a problem."

"But I was transsexual. And I was sort of gay."

"Neither of which is a sin," I said without looking up. "They were defending homosexuality before I was even born. Transsexuality? The precedent was established quickly to eliminate it as a sin."

Shalmana leaned close to Alex and pointed to me. "She's the one who did it," she whispered.

For the first time, he straightened, craning his neck a little towards me. "Really?"

I smiled at him. I had him right where I wanted him. "You did enough right, you didn't really do anything wrong that repenting won't fix. You had some confusion over your identity. It's uncommon, but not unheard of, and is not grounds to deny petition. I'd say you're a shoo-in, kid."

We talked some more, explaining things about trial procedure and how he was on his way to Heaven. I didn't realize the Churches would soon be putting things in motion to attempt to prove me wrong and destroy the precedent I worked so hard for.

I came out of the Equilibrium, the life scroll in one hand, my pint glass in the other. It had been refilled and given to me as I was on my way out. I got outside and stepped on the grass, reminding myself that the Equilibrium is not how it's supposed to be for me now. I sighed, then took a swig from my glass.

It didn't register that the contents of the glass didn't smell like jasmine until I had a good amount of liquid in my mouth. It tasted like motor oil and chicken grease mixed together with a splash of aftershave. I spit it out and dumped out the glass. It actually turned the grass brown.

I started looking around. "*MICHAEL!!!*"

St. Michael suddenly appeared next to me, the speed of angels making it look like he simply materialized. I'm used to his sudden appearances, so I didn't jump. He was jumping, though. "Oh, that was a good one!" said the

World's Biggest Prankster. "You should have seen the look on your face! It was like you were watching Yoko Ono's Broadway revue!"

St. Michael the archangel was the head of the Celestial Courts and my boss. We quickly became best friends when I first turned up and was on trial for being an Atheist. On the bright side, Michael acted like my big brother. The downside? Well...Michael acted like my big brother.

Michael was wearing a fairly sedate look for himself, jeans with rips in the knees and a T-shirt that declared, "The man, the myth, the legend." I looked back at the grass. It was actually taking longer than usual for it to return to normal. "What in the name of God was that?" I demanded.

"I don't know, but humans are paying big bucks for it at coffee shop chains," he said with a smile.

I just stood there, trying to keep my will in place.

Michael leaned up in front of me. Being over a head taller than me, he had to crouch a little. He extended his finger and started maneuvering it towards where my dimple would be. "Do I see a smile peaking out in there?"

"Burn." I batted his hand away. I didn't need to see it to know it sprung right back.

"Come on, Hannah. Give us a smile, as you Brits say."

"No." It was getting harder to maintain my grimace.

Michael brought up his other hand and put his index fingers on the corners of my mouth. He started lifting. Soon I was smiling. He pulled his fingers away, but I couldn't force the smile away.

"There," he said as he straightened. Looking down at me, he said, "Was that so bad?"

I can never stay mad at him for very long, much as I might occasionally like to otherwise. "So, what brings you around?"

"Making sure you're happy," he said, eying the Equilibrium. "Despair can be a powerful force."

"I wasn't there for me, you didn't have to worry," I told him, holding up the life scroll. "The guy is just worried. Needed some reassuring. He'll be petitioning before we know it."

Michael took the scroll and started reading it. His head tilted from side to side once in a while. "He's worried about this kind of life?"

I held up my left hand. "Transsexual." I held up my right hand. "Suicide." I clapped them together. "Smash."

"Well, he'll be on his way for sure. Although you might not get the case."

"It might make him feel better to have the ace in his hand."

"Your case load is really high right now, and there's nothing here that any grey that isn't green can't handle. I'll keep you in mind, but I doubt you'll need to get involved."

I pretty much pushed Alex from my mind after that, getting back to my cases. They were simple and easy, and I enjoyed those. I get the toughest cases, so having times where there was nothing to it was a great relief. After all, I never knew when a storm would blow up.

One blew up quick.

I just finished my last of five cases in a row and was heading to return my scrolls when a putto, David, flew up to me in the court hallway. "Miss Singer? St. Michael needs you in his chambers immediately."

"Tell him I'm coming," I said. The childlike angel flew off as I ran. Humans aren't as fast as angels, so I could only do my best.

When I got to Michael's chambers, the door was wide open. He didn't want me wasting any time by knocking. I walked right in, and saw Michael at his desk, looking over a document. "Hello, Hannah," he said without looking up.

I shut the door. Michael promptly flicked his hand at it, and it vanished into the wall. No one else in or out except angels. I went to the front of Michael's desk, where he had two highback chairs. Michael was all business, but force of habit made me check for a whoopee cushion before I sat. Some habits, you just never get rid of.

I sat, but didn't lean back. I leaned forward, my elbows on my knees, looking at Michael levelly to discern whatever was coming. Michael looked at me and cocked an eyebrow. "Churches are contesting Alex Sayles' petition."

"Not a surprise," I told him. "They still contest transsexuals once in a while, even though they never win."

Michael delivered the bad news. "Here's the request for trial. Jeff Fairchild is going to lead."

My eyes popped. I held out my hand to Michael, and he put the trial request there. I pulled it over and just stared at it, trying to divine answers. "Why?"

"Only one thing I can think of."

"Yeah," I said. "Fairchild is trying to establish a precedent where transsexuality is concerned."

"The question is, how does he intend to do it?" Neither side was required to disclose their trial strategy beforehand. As such, when secrecy worked in your favor, you took it.

"I don't know," I said after some introspection. "I led the first trial. I sewed that thing up. Fairchild thinks he's found some angle. What is it?"

"Got me," Michael said. "All your other cases are being reassigned. Find out what this is and shut it down."

I stood up. "You got it."

"Keep me posted, Hannah," Michael said, making the door reappear.

When preparing for trial, any Advocate worth their salt starts with the Petitioner's life scroll. Alex's was pretty straightforward. If anything, he suffered far more than other transgenders because of one tiny little problem.

Alex never had a gender identification problem.

One of the most important things to people is their identity. People don't like being known as what they are. It's either not exciting or it's embarrassing or any one of hundreds of reasons. People would rather be known for what they want to be, where their ambitions would take them if only things would turn their way. How they present themselves is sort of a down payment on the genuine article.

Identity carries a problem. There are people who accept what their identity ultimately is, and those who do things based on what it should be. For example, there are men who enjoy reading romance novels. They don't admit it, but they do. Most of them are perfectly content to think to themselves, "I like romance novels," and that's the end of that. But there are some who think the fact that they like romance novels means something different about their identity, that it indicates they are a lot more different than they think. This latter group will do things, not based on whether or not they like them, but whether or not they think they SHOULD like them. There are people who watch cartoons because they find art inside them, and those that watch them because they figure they should, that it's some way to connect to what they truly are. Even if they hate what they are doing, they do it just because they think they are supposed to.

Alex fell into this second group. Alex had grown up with a different view of women. Because of gender differences, both sexes start off regarding the opposite as "The Other." They eventually get over it, usually because the yearning for love and the desire for sex forces them to get past that. Alex was a sensitive soul. He could actually appreciate things that were considered "girly" by modern society. Eventually, he started trying to put the pieces together. And the results said one thing to him loud and clear: he was supposed to be a woman.

Nobody much bought his conclusion. They figured he was just a guy with different interests. But Alex started convincing himself that he was a woman trapped in a man's body. Eventually, he stumbled on the alternative lifestyle communities, groups of people whose sexual identities formed the basis of what they were. Their conclusions about Alex were unanimous – he wasn't a woman trapped in a man's body. They knew such people. Alex was reading waaaaaaaaaay too much into things, and instead of just accepting what he was and being happy with it, he was determined to change himself in ways that even transgenders are advised not to do.

Alex dismissed them as not knowing the truth for whatever reason. It didn't help that doctors refused the operation he sought that would turn him into a woman. And then, he discovered the Internet. With some diligent research and talking with others while keeping his true motivations to himself, he soon learned what he needed to say, how he needed to react, everything to make the doctors willing to go along with this. He began the hormones, and eventually went under the knife.

Unfortunately, Alex completed the operation before he figured out the truth. He actually was male. In his new body, he started feeling uncomfortable and ill at ease. He soon wanted to reverse the operation. Everyone refused this time. He felt more separated and isolated from humanity than ever. Despair became stronger. He couldn't take it any longer. He went up on a bridge and took a flying leap. Hitting the water started everything, and the undertow finished it.

Alex turned up in the Valley Of Death and wandered around. Unfortunately, a group of Churches found him first. Alex, being an honest guy, answered their probing questions until they learned the truth, and out came the fire and brimstone. Alex was already scared what would happen to him, this pushed him over the edge. He ran, collapsed, and just started crying in anguish. This alerted an angel where he was. Alex saw the angel and curled into a fetal tuck, thinking this was the end. The angel instead took him to the Equilibrium. And that was when Shalmana decided to introduce me to him.

I rolled up Alex's scroll and tied it shut. I sat it on the far end of my couch, just looking at it. Whatever angle Fairchild was after, I wasn't seeing it.

There was really nothing more to be learned from the scroll, so I got up to return it to Russell at the Office Of Records. I was about halfway through the Archives when I saw him.

Fairchild.

He was smiling.

I had stopped dead in my tracks. Fairchild saw me, and his smile got even wider. He sauntered up to me as I fought to keep my anger under control.

"Greetings, Singer," he said brightly.

"I ought to throttle you," I said, my voice actually dropping an octave.

He craned his head out to me. "Go ahead."

Attacking an on duty officer of the court is grounds to automatically Cast Down. "Burn."

"Too bad," he said, pulling his head back. "I really wanted you to try."

"Want in one hand, puke in the other, and see which one fills up first."

"So, you've figured out I'm going to overturn your precedent," he said. Fairchild knows I'm not usually this furious at him unless he's playing fast and loose with God's mercy.

"You won't succeed."

"Sure, I will," he said simply.

I carefully stepped around him, as if coming too close to him would infect me with something. I heard him chuckle as I did. I forced it from my mind. I had bigger problems right now.

When I got to the Office Of Records, Russell was at the window. He usually greets me brightly, but he knew from the look on my face that I had a real bad one on my hands. "What can I do for you, Hannah?"

I started to hand Alex's scroll back, then stopped. I pulled it back and said, "I want the life scroll for Maurice McCree, and the trial record."

Russell took off and was back in record time. McCree's trial was relatively recent, so it was nothing to locate. McCree wasn't the first person to have a sex change operation, but he was the first to petition. Everyone else had been frightened into straggling by the Churches. McCree was bold, however, and petitioned. Michael made me his Advocate, trial happened, and the precedent was set. At the time, I had been surprised how relatively smooth it went even with Fairchild and five juniors against me. And everyone was safely in Heaven, they couldn't be retried. Apparently, there was some aspect that was different with Alex. There had to be. Fairchild would have tried this by now otherwise.

I went back to my quarters, put on the kettle, and started reading, stopping only to keep the flow of jasmine tea going. I did a quick review of McCree's trial record. I had acted alone on that case. Anyone who was willing to junior for me was too green for such a pivotal case, and those with experience were kind of...squishy on the whole transgender thing. They knew how they were supposed to regard it, but they were having problems processing it. Sexuality makes people behave in strange ways they wouldn't otherwise.

I spread out McCree's life scroll, then Alex's. I would read them in bits and pieces, jumping from McCree's to Alex's at certain life points. I would read the trial record and examine what was said, returning to the life scrolls to compare them. I read them start to finish, then started making connections again. Eventually, I felt my mind starting to wander. I forced myself to focus. I was becoming so familiar with what was laid out in front of me, I was filling things in subconsciously. It meant I was seeing what I thought should be there, not what was there. I'd lose that way for sure.

And then, after starting yet another pot of jasmine tea and sitting back down, I looked over Alex's scroll and went over his time as a transgender.

And as I reached my hand back into the haystack, I felt the needle stick into me.

I saw it. I saw the difference. I saw exactly what Fairchild was going to build his case around.

I quickly rolled up the scrolls and tied or clasped them shut. I turned off the kettle, and bolted from my quarters, on a dead run for Michael's chambers. Michael wasn't in at that moment, he was leading a case, so I just paced around outside his door.

Eventually, Michael turned up. He came around the corner, saw me, and his face twisted into a sinister expression. "Oh, I never get tired of that look," he laughed.

We ducked into his chambers and I laid everything out. Michael liked the direction I was going in. I filed my request for trial, selected my juniors, and got ready for an epic battle.

Word got around quickly of what was at stake in this case. Between Fairchild making it known he was trying to overturn my precedent and my complete and utter lack of concern, everyone was expecting a fireworks display that would make the Chinese New Year look tame. And I mean everyone. Almost as soon as trial was set, it was assigned to the Grand Courtroom. The Grand Courtroom is the biggest courtroom, the only one with a Gallery that occupied two floors.

I strode through the Celestial Courts, my gaze sharp as a knife. There was no lightness to my step, it was heavy slaps of my feet on the stone floor. My juniors would have all the trial scrolls I requested by the time I got there. I wanted to be dramatic today.

When I got to the doors of the Grand Courtroom. I could actually hear the buzzing of everyone talking inside there. A Guardian on either side of the doors saw me and nodded as if to say, "Here we go again." I held up my hand, indicating they should not open the doors for me. They stood straight as I went for the center and forced the doors with enough strength to make them swing all the way in. I was past them by the time they started swinging back, and already halfway down the aisle when they closed. Every eye in the courtroom was focused on me and the talking vanished.

The Gallery was huge, and still not big enough. Angels and Advocates were packed like sardines in the seats. Michael was already here, the seat directly behind where the lead Celestial sat in the courtroom. His left leg was sticking out into the aisle. Michael is a giant of a man who usually doesn't get crowded. He looked at me with a, "Whatcha gonna do?" smirk and shrugged his shoulders as well as he was able to.

I got down the aisle and past the divider that separated the Gallery from the court. Despite being dwarfed by two floors of onlookers, the court had its own presence, gave its own vibe. It wasn't swallowed up by the hustle and bustle going on around it. Coming into the courtroom and getting past the divider, the Church table was on the left, the Celestial table on the right – in a regular sized courtroom, the Celestial table was situated in the exact center. Each table had four stools to sit at. To the right was the Tribunal box, where twelve angels would enter the door behind it and sit in judgment. Directly ahead was the judge's bench where the presiding angel sat, his own entrance to the left of it. The dock where the Petitioner stood during trial was right next to the judge's bench on the side with the Tribunal. It was a small, square area ringed with banisters except on the side where the Petitioner entered or exited. On the left was the Petitioner's exit – when the judgment was made, the Petitioner went through it to whatever fate was coming next.

Things had changed in the intervening years. On the Celestial side, Alex was already here, sitting in the Petitioner's seat, second in from the aisle. Next to him, in the third seat, was my first junior, Harold Kowalski. Kowalski, also known as "Smack", was a sportswriter when he died at seventy-five. He was one of the fastest thinkers I ever met and was dangerous to argue with if you didn't have your facts ready. He was usually my first choice for the really difficult trials.

In the fourth seat was my other junior, Vincent Huda. Huda was our most recent gay Celestial. We've actually had a few of them over the ages, he's the eighth. Huda was a bit different from his predecessors, though. The others were quiet and reserved about their sexuality, Huda was out and proud. I lead his defense when he petitioned, and he actually corrected Fairchild and I from the dock.

"Drag queen," he said.

Fairchild and I stopped short. Fairchild called him a transvestite. I attempted to keep things dignified and called him a gender illusionist. Huda was having none of that. The presiding angel reminded Huda not to speak unless addressed, but at that moment, I knew he'd be a great Advocate, and he jumped at the chance.

The Church table looked fully stocked. Jeff Fairchild sat in the lead spot right by the aisle. With him were his two regular juniors, Burke Finley and Edward Fiedler, and a bonus, Neil Amacker. Fairchild had created a hierarchy where those who rose through the ranks were similar to him. His juniors rarely provided more than moral support, reaffirming who The Boss was. I always kept sharp just in case, but for the most part, they were afterthoughts. The fight had to go through Fairchild.

I went to the seat for the lead Celestial, first in from the aisle. I had been hoping my juniors would keep Alex calm. He and Smack were engaged in a very animated discussion. Smack's fedora was angled low and his substitute for a cigarette, his pen, was in his hand and being used as a pointer. I couldn't help but overhear.

Alex said, "No, Chamberlain was the best! They changed the rules because of him!"

Smack shot back, "Which proves Jordan was the best ever! He was always playing with the tougher rule set!"

"Jordan was surrounded by a bunch of stiffs!"

"Further proof!"

Huda raised his finger politely. "What about LeBron?"

Smack glared at him. "Stay out of this, rookie!"

"Yeah!" sneered Alex.

I leaned over to see the debating duo. "Excuse me...."

Smack and Alex both turned to me and said in unison, "Not now!"

They resumed arguing with each other as I sat there in bemusement. I slammed my fist on the tabletop, making both of them, Huda, the Churches, and a significant portion of the Gallery look at me. I simply cleared my throat and said, "Excuse me."

Smack shot to his feet, pulling his fedora off his head and holding it over his heart. "Sorry, Hannah. Just got a little caught up is all."

I looked around the tabletop. Scrolls were set in specific spots. "Everything organized the way I wanted?"

"Yes, ma'am," Smack said.

"Clear on your instructions?"

Both he and Huda said, "Yes, ma'am."

I saluted Smack, palm out like a proper Brit. "Carry on."

He sat back down and he and Alex continued talking, although a lot quieter than before and Smack didn't bother replacing his fedora. Huda could only shake his head.

I took a good look at the Church table. It was covered with all kinds of scrolls. No way of telling what was inside, but I smelled a bluff. Fairchild knows I look and make conclusions based on what I see. This was his first challenge to a precedent that was decades old. He had something immediate, the past was no help to him.

I faced forward, locking my thoughts in their own little world. I was going over contingencies and other ideas just in case Fairchild's train of thought switched tracks on me. Unlikely, it smelled like Fairchild was wagering all his chips on one number, but I didn't become the best by not considering all the angles.

The chimes sounded, signaling the start of session. Everyone stood and we Advocates deployed our wings. Those of us that are human have artificial wings – they aren't attached to us, but they move with us as if they were. My wings are the plainest of all the Advocates. Each one looked like two upside down teardrops with a flat top, the smaller one on the outside. I just didn't feel like I deserved a more angelic looking set. Wings are a reflection of their owners.

The door by the Tribunal box opened and twelve angels entered. For a moment, I forgot about everything, lost in an eternity of wonder. I know I keep saying I'll never be an angel, but that doesn't stop me from wishing for it.

The door at the back of the court opened and the presiding angel entered. Oh, good. It was Barachiel. He was a real pro, his expert hand kept things running smooth. There was virtually no risk of mistrial with him. If I could shut Fairchild down, the precedent was as good as upheld.

Barachiel went to the bench and looked out over the court. He was carrying a record scroll, which he unrolled and checked over. Satisfied everything was in place, he hit the gavel and sat at the same time as the Tribunal and the Gallery. He interlaced his fingers in front of him, closed his eyes, and called, "Who is the Petitioner?"

"The Petitioner is Alexander David Sayles," I called back.

"And who are his Advocates?"

"Vincent Huda, Harold Kowalski, and Hannah Singer, acting as lead."

"And who Advocates for the Church?"

"Neil Amacker, Edward Fiedler, Burke Finley, and Jeff Fairchild, acting as lead," came the call from my left.

"Will the Petitioner please take the stand?"

Alex looked at me one last time. I smiled at him, willing what strength he would take. He walked out and climbed into the dock. He was leaning on the banister and looked like he was ready to start shaking. Barachiel noticed this.

"Brave heart," he told Alex. Alex simply nodded nervously at the angel and faced the Advocates.

With the Petitioner in the dock, my juniors moved over one seat and all the juniors sat down, leaving just me, Fairchild, and the two Guardians in front of the bench standing. Barachiel looked at me and said, "Advocate for the Petitioner goes first. Miss Singer, your opening arguments, please."

I was originally going to throw my turn, simply stating my position on the case and get Fairchild to establish his position. But once I figured out his angle, I started coming up with opening arguments. My goal was to force

Fairchild in a certain direction, cut off other avenues he could take to bolster his argument. He would know I was up to something, but hopefully, his arrogance would make him think I wasn't on the scent.

It's star time.

"One of the things you get used to in Eternity is deja vu," I said. "The feeling that all of this has happened before. We see so many cases with so many Petitioners that aren't all that different, we wonder why we are going through this. Especially when the ending is not in doubt. This may be Eternity, wasting time may not be a crime, but it's still pointless.

"We don't suffer for this. We just get annoyed. But Petitioners suffer. They have to deal with the uncertainty of their fate. The waiting. The fear that they may be Cast Down. Alex Sayles is one such person. He has done NOTHING to warrant being put on trial."

Amacker started to talk. "What about the --"

CRACK! The gavel interrupted him. Barachiel glared at him. Opening and closing arguments are the only times Advocates are allowed to speak uninterrupted. Blow that rule, and it is the presiding angel's discretion what to do with you. Barachiel said, "Barred from advocating this case. Guardians, remove Amacker from court."

Amacker's eyes flew open. Fairchild rolled his. One of his juniors just sniped himself, removing him from the trial. Amacker wasn't that important, Fairchild could have plead for mercy, but he didn't. He was happy to be rid of a junior that could undermine his case. Still, Amacker's interruption could cause problems for my opening arguments. If I acted like nothing happened, it left a cloud of mystery over things. Easy enough to fix, I'd simply talk like what his statement was going to be. Eliminated the mystery and kept Fairchild from seizing on it.

"As I was saying," once Amacker had been removed from court and the Guardians returned to their spots, "Alex has done nothing to warrant a trial, let alone Casting. The precedents for suicide have been well established. The precedents for transsexuals have been well established. The Churches need to make some unique argument, one that hasn't been made before, if they want this to be taken seriously. Without it, Alex is just like the others who wound up here before going through the Pearly Gates. He should be allowed into Heaven. Thank you."

This was it. I turned my head to Fairchild as he started speaking. "Singer is making a foolish assumption about this case. She says that we need to present some new stance, new argument, something that hasn't been tried before.

"We have that.

"There is a fundamental difference between Sayles and the previous...transsexuals," Fairchild sounded like the word was being dragged out of him. "Not only does this difference render the precedent my learned colleague achieved moot, but the situation itself does, as well. There are constantly new motivations, new situations, a precedent is no good because it cannot change with the times. It cannot take everything into account.

"Sayles' circumstances cannot be covered by precedent. They are different. They illustrate the flaw in the precedent. By the time closing arguments are made, the only reasonable conclusion anyone will be able to reach is to Cast Down. Thank you."

I didn't want to attack him directly. Not yet. Fairchild is very clever. Attacking his points now gave him too much to argue with. And with the precedent at stake, it was too risky. The best course of action was to continue to act confident, like I had the utmost faith in the precedent. If I could make Fairchild advance certain arguments, it would confine him later. If he changed what he was arguing, it could be struck.

And so, the two boxers stepped into the center of the ring, keeping their guards up and watching very carefully for openings. I started. "The precedent very much applies to Alex."

"No, it doesn't," Fairchild said.

It was too early to ask him why. I needed to close off some of his venues first. "Alex was a churchgoer."

"So what?"

"The church that he attended was a branch of the Episcopalian church. One that stayed within the order when the fissure over the gay bishop happened. No one in the chain of command condemned Alex for his sex change."

"They didn't know to condemn him," Fairchild responded.

"Immaterial," I said. "Sexual concerns and politics are a part of modern churches and they will make blanket statements to cover things. The Mormons condemn homosexuality. The Catholics condemn birth control."

"That last one has been disallowed several times, by you and just about every other Celestial."

"If the church authorities don't have a problem, why should you? Do you not represent the earthly churches up here?"

"We do. We can't help it if they're wrong."

"The covenant says they are right. God said, 'What is held true on Earth, He will hold true in Heaven.' They don't have a problem. So you're right, the precedent isn't necessary for this case."

Fairchild looked at me, weighing his options. He then made the absolute worst choice. He looked at the bench and said, "Move to strike the covenant from consideration."

Time for my Oscar moment. "Motion should be denied!" I yelled, putting panic in my voice. Fairchild smirked at me. Barachiel just looked at me in challenge. He knew what I was doing. I needed to present an argument that Barachiel wouldn't rule in favor of but wouldn't tip off Fairchild that I was setting him up. "The covenant is at the very heart of this!" I continued. "The churches of Earth never told Alex not to do this!"

"Because it is not part of their jurisdiction," Fairchild countered. "Sayles make his choices without input from the church, without their permission, without their council. As the church had no involvement, in all fairness, they cannot offer their protection."

"The churches offer their blessings to those outside their faith! 'Come worship with us, even if you aren't the same faith we are!'"

"Once again, only for those who actively seek the church. In fact, people frequently do things without the church's authorization. It is the whole reason for the Celestial Courts, for those things not covered. The covenant should not be allowed to extend protection to Sayles."

I gave Barachiel a desperate look. He cocked an eyebrow at me, then hit the gavel as he declared, "Struck."

I didn't drop my act. If I pulled anything now, Fairchild would move to have the covenant reinstated. I needed to make sure that bridge couldn't be rebuilt. I fought the urge to yell, "Sucker!", looked around while feigning uncertainty, then moved ahead, flapping my cape to make Fairchild charge.

"Well, Singer, what now? Can you actually present a cogent argument without abusing the shield of the covenant?"

"You bet," I said. "Simply put, there's no objection."

Fairchild reeled back. "What do you mean, no objection?"

"This isn't like normal trials," I told him. "Usually, it's the Celestials trying to establish an exception is to be made. This time, it's you."

"Do you ever get tired of being wrong, Singer?"

"The precedent is set. I've won. You have to establish the precedent does not apply here. Your move."

Fairchild looked a little uncertain. He clearly wanted to whittle me down some more, but I just backed him into a corner. He advanced nothing, and if I called for closing arguments, he would only have that time to make his points. And then, I would have my closing arguments to turn them upside down and he couldn't say or do anything. If he wanted this, he had to present his idea now.

"It was wrong for Sayles to change his sex."

"No, it's not. People have been changing their sex and getting into Heaven for decades now."

"It's not me who says he's wrong."

"Who does?"

"Sayles does."

I acted surprised. In truth, this was exactly what I figured Fairchild would do. "What does that have to do with it?"

"It's all about the why of your actions, not the what," Fairchild said, smiling at Sayles. "The difference between all those other transsexuals and him? They honestly believed they had to change their sex. Sayles never should have done it. He admits it himself by trying to have the operation undone. The why of his actions is a bad reason, one that he should not have done, and he knows he shouldn't have done it. Combined with altering the body God made, Sayles has committed a mortal sin and should be Cast Down. He was mistaken, and he knows it."

"And that gives you the right to cast judgment on him?"

"Yes. He should have stayed the way he was and just accepted himself.

Instead, he sought to make himself over into something he wasn't."

Huda made a quiet clearing his throat sound, indicating he was ready to jump in. I held my right hand down by my side, blocking its view from Fairchild. I tapped my outer thigh twice with the two middle fingers, signaling to Huda it wasn't time for him yet, he'd get his chance soon enough. I first needed to force Fairchild into a specific stance.

"Lots of people are guilty of making themselves into something they shouldn't be. Something that conflicts with their basic natures. Something they regret."

"Sex changes are not that common," Fairchild countered.

"I'm not talking about sex changes. I'm talking about a person who gets an accounting degree but can't stand it. He changes jobs. No sin. A couple gets married and realizes they didn't know each other that well and can't stand each other. They divorce. No sin."

"We're talking about sex changes, not life changes."

"You deny changing something that fundamental is a cakewalk compared to those other things?"

"Doesn't matter. We are not talking about those things, only sex changes."

"You can't have it both ways, Fairchild. The reasoning you provided can be applied to many things that are forgiven or allowed. What makes a sex change so different that those same considerations can't be extended to it?"

"They are not how things are supposed to go. Humanity has certain general characteristics."

"They are general characteristics, not how everyone is supposed to be."

"There are plenty of bad behaviors that are not considered general characteristics."

"I see. So you aren't saying sex changes are wrong because they aren't characteristic, but because they are evil acts."

"That's exactly what I'm saying."

My hand still at my side, I pointed the two middle fingers of my hand to Huda. He jumped up. "Sex is not evil."

"It is too evil," Fairchild said, looking at Huda with obvious discomfort. "It corrupts. It holds power. People desire it over love. It's why virginity is so important."

"The world is full of things that corrupt and people desire over love, but your precious churches don't crusade against them."

"We always condemn such things."

"You didn't condemn Jim and Tammy Faye Bakker for their excesses. All that money from their followers, and it went to solid gold faucets and an air conditioned dog house."

"Those aren't excesses," Fairchild said tersely. "Being a success and having nice things is not a sin."

Smack piped up. "Just ask the Vatican."

Fairchild glared at Smack and was clearly ready to tell him to go burn.

He then looked at the bench. Barachiel was holding the gavel at ready and just looking at Fairchild as if to say, "Go ahead, I dare you."

Fairchild smirked. He looked to the bench. "Move to strike Kowalski's last comment."

Barachiel set the gavel down. "On what grounds?"

"Irrelevancy," Fairchild responded. "He's making cheap jokes in the middle of arguments."

Smack joined Huda and I on his feet. "It may have been a joke, but it also had a point."

Barachiel looked at Smack. "What point is that?"

"Scripture says to live humbly, and there are clearly people who studied this stuff who do otherwise. Clearly, scripture and ethics can be disregarded for far less valid reasons and left uncontested than someone who was confused about his life."

Smack's argument was beautiful. It had everything needed to mislead Fairchild. Sure enough, he took the wrong path. "They are not violating scripture," Fairchild said.

I moved. "Move to strike Fairchild's argument."

"On what grounds?" Barachiel asked.

"Fairchild is a Protestant. Kowalski is Catholic. Kowalski has every right to criticize the Vatican, Fairchild has no standing to defend it."

"Motion should be denied," Fairchild said. "Not only should we look out for our brothers and sisters in Christ, but by that logic, Singer has no basis to argue for God's mercy, since she was an Atheist."

"Motion denied," Barachiel said.

Smack was right back in things. "You mean to tell me that all those riches is not living humbly?"

"It's humble for them," Fairchild said.

Huda was in it, too. "And what these people do makes perfect sense to them, just like living those lifestyles somehow is humble."

"That is a difference of interpretation," Fairchild said. "The Bible says to live humbly, it doesn't say what constitutes that. By way of contrast, the Bible says for a man to lie with a man as he would a woman is an abomination, that our bodies belong to God so we should not alter them, that deviant sexuality is a mortal sin."

Huda propped his chin up with his finger. "Gee, there's some flaw to that, I wonder what it is...."

Suddenly, all three of us, in perfect unison, snapped our fingers and said, "Thaaaaaat's right!"

Smack and Huda sat as I said, "Move to strike Fairchild's arguments."

"On what grounds?!?" Fairchild screamed.

"Covenant was disallowed."

Fairchild's jaw dropped so low, I wondered if it had been unhinged. All he could do was stammer as Barachiel lifted the gavel and smashed it as he declared, "Struck!"

23

I gave Fairchild a smile of pure evil. He had wrapped so much up in arguing doctrine, he had nothing prepared for its absence. He gambled. "Move to reintroduce the covenant to proceedings."

I could argue against that, but if I did, Fairchild would be free to try Casting someone else who regretted having a sex change. If I wanted the precedent upheld, I had to take on all comers. "No objection," I smiled.

I eased up the pressure on myself, just a little. I had the wind at my back. If Fairchild tried to incorporate too much doctrine, I could easily undermine it. I did a quick read of the Tribunal, they were on my side. Fairchild had his back against the wall, and he was going to get desperate.

"I don't need doctrine," Fairchild declared.

"That's why you tried so hard to get it reintroduced, right?" I smiled.

"Doctrine is based on human nature. Don't steal. Don't kill. Things like that. Doctrine says that sex changes and homosexuality and all that is wrong."

"Why?"

Fairchild searched for the right words, then came up with, "...because it's icky!"

Huda held his hands out, wiggled his fingers and said, "Eeeeeeeeeeeeeew!"

CRACK! went the gavel. Barachiel gave Huda a look like, "This isn't the time for that." Huda stood up, bowed deeply and said, "I apologize, your honor. It won't happen again."

"Good," Barachiel said, still smiling. He then looked back at me. "Please continue, Singer."

I bowed to Barachiel then returned my attention to Fairchild. "'Icky', as you put it, is a relative measure."

"Some things, everyone finds disgusting, like killing a puppy."

"And some things are relative. Some people don't see how others enjoy drinking beer. Or like certain movies. If it doesn't affect anyone else, what difference does it make?"

"It does influence," Fairchild said. "His action can encourage others to try doing what he did."

"A sex change?" I raised my eyebrows. "This isn't like trying a drink or something, we're talking hormone injections and surgery. And money. Gobs and gobs of money."

"Those motivated enough will find a way."

"Those motivated enough will do it whether or not he did. There are lots of people having gender reassignment surgery. They don't know each other. Ergo, they came to the conclusion themselves."

"They came to the conclusion because they were aware it existed."

"If that were true, everyone would be divorced. Everyone would be having abortions. Everyone would be committing justifiable homicide. People will imitate relatively harmless things like double parking. As the risks and effort goes up, the likelihood goes down."

"Allowing it to exist is endorsing it," Fairchild said. "The church has no choice but to denounce it to protect the flock."

"Yeah, that's worked real good with extramarital sex."

Fairchild just blinked at me. "We must uphold scripture."

"You mean like the one you quoted about looking out for our brothers and sisters in Christ?"

"We are looking out for most of them."

"And providing nothing to the one who needed it."

Fairchild just kept looking at me. He quietly said, "Move for closing arguments."

I smiled at Barachiel. "I concur."

Barachial nodded to us. Fairchild went first. "Don't you ever get tired of this?" he asked the Tribunal. "God gave us instructions on how to live life. He gave us commandments. He gave us laws. He made it very simple for us to gain eternal life in Heaven. Just do as He says. These aren't great sacrifices being asked. They are part of human nature. Don't be cruel to others. Respect your fellow man. Praise Him and His glory.

"People like Sayles defy those simple rules. Life isn't supposed to be easy. Life is very hard. Sayles' actions made it harder for himself. In fact, had he not gone through with the sex change, he would have lived a happier life. He was what God made him to be. He changed that because of ill considered logic and faulty reasoning. Reasoning that his own actions testify are wrong.

"God gave no explicit instructions for alternate sexuality or things like that because it didn't exist then. No one could foresee a day when this would be possible and people would feel that was better than living as they were. This is a violation of God's purpose.

"So many souls enter Heaven without adherence to the precepts of God. Mercy? No. It is shielding people from the consequences of their actions. We are responsible for what we do. It is the reason for penance. To atone for our misdeeds. By continuing to allow people into Heaven, it makes what God established for us, for our lives, into a joke. Stop the joke now. Sayles was wrong. He knows it. You know it. Everyone knows it. He violated the body God made and the order God established. He should be Cast Down. Thank you."

Fairchild looked at me. He had that look in his eyes. He knew he'd done good with his closing arguments. But he also knew I was too sharp to let any of those points stand. All he could do was watch as I demolished them all.

"God gave us laws. God gave us commandments. God gave us instructions. God gave us rules.

"God gave us mercy. God gave us compassion. God gave us the ability to find what makes sense to us instead of what we are told should make sense to us.

"This is the whole reason for the covenant. What is held true on Earth would be held true in Heaven. Because times and people change. The things God laid down for man were not intended to be absolute. They were meant to guide through times when man did not have the knowledge to figure out what to do.

"As man advances, he has an obligation to learn, to adapt, to understand how what he does relates to God. People do it all the time. Martin Luther struck out on his own because he felt the church was no longer effective. People practice birth control even though their church may say it's wrong. Alex struck out on his own, changing his sex because he thought he couldn't live with himself any other way.

"What's the difference between Alex and other people who don't get in trouble? What's the difference between him and Maurice McCree, the first transsexual to petition? Since I led that case as well as leading this one, I'll tell you the difference. McCree felt he was in the right to do what he did, Alex felt he was in the wrong.

"It is very easy to defend someone who sticks to their guns, who won't view what they did as a mistake, who doesn't think, 'Oy, I never should have done that.' Those that try and fail? That find out they shouldn't have done it? It is very easy to look at them and go, 'You shouldn't have done that.' Because, unlike in the first example, they think the same thing themselves.

"Failure is not a sin. Mistakes are not sins. Alex did nothing to hurt anyone but himself. He took a risk, thinking it would end his suffering. It didn't. Despite Alex doing the best he could, making the best choice he could, one that ultimately didn't work out, you are being asked to disregard his human situation and Cast him Down. People make mistakes and regret them all the time. Those that atone, those that make good, those things are NEVER held against them. They are greeted with open arms, with love, that they have figured things out and made it to their Heavenly reward.

"Fairchild's statements are dangerous. Lots of people do things that seem like good ideas at the time. They fall in love. They have kids. They start career paths. They move to new neighborhoods. Each of these things are events that cannot be simply unwound. They turn life from something joyous to simple survival, working for a better tomorrow, or at least a tolerable present.

"The only difference between Alex and such people is the nature of the change he sought. He didn't have a baby to keep his marriage together. He didn't marry someone just to make others happy or impress them. He didn't do things to make money at the cost of other's humanity.

"He made a mistake. He is not denying that. The Celestials aren't denying that. But making mistakes is not only human nature, God expects us to make mistakes. It is the reason for the covenant, because His will could be misinterpreted. It is the reason for the Celestial Courts. It is the reason for confession. It is the reason for apologizing.

"It is the reason mercy exists.

"The only reason we are debating this is because of the 'ick' factor. Some people never get over their reactions to things outside their comfort zones. But it is precisely because of this that angels decide fates, not humans. Angels see. They understand. They recognize the confusion, hope, and fear that can make people do stupid things. Alex isn't a murderer. He isn't a thief. He was sexually confused and forced something that shouldn't have happened. Casting is completely out of proportion to what he did. He was confused by his impulses and himself in life. End that confusion. Grant his petition. Thank you."

Barachiel looked to the Tribunal. "You have heard the Advocates for Alexander David Sayles state their recommended fates. You may now make your decision. You wish to confer?"

The angels leaned together for a moment and whispered amongst themselves. Finally, the lead Tribunal stood and said, "We are ready to rule."

"And what is your decision?"

"Petition for entry into Heaven is pending."

My eyes popped. I looked at Fairchild. He was shocked, too. I didn't get it. I mean, I had this in the bag! What did I do wrong?

There are three ways to approve petition. If the Tribunal simply grants it, you are on your way to Heaven. Suspended meant that you had some duty to attend to first, like atoning for your misdeeds, and there was no way to be sure exactly how long it would take. If the petition was pending, though, there was something simple involved, and the Petitioner would be in before too long.

"What are the conditions?" Barachiel asked.

The lead Tribunal stated, "The Petitioner is to be reincarnated and live a happy life. Once that life is over, he may enter Heaven."

Barachiel declared, "So be it!" and slammed the gavel, ending the court session. He and the Tribunal exited their respective doors. I looked at Fairchild again. His face showed mixed emotions. He was thrilled I didn't get my way, but disappointed he didn't upend my precedent. He simply walked out, leaving his juniors to gather up the scrolls and clean up.

Alex walked up to me from the dock. "Thank you," he said.

"Don't thank me," I said, not bothering to hide the bitterness in my voice. "I didn't win."

Alex was silent for a moment, then said, "I'm glad you didn't."

I looked at him strange. "What?"

He looked to the side, took a deep breath, and said, "I get to live again."

"Which means you don't get into Heaven for another lifetime."

He looked at me and smiled. "I remember what it was like before. Before I wanted to be...different. I want to feel that again."

I let out a very long sigh. Life is precious, and he appreciated it. Going back to life wasn't going to be bad for him under normal circumstances. And by court order, he was going to have one that definitely wasn't bad. We shook hands, said our goodbyes, and Alex went through the Petitioner's exit on the left side of court.

I exited the courtroom, shrouded by my frustration. I didn't really hear anything. I know I told Smack and Huda to take the scrolls back. They did react. Usually, I take them back, I consider it part of my duties and I don't like treating my juniors as my servants. If I did that, I needed some time with my thoughts.

Unfortunately, I found myself spending time with Michael, too. I was heading to get some cases to advocate, something to distract me. I walked straight into Michael. It actually took me a moment to register who I had bumped into.

Michael smiled down at me. "Want to talk?"

"Nope."

Michael let out a short laugh. "Seven hundred years we've known each other, and you still think you can bluff me."

"It's not a bluff."

Michael promptly put his hands on my shoulders, turned me around, and started pushing me. Fighting Michael is a waste of effort, so I just walked in the direction he was steering me in. Eventually, we got to the Residencies, where the Celestials have their quarters. He guided me to my door and waited as I opened it. He then steered me back inside, only removing a hand long enough to shut the door and vanish it.

Michael then steered me over to my couch. We stopped in front of it, he turned me around again, and he pushed my shoulders down. He then sat next to me and asked, "What's on your mind, Hannah?"

I didn't even look at him. "Couldn't you think of a less dignified way to travel?"

"You have obviously never flown coach."

I wasn't going to get anywhere until Michael was satisfied. I threw myself against the back of the couch and started rubbing my face with my hands. "I hate it when I fail."

"You didn't fail, Hannah." I heard the change in Michael's voice. It was no longer the goofy big brother. It was the concerned big brother, the one that wants to make sure you're all right.

"Alex isn't in Heaven. He's going around again. He didn't deserve that. And Fairchild has thrown doubt on my precedent."

"Wrong on both counts," Michael said gently. I took down my hands and looked at him. He was smiling, comfort and reassurance radiating from his expression. "And the reasons why tie in to each other."

"Okay. What am I missing?"

"Even without the sex change, Alex wouldn't have been allowed into Heaven. You know that. He's not like a homeless person or a drunk or anyone whose misery can't be fought. He brought his misery on himself. He never really lived. No one gets into Heaven until they have actually lived."

"So what? His petition wasn't outright approved. Fairchild can undermine the precedent with it."

"No, he can't," Michael countered. "You are so focused on the travesty of justice you didn't prevent, you aren't seeing what really is. The precedent is safe. The petition isn't pending because of anything to do with his transsexuality. It's because he didn't really live. Fairchild would be misrepresenting what happened. It'll never work. The precedent has nothing to do with the verdict, the Hell Alex made for himself does."

"You don't think Fairchild will twist that? Continue to play the, 'He knew he did wrong' angle?"

"No. He can't. People regret their actions. Everyone does. Even that happiest person has something in their past that they don't want to revisit. That they don't want to talk about. That, if they could erase it from history, they would. His precious religious leaders have them all the time. Advocates would have a field day with them. They don't even have to be you. If he pushes, he'll get shoved. And he knows it."

"He'll establish a precedent that can be used against him."

"Remember, Fairchild works and protects those he approves of, not those who genuinely need or deserve it. Lots of church leaders do, because they figure their authority gives them the right. They see what they do as power, not responsibility."

"Thank God for Celestials, then," I told him.

"Exactly," Michael said with a flourish of his hands.

"I guess I'm just edgy," I told Michael. "I mean, people can be so reactive about sex."

"Times are changing," Michael said with a smile.

"Not fast enough," I told him. "Fairchild and them are from eras when sexual identity wasn't an issue. And now they are the ones who get to determine if someone gets Cast or not. All because of their times."

"It's not their times, Hannah, it's them. It's a matter of their hearts and what they are willing to accept and believe. They are the ones who are biased, not the eras they live in. Everyone always has the choice."

I smirked at him. "Prove it."

He smirked back. "You come from Medieval times, and you're doing just fine."

I felt myself calming down. Good thing, too. There were always more cases to hear. There were always people who needed help.

And as long as I was around, I was going to help them.

ARC ENEMIES

There are people who believe that everything happens to them for a reason.

This is correct.

The flaw in their logic is oversimplification.

They assume everything happens to them for a GOOD reason.

There are times when bad things happen and it isn't because it's to guide them in their proper life direction or to save them from danger. It's because someone else made something bad happen to them. Man does not live in a vacuum. For example, someone elbows his way in front of you for a promotion at work. God did not do that because he has a better gig lined up for you. This guy did it to take what was yours.

Most people at this point ask, Why does God allow that to happen? The simple answer – God is not your bodyguard. He is not to protect you from everyday life. He can help with certain things once in a while, but He cannot live for you. Otherwise, there'd be no point to life at all.

So, the result of this inequity is resentment. Anger. Hatred. Let me tell you something about hate.

Hate isn't necessarily a bad thing.

I can tell some of you are gasping and some of you are wondering if I've lost my mind.

You have to understand that God allows us to feel hate. Believe it or not, it is part of His master plan. The basic human tendency is to love. Well, for the most part. Some people tend towards selfishness. Some tend towards greed. There are other negative emotions, and they all exist at the cost of love.

And this is the reason for hate. Man is not meant to be miserable. Man is not meant to be taken advantage of. All the talk about rising above frustrations and being Zen is all well and good. But some things, action MUST be taken. Fairness demands it. Hate exists in the vacuum left by love.

Hate is allowed to exist because it is a powerful motivator. But there's a catch. People aren't supposed to enjoy hate. There's a reason hate feels so bad. Hate is supposed to spur you into making things better. You are in a situation where just putting up with something is no longer possible. Something must be done. Because, the sooner you fix it, the sooner you won't feel that hate anymore and can enjoy love again. Some people, however, value hate more than love.

And they love that hate.

It was 1424, still the early days of my career as a Celestial Advocate. I was already leading regular cases and even leading some greys. Not bad for less than a hundred years on the job. I was junioring on some of the more interesting ones, as well. Noah Holman was senior Celestial and senior grey (it's very unusual for one Celestial to not possess both those titles at the same time). He was originally the lead for my own trial before St. Michael took over and then I did. Great guy. He was about sixty when he died, really remarkable for medieval times. He had been a monk and was very familiar with religious philosophy and human nature. I felt incredibly lucky to have him as a mentor.

"I feel incredibly lucky to have you as a student," he told me happily.

I could feel myself start to blush. "Oh, go on."

"Really," he said. "I'm telling you, you are going places."

"If that is God's will." I was trying to be diplomatic. I had been an Atheist before I died. God loved me. In fact, He never stopped loving me, even when my philosophy told me He wasn't real. But I still felt guilty about it, and had trouble believing God would simply look the other way about it. I mean, He hadn't done anything to me, but it's not like I was trying to be anything more than a Celestial Advocate. I really wanted to be an angel, but was content to just dream about that.

"Humble as always," Holman said with a laugh. "Any chance of some of that rubbing off on Spire?"

"Anything I try to rub on him is the wrong way," I said with a laugh of my own. Victor Spire was the senior Church and he hated me with a passion. He had tried using my Atheism as a way to destroy the Celestial Courts. The last thing he expected was that I would take over, rise to the occasion, and win, alone and without a leader, and protect the Celestial Courts. He did not like me becoming a Celestial. I didn't run into him much at first. But as I started taking on grey cases, I was coming across him in court more and more often. He was my opposition in my first grey case I led. He ramped things up then. My success and my continual presence was an affront to him. I'd feel bad about it if he wasn't such a jerk.

Holman was nodding at what I said when a Putto, John, came flying up to us. "There you are, Lady Singer," the childlike angel said. "Michael wants to see you. His chambers, please."

Holman and I were both standing up as I said, "Tell him I'm on my way, please." John gave me a salute and took off.

Holman and I said our good-byes and walked in opposite directions. I got to Michael's chambers. The door was shut. I knocked politely.

"Come on in, Hannah," came Michael's cheery response.

I opened the door and walked in. Michael was sitting at his desk, smiling broadly while going over a scroll. He looked up. "Hannah! Great to see you! Please have a seat."

I went to one of the chairs, casually looking as I went to make sure there wasn't a tack there (a habit I got into really quick). There was nothing, so I plopped down. Michael smiled at me. "Hannah, do you remember the reason you decided to become a Celestial Advocate?"

"Absolutely. I want to help people facing nearly impossible odds and see that God's mercy is not taken away from them."

"Basically...."

"I want to help the next Hannah Singer."

"How would you like to see her?"

My eyes popped. "What?"

"You can't meet her yet. She's still alive. But, she's going to be given a very important charge. You'll like her, Hannah. She's strong. Fierce. Smart. Determined. She's almost like another you."

I finally figured out the look on Michael's face. It was like a kid with a new toy that he can't wait to show off. Michael generally likes humans, and when it's someone he really likes, you can tell. That intrigued me. "I would love to see her."

Michael jumped up and started rubbing his hands together. "Great. I'll come and get you when it's time. It won't be long. Just go back to your quarters and wait for me there."

I stood up and smiled. "Sounds good. See you later, Michael."

I had just gotten back to my quarters and was considering what book I would read when I heard a knock at my door. From the height and strength, there was only one individual it could be. "Come in, Michael," I called.

Michael entered, smiling wide. "You ready, Hannah?"

"You bet," I smiled.

Michael came up to me and touched my shoulder. Everything around me shifted and swirled. When it settled, we were in the countryside on some sort of farmland. I wasn't sure where. All I knew was the temperature and atmosphere was telling me it wasn't my native England. "Where are we, Michael?" I asked.

"Domremy, France," he smiled. "Follow me."

As Michael marched off and I raced to keep up with his long strides, he talked. "How familiar are you with what is going on here right now?"

"Not very."

"How about England? Any ideas?"

"No. Is one connected to the other?"

"Yes. England has basically been trying to take over France through royalty."

"How?"

"Due to palace intrigue, the English monarchy is claiming authority over France. Many in France don't want a dual monarchy and have their own sovereign that they will follow. There has been warring off and on since 1337. But tonight, things are set in motion so that that will not go on much longer."

"What are the results you are after?"

"The French are to be their own country. Their own culture. Their own people. The English are to be driven out." Michael looked at me slyly. "What do you think of that, Hannah?"

"If you're asking because I'm English, I will simply remind you – I don't argue with God."

"And if it wasn't God?"

"People have a right to be free, don't they? And they are clearly willing to fight for it."

"Well, fighting for it is a problem," Michael said, going back to facing ahead. "The French are in complete disarray. They need help. They need a leader."

"They need hope," I added.

"Yes. And this woman is going to be the one to make it happen," Michael said, beaming with pride. Michael has a lot of love and respect for soldiers and warriors. Whoever she was, she was going to be big.

I was going to witness history in the making.

We traveled along the farmland, eventually coming to a field. As we walked, I could see a lone girl in the distance. She was young, not even a teenager, from what I could tell. She had a weary look in her eyes. She clearly did not like living in this era.

I suddenly noticed that Michael was heading right for her. Was she....

I wasn't sure what to say. Like I said, I would never argue God's will. But this girl was just a child....

...I stopped dead in my tracks. Michael must have noticed, because he turned to me and smiled. "You feel it, don't you?"

I did. I stared at the girl in amazement. I felt it. A fighting spirit. This wasn't an angel born as a human to help nudge the world in the right direction. This was a human, full of fire and energy. No matter what God had in mind, I suddenly had no doubt she could do it.

Michael came up to me and waved his hand in front of my face. "Hannah? You okay?"

All I could do was stammer, "...I feel it. I feel her spirit."

"Such strength is very rare. Angels," and he leaned down until his eyes were all I saw, "and humans of a similar level of strength," and he smiled as he straightened, "can detect it. It is precious, Hannah. As precious as love."

I looked at the girl. "Then why don't all humans have it? Wouldn't the world be better if everyone could be like her?"

Michael laughed. "You mean, like the two of you. No. The world would not be better. The will you two exhibit is many things. It is a forge. It is a farm. Those with it create better things for others, by their actions or by their love. They create objects, thoughts, they encourage others, they feed souls with their acts and their presence. Their own inspiration inspires others. Many humans are limited simply because such power is easy to abuse. It has to be this way. It's for everyone's own good."

"They still have access to such power, but only through someone God trusts."

"You got it, Hannah. That little girl," he said, pointing specifically to her, "is going to change the world." He then resumed walking towards her.

We got a distance away from her as she continued to walk, unaware she was heading straight for us. I looked at Michael. "How old is she?"

"She's twelve. A very sacred number. The number of the tribes of Israel. The number of the Disciples. The number of...."

"Sorry we're late."

Michael and I looked behind us to the new voice. My jaw dropped.

Standing before me were St. Catherine of Alexandria and St. Margaret the Virgin. I felt in them the same spirit I felt in this girl. I dropped to my knees and bowed my head to them. After a few moments, I heard Catherine say, "Please rise, Singer."

I squeezed my eyes shut. "No. I'm not worthy."

Suddenly, I heard Margaret's voice, seemingly right over my head. "Rise, little one."

I felt a determined fingertip go underneath my chin and start to lift my head. I saw the imperious but somewhat mischievous smile of Margaret. She didn't stop lifting, and I started rising up onto my haunches. She continued to lift my chin, and I was unfolding my legs and standing before I knew it. I could only stare at her as she tapped my nose with her finger and walked back to Catherine. "Thank you, little one, for not disobeying your superiors."

Catherine shot her a bemused look. "Please go easier on her."

"Privileges are earned, not given," Margaret stated, tilting her head back. It was tough to say if she was just giving me grief or if she really meant it. I don't know either of them that well. I try not to be where they are.

Michael's voice cut through, helping me relax. "Well, it is almost time, ladies. Will you please stand over here?" And he gestured to his right.

Catherine shook her head. "You are St. Michael. You are the leader of the angels. You should be in the middle of us."

Michael looked a little let down. "But I want her to see my best side."

Margaret simply took up a position on Michael's left, facing the approaching girl. "She's about to meet a real archangel, Michael. I don't think she's going to notice a best side."

Catherine went on Michael's right, facing him, waiting. Michael's gave a quirked smile, then turned around. Now, all three were facing the girl. I quickly dashed around to the side so I could see everything.

The girl had just about gotten up to them when Michael said, "Now."

The light of God that was within the three of them suddenly blazed through their bodies, illuminating them, but I could still see them. Their faces, their expressions, their postures, Michael's mighty angel wings sweeping high and wide. And so did the girl. She had stopped dead in her tracks, staring at the three beings of light in front of her.

"I am St. Michael."

"I am St. Margaret the Virgin."

"I am St. Catherine of Alexandria."

The girl fell to her knees in front of them and bowed deeply.

"Look upon us," Michael ordered, "and be glad."

Slowly, she tilted her head up. Tears were forming in her eyes, a rapturous smile on her face. All she said was, "So beautiful...."

"We have come because God has chosen you for a sacred task."

The girl suddenly rocked back so she was sitting on her heels. Her back was ramrod straight, and a fiercely determined look appeared in her eyes. "What is His bidding?"

"For the English to leave France."

"How do I accomplish this?" If she had any doubts, she didn't let on.

"First, you must weaken their military grip. When that is done, you are to bring the Dauphin to Rheims for coronation. With the military defeated and a proper king in place, your nation will be restored."

"It will be done," she said.

"You have much preparation to do, and we will always be by your side," Michael said. "Be strong. Be brave. The history of your countrymen depends on you."

The lights from the Heavenly figures grew brighter again. When they faded, the saints had dematerialized, but were still there in spirit and could see the girl. She just kept staring where they had been and saying, "So beautiful...."

Margaret turned to Michael. "Why do you get to do all the talking?"

Michael looked at her. "Because I'm St. Michael, that's why."

Margaret turned on her heel and threw her nose in the air. "Hmph. How an archangel who acts inferior to me continues to lead me, I'll never know."

"Rank has its privileges," Michael smiled as the figure continued to face the front and vanished.

Catherine looked at me. "Any chance you can teach Margaret how to bicker with Michael? You are so much more entertaining than she is."

I started stammering. Was she suggesting I teach someone how to be insolent to Michael?!? Wait a minute! I wasn't being insolent to Michael! He teases me like a big brother and I tease him back like a big brother! I....

Catherine turned to Michael. "You best calm her down. She looks like she's about to have a nervous breakdown." And she vanished in a flash of light.

I turned to Michael. "I'm sorry! I didn't know they took it that way! I wasn't being...."

Michael held up his hand, indicating I should stop. I did so. "She's teasing you, Hannah. She knows better. Don't you think, if I had a problem with your behavior, I would have done something about it by now?"

I relaxed. My big brother, my best friend. He was right. It was never wrong for me to be who I was with him.

Michael came up to me and put his arm buddy-style over my shoulder. He turned me so we could both see the girl. She had gotten up by now, and was walking across the field, returning to her home. I could sense the emotions running through her. She was overwhelmed. But there was also determination. She would find some way to make this happen. You could count on it.

"Take a good look at history, Hannah," Michael whispered reverently. "Take a good look at Joan Of Arc."

Jeanne d'Arc, or as she is known in the English vernacular, Joan Of Arc, had been given a mighty task. However, she was more than up to it. She spent her time preparing herself. Michael and the others kept a close eye on her. Michael couldn't wait to tell me about the progress she was making. I didn't need a life scroll to know her.

When Jeanne was sixteen, her efforts began in earnest. She requested a meeting with the French royal court. Naturally, the men dismissed this woman claiming Divine Guidance as delusional. She needed an edge. Michael provided it, telling Jeanne about an upcoming military reversal in Orleans (one which he helped make sure happened). She made the bold prediction Michael told her, and when it came true, the royal court flipped. Charles VII granted her an audience. From there, as they say in modern times, the product sold itself. Jeanne convinced him that this was no joke. He granted her authority, and Jeanne got to work.

Jeanne's intelligence and boldness, especially in the face of the ingrained gender roles of the times, enabled her to start turning things around. The British found themselves being outmaneuvered, and the French loyalists found themselves winning. On July 16, 1429, the city of Reims allowed the French army under Jeanne's command to enter, and Charles VII was crowned the next day. A regular person would have called it a day. Not Jeanne. She was not done until the British were gone. She didn't rest for long.

However, as Michael likes to point out, humans are unpredictable. A series of events that no one could have foreseen began, events that would ultimately cut short the remarkable mission of Jeanne d'Arc.

I knew when the trouble started. I had been walking through the Archives, on the far side that led to the Ancient Forest. I had just finished a couple of cases, winning one, guardian angel duty for the second. I was replaying the second trial in my head, trying to figure out what I could have done different to have won when I heard it.

It was Michael's voice. Coming from the Ancient Forest. He screamed, "NO!"

Everything on my mind vanished as I dashed for the Ancient Forest. I didn't know what a lowly human soul could do, but if Michael needed help, he had it, and I'd find a way to do it.

Michael's voice indicated he wasn't very far in the Ancient Forest. I heard a couple of other voices. Female. I recognized them as St. Catherine's and St. Margaret's. There was more here than I realized. Rather than just barging in like the cavalry, I snuck around the trees until I found a clearing.

Standing alone in the middle of it was the trio. Catherine and Margaret were facing my general direction. Michael had his back to me, but I could tell from how he was standing that he was enraged. Wrathful angels are scary enough. When Michael is angry, it's terrifying, possibly more than Lucifer himself. I returned back around the tree, hiding behind it, just listening.

"Come out, little one."

Margaret had seen me. The command was her usual style, but there was something else to it. A pleading quality. If I stalled, Michael would simply call to me anyway. Given it was the three of them, there was only one thing I could think it would be.

I came slowly out from behind the tree. The three of them were looking at me, concern on their faces. "I'm sorry," I said. "I wasn't trying to interrupt."

"You aren't interrupting, Hannah," Michael said, his voice rumbling like a volcano. "I'd be telling you about this sooner or later anyway."

"What's going on?" I asked. "Is it Jeanne d'Arc?"

"Yes, little one," Margaret said. "She's going to die."

I felt my mouth fall open and tears form in my eyes. I couldn't form any words.

Margaret swooped up to me and took me in a comforting embrace. "I know, Hannah. I know."

I could only hug her back. "How? How long does she have?"

"We don't know," said Catherine. Michael's jaw was working back and forth, trying to keep the words from lashing out. "She was captured," she continued, "felled by an archer. She led an attack on Burgundian forces at Margny."

"She was the last to leave the field," Michael grumbled, tears forming in his eyes.

"King Charles VII has done nothing to get her back," Catherine continued, anger rising in her voice as well. "She's fought harder for her freedom than he has. She's tried escape several times. Duke Phillip of Burgundy has sold her to the English. She is to stand trial for heresy."

I suddenly broke from Margaret's hold. "I can save her."

"No, you can't," Margaret said.

I shot her a defiant look. "I know ecclesiastical law. I have to in my position. Send me as an agent. Replace whoever you can with me, I'll have her out in no time."

Margaret shook her head. "You can never win this case."

"Wrong, and I'll prove it!"

"It's not actually going to turn on ecclesiastical law. It's a political ploy to cost King Charles VII standing. The outcome is already decided, and they will not rest until they get it."

"That can't be! It *can't* be over!"

"Bishop Pierre Cauchon has no authority under ecclesiastical law, and he's leading the trial. He became bishop because of the English royal family, which bought d'Arc's freedom."

I covered my mouth with my hands. It was overwhelming. The anger. The fear. The despair. The frustration. The *wrongness*. They had no right to do this. Divine Guidance or not, this was an abuse of justice, just so the English could keep another country under their thumb.

A thought struck me. I looked at Michael. "Divine Guidance. She has Divine Guidance. Can't we somehow get her out?"

Catherine spoke for Michael. "Divine Guidance only works on those who will listen to it."

I couldn't believe it. I wanted to scream out in rage. In fury. The cry of a fallen angel would sound like a symphony compared to the sound ready to erupt from my throat. Our hands were tied. We can't save people from human events. Mankind has dominion over the Earth. We could not interfere. No matter how much we wanted to. The Divine couldn't save Catherine from her fate, and they couldn't save Jeanne from hers.

Margaret lightly placed a hand on my shoulder and guided me over to Michael. "Listen, why don't you two go and talk. We'll catch up with you later."

I looked at Margaret. All my defiance was gone. I could only say, "I think he'd rather be with his fellow saints."

Margaret just looked at me. "I think he'd rather be with his closest friend right now."

I looked at Michael. He was refusing to crack, but I understood what was going through his mind. I wanted his company right now, too.

"Come on, Michael," I said, holding my hand out to him. "Let's go to my quarters. We can talk there."

Michael took my hand, a smile of thanks appearing on his face. The forest around us shifted, and we were in my quarters. Because Michael is so huge, I could reach over to my door and vanish it into the wall without letting go of his hand. We then walked over to my bench next to my reading light and sat.

Michael was silent for a while. So was I. When he finally spoke, I knew the dam was about to burst. "It wasn't supposed to end like this for her."

I gripped his hand in both of mine. His other giant hand closed around them.

"She was supposed to end this in a couple of years. While she was young. She was supposed to have a husband. Children. A life. She was supposed to get to a place where she could be happy. She wasn't supposed to live a life of war...."

I pulled my hands from his and wrapped Michael in a hug. His arms went around me and swallowed me up. He was crying openly now. "She wasn't supposed to die now...."

An expert Celestial Advocate and an archangel fated to destroy the devil. And we were completely powerless to stop the travesty people were determined to make happen. We just held each other, our crying expressing what words never could.

Eventually, we pulled ourselves together. I asked Michael if I should stick with him so that I could be there for him...when the moment came. He said, no, he was fine now, so we went back to our duties.

The trial was a joke. I know. An angel went and kept records of the testimony for all of us to read. I had to struggle to keep my anger with my countrymen in check. Jeanne was extreme sharp. She'd make a great Celestial. I reflected how I was abused because of my Atheism. They said if I would just accept God's purpose for my life, they'd leave me alone. Jeanne had accepted God's purpose for her life, her every action was a testimony to His glory. And they were abusing her, too. Faith is incidental if people can use you to make themselves feel important.

I was sitting in my favorite spot in the Water Gardens, going over a couple of scrolls. The cases were sort of simple but a little tricky. I wondered if they'd be taken away from me and given to other greys or not. It was then that I saw shadows streaking along the ground. I jumped up and looked to the sky. The Water Gardens don't have overhanging structures other than bridges, so I had an unobstructed view of dozens of guardians, majestic wings out, streaking through the sky and heading for the Valley Of Death.

I felt sadness. There was only one person who would warrant this kind of attention. Jeanne d'Arc must have finally been executed. I sat back down again, my sadness tempered with relief for her. She was as good as in Heaven. Life is hard, but the uncertainty and the frustration of it was over for her.

I don't know how long it was, but I started noticing more shadows racing along the ground. I didn't tilt my head up, I just angled my eyes. More guardians were flying through the air, all heading for the Valley Of Death. This wasn't right. Something was very very wrong.

I quickly dropped the scrolls off in my quarters and raced outside of the Archives, just off the grounds where the Valley Of Death proper started and just stared. The sky was filled with guardians flying every which way and occasionally talking with each other. And I'm not talking casual. There were thousands of them. I waved to a group of them, hoping to get their attention. A group of seven of them came down to me.

"What's going on?" I asked.

"We are searching for Jeanne d'Arc. Nothing personal, Singer, but...."

"Priorities, I know," I said, waving my hand, and the guardians flew up into the air again.

I started thinking. There was no fixed point of entry for the Valley Of Death. Usually, where you turn up when your soul arrives reflects your mentality, your values, what you wish for and miss the most. The guardians can find anybody just wandering around the Valley Of Death. Usually. With thousands of them around, one of them should have found their target by now.

Jeanne was hiding.

I held up one hand with the index finger extended. A Putto, Zachary, flew up. "Yes, Lady Singer. How may I assist you?"

"Can you please locate Camael, and if he's available, tell him I need his help."

Zachary saluted and flew off. This was back in the days when Camael and I got along pretty well. Camael was a proud warrior and good soldier. He frequently sat at trials involving military figures. If anybody would be ready to help me find Jeanne, it would be him.

In a flash, Camael appeared before me. He was short and solidly built, like a bulldog. I was actually a smidge taller than him. Camael is sometimes referred to by Michael and others who have earned the privilege as "The Bouncer." He was the one who led the group of angels who gave Adam the bum's rush out of the Garden Of Eden. Camael wasn't subtle about it, he hated Adam for basically going to Eve, "Yeah. Eating the forbidden fruit sounds like a good idea. You first." He felt Eve had been used and walked her out, apologizing the entire time. His pitch black hair was cut close to his head, looking more like stubble than anything else. His flattened face and nose made him look like a scrapper -- if you tried to punch him in the face, you better pray you knock him out, or you won't like what happens next. The stern look in his eye spoke of his determination. You gave Camael a mission, you might as well plan what comes next, because he will get it done.

"You wish to see me, Lady Singer?"

"Yes," I said in a rush. "Jeanne d'Arc is hiding. I think I know where to find her."

"Where do you wish to go?"

I told him quickly. He understood my logic. He reached out, grabbed my shoulder, and with the speed of angels, we were on the edge of a forest by a field. The air, the smells, the view, everything was like the French countryside where Jeanne grew up. I figured the bond to it would be strong enough to pull her soul here when she died. It was how France was supposed to be. How she was supposed to make it.

Camael followed me a short distance to the trees at the edge. "If she is truly hiding from angels, I should wait here," he said.

"Just what I was about to suggest," I said, smiling apologetically.

"I'm not offended, Singer," he said. "She's scared. Bring her comfort. Bring her home."

I nodded, steeled up my face, and ducked into the cover of the woods.

I had to move carefully. Some angels were searching around here, darting to and fro. If Jeanne was watching for them, I didn't want her alerted to my presence. The element of surprise was the only thing I really had going for me.

I eventually got to what I was looking for – a rocky ravine. Lots of cracks, lots of places to hide from beings moving quickly and searching for a specific object instead of where that specific object could be. There was a stream and a small waterfall, not very big, but with enough noise to conceal casual sounds. I waited carefully for the angels to zip away, and dashed into the crack closest to the flowing water before they returned.

I crept through the passageways of the cracks, listening closely for any sign of Jeanne. I couldn't hear anything, but I doubted it was because of the masking environmental sounds. She would keep herself together to make sure she wouldn't be found. Just like I did when I first arrived in the Valley Of Death. Maybe Michael was right. Maybe she really was another me.

Wait a minute. Another me. She had the same fighting spirit I did. One I could feel.

I closed my eyes and reached out with my senses, hoping to connect with that feeling and it would lead me to her. It was doubtful. I had no way of knowing if it would work. I'd never tried anything like this before. We do really strange things in times of desperation without a single thought to whether or not they make sense or will work.

I just kept there, reaching out, trying to feel. I was starting to feel like an idiot. This was the stupidest idea I'd had since....

My eyes popped. I felt her! I could sense her direction!

I started moving again, paying attention to the feeling as it grew stronger or weaker depending on what path I chose. Eventually, I got to another passageway. And I heard something inside it. Breathing. Forced breathing. Whoever it was was forcing themselves to keep calm and measured. I prayed this was a dead end so she couldn't bolt from me and resumed moving.

This passageway was shorter than the others. I went around a couple of turns before I saw the wall enclosing the other side. The breathing had stopped. Jeanne had to be just around the bend. Was she looking to attack me to escape? Just to be on the safe side, I called out, "I'm off duty."

No response. She probably didn't realize the significance of what I said. Attacking an on duty officer of the court was grounds to automatically Cast Down. If you were unaware whether or not someone was, it did mitigate things, but I didn't want her bogged down in a quagmire in the Celestial Courts. If she was going to run, I wanted her to run with no consequences for her panic.

There was no one else it could be. No one else would have reason to react like this. I softly called, "Jeanne? Jeanne d'Arc?"

Nothing.

I spoke again. "I've come to take you to your Heavenly reward."

Still nothing.

I tried a hopefully forgivable bluff. "Would a Heavenly host lie about that?"

I heard it. A faint sob. A tiny voice said, "I have no Heavenly reward."

"Sure, you do," I said, not moving an inch.

"I...I failed...."

This was not going in a good direction. I said, "Listen, I mean you no harm. I carry no weapons. You have nothing to fear from me. I'm going to come around the corner and just talk to you. I won't block your escape. You could overpower me, anyway. You are free to leave any time you want. I just want to talk to you." A thought struck me. I swallowed my pride and said, "I'm just a woman. Please don't be afraid."

Complete silence. Please let her be so wrapped up, she doesn't feel the fighting spirit in me. I slowly walked around the corner, grinding my bare feet a little as I went, letting the sound tell her where I was and how I was moving.

Coming around the corner, I saw her. The twelve year old girl I had seen had grown up. She sat on the ground, feet back enough to bend her knees up. Her arms splayed out until her hands touched the ground. He head tilted forward, I couldn't see her eyes or even her chin with her bangs hanging down. She looked lost. Hopelessly lost.

I carefully moved over so that she had a clear shot at the exit if she wanted it. I wanted to be as inconspicuous as possible. I went against the opposite wall, never taking my eyes off of her. I carefully lowered myself and sat crosslegged across from her. She still didn't look up. She wasn't afraid of me exactly. She was afraid of her fate. And she was sure I was part of it.

I thought carefully, trying to figure out exactly what to say. I'm bold.

I'm not used to finessing my way through things. I tried an easy statement. "You know, you did really well down there."

She was silent. I continued. "You did more than anyone had a right to. Everything you were up against, everyone you had to fight, all the distrust for whatever reason. I'm frankly surprised you got as far as you did."

"Means nothing," she responded.

"What do you mean by that?" I asked. "I mean, you laid some good groundwork. Your people have a good chance of finishing what you started."

"They weren't supposed to finish what I started. I was supposed to." She leaned her head back, and I saw her face. My God, she still looked so young! She wasn't a child, but she wasn't a true adult, either. How old was she again? Nineteen? The feelings Michael had the day she was to be put on trial washed over me.

Jeanne took a deep breath, then continued. "I wasn't told, 'Do your best to chase the English out,' I was told, 'Chase the English out.' It wasn't something I was asked to try, it was something I was told and expected to do. I let God down. I failed Him."

My God! She really WAS another me! Michael was right! I thought quickly. I now had an understanding of her. What could I say that would get her to snap out of it?

I smiled at her. "I'm to bring you to your Heavenly reward. St. Michael told me to."

That got her attention. I made sure to include Michael's saint title. This wasn't the time for her to know how familiar we were with each other. "But...but I failed him."

"You didn't fail him," I said with certainty. "Bishop Cauchon and English crown failed him."

She looked at me, as if not wiling to believe anything other than what she feared would happen. "I thought...."

I smiled at her. "I know. You're scared. But you have no reason to be. You did more than anyone else could have. Leaping from your tower? Few have the guts to do that."

"I would think that would only make him more disappointed," Jeanne said. "'To him who much is given, much will be expected.'"

"It's not like you just sat around waiting for fate to come to you," I told her. "You did what you thought was right. You did what God wanted. You made a difference."

"Just trying isn't good enough."

"There are times when it has to be."

She tilted her head down again, hiding her features. "I really thought I could have done it."

"I know. I thought you could do it, too. Everyone here did. And you know what?"

When I didn't finish the thought, she lifted her head up. I smiled at her. I pushed myself onto my knees and crawled a little closer to her. "You could

43

have. That's why the English fought you so hard. They couldn't beat you fairly. They had to cheat."

I saw it. A faint hint of a smile. She was fighting to keep it down. I stood up and spoke down to her. "They are the ones who defied God's will. You upheld it. You have a wonderful reward waiting for you. You weren't supposed to die like this. Come. Let me take you where God really wants you."

I reached my hand out to her. She just studied me for a long, long moment. Then she pushed herself up and stood on her own. We walked down the passageways, heading for the exit.

Just before we got to the exit, I held my hand up, indicating she should stop. "Wait here one moment," I told her. I stepped further around a corner, giving Jeanne some cover to hide behind. I bent my arm at the elbow, holding up my hand with one finger extended.

Zachary appeared instantly. "Yes, Lady Singer. How may I assist you?"

"Please tell Camael that everything is fine, he should leave, and if he can get the guardians to break off their search, it would be wonderful. When you're done with that, please tell Michael I'll meet him in his chambers, and I'm bringing a guest with me."

Zachary gave me a salute and zipped off. I turned behind me. Jeanne was leaning around the corner, not exactly exposed, but not exactly hidden, either. I smiled at her. "Come on. We have a lot of traveling to do."

We got to the exit and peeked outside. We could still see the shadows of the angels flying overhead on their search mission. Then, without warning, every shadow stopped for a split second, then streaked along the ground, returning to the Archives. Eventually, the shadows became fewer, then stopped all together. "All clear," I told Jeanne. "Let's go."

We began trekking across the Valley Of Death. Jeanne was quiet for a long time, then she finally spoke. "How did you know where to find me?"

"I'm pretty familiar with this region of the Valley Of Death. When I first got here, my friend Artie and I explored a lot of it."

"Artie, huh? How is he doing?"

"Great. He's in Heaven, no doubt being obnoxious and waiting for me."

"You were close?"

"Close as friends can get."

"Oh. I thought he was your husband."

"No. I never married. And Artie was too much of a rogue to ever marry himself."

She nodded at this. She was quiet a while longer. Then, she asked, "So, you're English, then?"

"Yes, I am, but don't let that get in the way. I'm a big admirer of yours."

She looked at me strange. "You can't be an angel."

"Right you are."

"What do you do here?"

I smiled at her. "Basically, when your soul is in danger, I'm your knight in shining armor."

I gave her a detailed history of my arrival in the Valley Of Death and my trial (like I said, we had a lot of traveling to do). She listened with rapt fascination. When I finished, she asked, "So you're not an Atheist anymore then?"

"Kind of stupid to be one now."

She laughed at that. "Right, right, good point." She quirked her mouth. "Sounds like this Victor Spire and Cauchon have a lot in common."

"Sounds like it to me, too. Then again, Spire can read your life scroll. He can see the truth." I smiled cheerily at her. "He might actually like you."

Jeanne looked like I just offered her a slice of horse manure pie. "When do I meet him?"

"Personally speaking? I don't think ever. Once we get to Michael's chambers, he'll guide you through the petition process. Michael files No Contest, Spire files No Contest, and you're getting robes and a harp before you know it."

We continued to talk about our lives, her with her family's farm, me working as a peasant in the fields. For a moment, I was scared. We were becoming fast friends, like we'd known each other all our lives. But I not only just met her, but she would be on her way to Heaven in no time. I really didn't want to bond with her. Eternity only makes loss feel that much worse. No matter what, though, I hated that her life was over. But I was glad she was going to find everlasting peace. She deserved it.

We got to the Archives and headed for the Court buildings. Strangely, there wasn't a soul around. Well, sort of. Everyone was hiding off to the side, peeking around buildings or from behind pillars or whatever to get a view of the Messenger Of God. If Jeanne noticed it, she didn't let on. She just kept walking with purpose at my side as I led her to Michael's chambers.

We got to the door, and I politely knocked on it. "Come in!" Michael's voice called out in joy.

The door opened. Michael was sitting at his desk. He saw Jeanne, and the look of anticipation on his face was replaced with exuberance. "Jeanne d'Arc! Welcome!"

He leapt from his seat and started walking towards us, then stopped when he got to the end of his desk. He quickly dashed to the two highback chairs in front of his desk, the ones he had for guests. He picked up a tack from the seat of each one. You son of a...you don't do that for me!

He then came over to the door and wrapped Jeanne in a huge hug. She was practically swallowed up by the archangel, and she returned the hug as best she could. Michael unfolded her from him and escorted her inside. As he did, he looked back to me. The last he saw was me smiling and waving to him through the narrow crack in the door before I closed it completely.

I got just outside the building with Michael's chambers and looked at the court grounds. Everyone was back, milling around, doing their business. I smirked and walked further, ready to move on.

I got sidetracked when I heard rapid footsteps heading right for me from behind. They were human footsteps, and they were rushing to catch up, not charge at me. Whoever it was meant me no harm. I turned to face whoever it was....

...oh, Jesus, Victor Spire was making a beeline for me.

I barely had time to pinch the bridge of my nose when he got up to me, stopping a few feet from me. Wide smile, open arms, excited buddy demeanor, what we now refer to as "the full Vegas." His shoulders were bubbling up and down as he spoke. "She's here, right? You brought her to see Michael?"

My eyes popped. I quickly shot both my hands in the air with their index fingers extended and crossed them above my head. Immediately, seven guardians appeared around us. I wasted no time. "Michael has Jeanne d'Arc in his chambers. They aren't to be disturbed."

All seven nodded and raced off to Michael's chambers. Two of them could have kept anyone from getting in the door. Seven giant and heavily muscled angels? Good luck even fitting in the hallway with them.

"Aw, why'd you do that?!?" Spire screamed.

"Because you're Victor Spire, that's why," I said, contempt dripping from my words.

Spire leaned back like I just fired an arrow into his chest. "You wound me!"

"If only."

"I am not going to hurt Jeanne d'Arc," he protested. "I would never do anything to a Messenger Of God."

"Why am I not reassured?"

"If you will try to focus that mind of yours, Singer, you'll see a big difference between her and you. She lived for the glory of God. You ignored Him."

"Well, when you're on the run from Christians trying to prove their love for you by killing you, you don't have much time for philosophy."

"It's not philosophy, it's fact," he said, anger creeping into his voice.

"Not down there, it's not," I countered.

"As much as I enjoyed your trial," he said with a roll of his eyes, "I'm not here to rehash good times. I would like to meet Jeanne d'Arc."

"Why are you asking me?"

"Because Michael has been ignoring my requests since she died."

"And you think I can help bridge the gap, huh?"

He leaned close to me. "Okay, how about a public apology? In the center of the Archives where everyone can see and hear me say I was wrong to put you through your trial?"

"It's easy to apologize when it means nothing to you."

His face darkened. I leaned in close and lowered my voice to a whisper. "Understand this, Spire – I don't trust you. At. All. I don't trust you any further than I can throw a bull by the tail. You're up to something dangerous for her, and

I will not be a party to it. And I will be at that trial, sitting next to Michael and watching Holman beat you like a drum."

Through clenched teeth, Spire said, "I'm not up to anything."

I simply walked away, leaving Spire to fume. I headed for Holman's quarters, so I could warn him Spire was on the scent of something. Jeanne was going to need the best Celestial, so he had to keep sharp.

Jeanne acclimated pretty quickly to the Afterlife and was making plenty of friends. Well, general friends. Michael noticed how well she and I got along. "Like two peas in a pod," he said happily.

"It's just that kindred spirit thing," I said, not looking up from my scroll.

"Like mentalities gravitate towards each other," he shrugged. "Had you been alive, you'd have been fated to meet."

Michael figured from the beginning that Spire was going to try to seek out the Messenger Of God that turned up in our midst, but he couldn't keep her isolated forever.

"I'd still try," I told him.

"What good would it do?" Michael shrugged as we watched Jeanne walking around the Archives, taking in the sights. "It basically says that she's too weak and has to be protected from every threat no matter what. She has to be allowed to interact with the bad as well as the good. Humans have faith in us to ultimately do right. We have to have the same faith in them."

As soon as he said it, Spire dashed past us on a dead run to Jeanne, moving with the certainty of a hawk spotting a field mouse. Michael and I just settled in and watched. Just because we were going to let her handle things didn't mean we weren't going to have her back.

The encounter was odd to watch from a distance. I couldn't exactly hear the words (Michael could. Angels with their enhanced senses can be really annoying sometimes), but I could see the reaction. Spire fell to his knees in front of Jeanne and started praising like a modern minister at a revival meeting. Jeanne looked at him with complete revulsion. Given that Spire was a high ranking church official, and English to boot, I could see why she reacted that way. It continued along those lines until Jeanne decided she'd had enough. Spire didn't think she had enough, though, lunging forward and wrapping his arms around her leg like a kid who doesn't want daddy to go to work on Saturday. Jeanne was actually taking steps, dragging Spire with her. It was comical, but we figured she'd suffered enough, so Michael and I went to break it up.

We got close enough to hear Spire wailing, "Praise God! Praise God for you!"

Jeanne looked right at me. I thought it was odd she wasn't looking at the archangel who was also the head of the Celestial Courts. Each word fell from her mouth like a hammer – "Get. Him. OFF. Me."

I leaned close to Spire and said, "If you want something to cling to and worship, I'm sure there's a golden calf around here somewhere."

Spire's eyes popped. After all, what I was implying about his actions wasn't exactly complimentary to him. The only thing stronger than his love for God was his hatred for me. He shot to his feet and brought himself up to his full completely average height. "How dare you suggest such a thing!"

"You've tried to Cast several people for worshiping false idols, robbing God of His rightful glory. Do I dare hope you've gained some understanding for others through this?"

"This is different! I am not denying God's glory! She is a vessel for that glory! I am praising Him through her."

I looked past him. "You disagree with that, don't you, Jeanne?"

He spun to address her, then froze in shock. Jeanne was gone. And, by no coincidence, so was Michael.

Oh, he didn't like that at all. "You really must think I'm evil to think I'd do anything terrible to a Messenger Of God."

"No argument from me."

"I would never defile her! Doing so would defile God Himself!"

I just looked him knowingly, smiled, and walked away. I just knew something crooked would come out of that mind. It turned out to be a depressingly accurate prediction.

I was walking across the Archives, looking for Jeanne. I hadn't seen her since Spire made a spectacle of himself, and wanted to see how she was holding up. She had filed her petition, and Michael filed No Contest. She was going to be in Heaven before I knew it. It was strange. I was already thinking of her as a friend and how I'd miss her company when she crossed over. I was hoping for a few more memories to occupy my mind for when she was gone.

When I came across her, she was engaged in a spirited philosophical debate with Saint Thomas Aquinas. Oh, this would be interesting. Aquinas has very definite ideas about gender roles. He never gave me any grief, but I did sometimes wonder if he found me an affront to his beliefs. We talked and discussed things, and rarely did that particular subject come up. But that was just casual. For actual debates, whether philosophical or mock trials or anything, I had never beaten Aquinas, he was just too good. But Jeanne looked like she was keeping up with him just fine in an apparently heated debate. Not only that, but from the look on his face, she might be holding a slight edge over him.

"Hello, you two," I smiled as I approached.

The two of them stopped talking and looked at me. They then eyed each other carefully. They immediately straightened and acted like they had been doing anything other than locking horns. "You are lucky, child," Aquinas sniffed. "I was about to put you in your place."

"Spirits don't sleep. How is it you are still dreaming?" she retorted.

I listened close. I had never heard Aquinas tell anyone to go burn before, and it looked like today was going to be the day. But no. They simply spun on their heels and started walking away, faces stern, but you could tell from how they were fighting to keep them that way and from how they walked that they had actually had more fun egging each other on than they had in ages.

I caught up to Jeanne. "You had him going, didn't you?"

"I'm sure I wasn't as impressive as you are with him."

I laughed in a very unladylike fashion. "I haven't beaten him yet."

"Ah, of course. You respect him too much."

I arched my eyebrows. I refused to think she might be right.

"So, what brings you around?" she asked.

"Just saying hello," I said.

"You really are impressed with me, aren't you, Singer?"

I took a deep breath. "Well, I admit I'm a bit jealous."

This caught her attention. "Jealous? Of me? Why?"

"You were a Messenger Of God. I wasn't. I could never be."

"Beating yourself up for being an Atheist?"

"Not beating myself up. Just...owning up to my mistake."

Jeanne stopped at that moment and just stared me in the eyes. I had to stop before I bumped into her. I wasn't sure what she was doing. It was like she was trying to see what was behind my eyes, to look at the mind and the soul they served. "What?" I finally asked, sounding a lot more casual than I felt.

"For someone so smart, you sure do miss some obvious things," she said, turning and resuming walking.

I followed, the two of us continuing on in silence for a while. She eventually started just sightseeing, asking me questions about the buildings that occupied the Archives and what I knew of their history. I answered everything I could. I wasn't anxious to revisit the discussion and find out what she was getting at.

Things were going well, she was attentive and a perfect audience. It was when we got to the Great Fountain at the center of the court grounds that I noticed him. Holman was standing on the other side. It was a specific look he gave me. To anyone else, he just looked interested in some inner thought. But I knew what it meant. He needed to talk to me and didn't want to cause a scene.

I somehow kept from gasping as my breath caught.

Something had gone wrong with Jeanne's petition.

I politely excused myself, saying I had a case consultation that I needed to attend. She had no problem and just stood against the wall of the fountain, watching the streams of water arcing gracefully everywhere. I walked easily up to Holman, who fell into step with me. We got around the corner of one of the buildings when I leaned my head towards him before he could speak. "What's going on? It's about Jeanne, isn't it?"

"The Churches are contesting her petition."

I stopped dead and just stared at Holman. If we weren't in public, I would have screamed a "What?!?" that could have been heard in Hell. "Please tell me this is another one of Michael's jokes."

Holman rolled his eyes. He didn't have to say it – Michael doesn't make jokes like that. "Michael and I need you in his chambers right now. I'm leading, and I'm choosing you as a junior."

I nodded without hesitation. We broke into a light jog, heading for Michael's chambers.

By the time we arrived, my shock had been replaced with outrage. We got to the door, and before Holman could knock, I slammed the bottom of my fist against the door three times.

"Come in, Hannah," Michael said immediately.

We went inside. Michael was in his chair, looking fit to be tied. He saw me, and the corner of his mouth quirked up a little. I stepped in just enough for Holman to fit inside and close the door. Once the door was shut, Michael flicked his hand at it and it vanished into the wall.

"That! Slime!" I bellowed. I marched straight over to one of the chairs in front of Michael's desk. It was business time, so I knew I didn't have to check for a tack before I sat.

"What did Holman tell you?" Michael asked as Holman took the other chair.

"Only that the Churches are contesting," I answered. "Recommended fate?"

"Reincarnation."

My rage vanished. I wasn't sure I heard right. "What?"

"Yeah, that was our reaction," Michael said, reaching into his desk drawer and pulling out a document.

I took it and just stared at it as if, should I look long and hard enough, another image would appear. "They've already named a family."

"Yup. Another farm family in France. Not a bad life they have set up for her."

Holman was watching me. "Stinks, doesn't it, Hannah?"

"Enough to knock a buzzard off a goat wagon," I said, rolling it up and handing it to Michael. I then looked at Holman. "Who else is junioring?"

"Don't know yet," Holman shrugged. "You were the first person I asked."

That caught me by surprise. "Really?"

"You're very fast on your feet. Clearly, Spire is up to something. I'm going to choose other juniors to handle the trial itself, but I want you focusing every last bit of that brain power on deducing what Spire's plan is. It could be the key to getting d'Arc her Heavenly reward."

This wasn't going to be easy. By going for reincarnation, they were giving Jeanne another chance to finish her sacred mission of driving the English out of France. How nice of them.

"You can count on me," I told him. I leaned back in the chair, then sat up, smiling. "I got it! Trial by God!"

Holman and Michael looked at me sadly. "No," they said in unison.

"What do you mean, 'no?' It's perfect. She is a Messenger Of God. There's no way He'll go along with whatever the Churches are planning."

"We have to preserve her legacy," Michael said.

"I don't follow."

50

Michael looked at Holman and smirked. Holman simply leaned back, letting Michael do whatever he felt was right. Michael said, "God is going to make Jeanne a saint."

My eyes popped. "That's great!" A beat. "Isn't it?"

"If she gets made a saint now, her legacy will be tarnished. Her petition will be granted because of her ties to God, not because of who and what she was. She can't be made a saint until she stands trial."

"Same thing with trial by God, then," I said. "It will be seen as a dodge instead of her facing up to her Earthly acts."

"Exactly," Michael said. "Much as we hate this, it has to go to trial. We have to face down whatever the Churches are going to throw at us."

"A Messenger Of God given a second chance to complete her mission? Tough to sell the Tribunal on anything else." Suddenly, a thought struck me. "Why aren't we supporting that ourselves?"

"Because then it is us or the Tribunal deciding the results of her mission, not God."

"Got it," I said.

"Every spare moment you have, I want you working on this case. Mock trials, brainstorming sessions, the works. I don't know why, all I know is we can't lose this one."

The time leading up to trial was insane. Holman wound up selecting the other juniors. There would be five Celestial at that table, ready to defend Jeanne's honor. I was the greenest one there. Everyone else was excellent. It was a bit intimidating, but I forced that from my mind.

It wasn't the level of experience that had me on pins and needles. Everyone's responsibilities were clearly defined. Everyone knew what to do and how to do it. Except me. I had no way of knowing if I was getting closer to the truth of whatever Spire was doing. The nebulousness assaulted my nerves. I felt like I was trapped inside an hourglass. Not only were the sands running, but it was burying me.

We had practiced and rehearsed until we had arguments and results repeating between sessions. Holman looked at me. "I guess there's nothing else to learn or deduce. We have to go to trial."

I had pulled out a case history scroll and started reading. "I'm all set." Actually, I wasn't. I was no closer to what Spire's scheme was. But the well was dry, it was time to move on.

Trial was assigned, and everyone headed for the courtroom. I was actually the last of the Celestials to arrive. I had just gotten in the courtroom when Michael stood up. He was sitting in the aisle seat further up on the right, directly behind where the lead Celestial sat in court. There were two empty seats next to him. I had a feeling they were for St. Margaret and St. Catherine.

Michael faced me, smiling a little. "Good to see you."

"Don't say that," I said, standing in front of him. "I got nothing."

"Right now, you have nothing," he said, his smile never wavering.

"That'll change."

"That's a lot of faith you have in me," I said, not entirely reassured.

"If you can't figure it out, no one can," Michael said, turning to the side to allow me to pass.

I got past the divider and saw the Celestial table. Holman was in the lead spot, Jeanne was in the Petitioner's seat directly next to it. Holman and her saw me and their faces smiled in relief. There are only four stools at each table, so I was expecting to stand. However, the seat directly next to Jeanne was open. Gideon Forrester and Jack Pidgeon were standing, motioning for me to sit. I motioned back for them to sit. I felt a tap on my shoulder. I turned to look behind me. Michael was smirking at me and pointing to the stool.

I carefully went to the stool and sat, fighting the urge to put my elbows on the table and my head in my hands. Jeanne just smiled at me. "Ready to seize the day, Hannah?"

I looked at her carefully, my panic just barely below the surface. "No."

"You will be," she said, facing forward. "You will be." Great. Another Hannah Singer fan.

I leaned back so I could see the Church table. Spire was there by himself. Him going for something other than Casting Down was unusual. This was even more so. I reached over and tapped Holman. He leaned back and looked at me. "Yes, Hannah? What is it?"

"Spire's gambling," I told him. "Whatever his scheme is, others will undermine it. He's keeping everything focused on himself. He's counting on no one guessing his true motives. Whatever they are, they'll sink his case. Do not engage him, force him to bring the fight to you until I figure out what he's up to."

"Got it," Holman said with a nod. We leaned back forward. I put my elbows on the table and put my clasped hands under my chin. Come on, Hannah. Time's running out.....

The chimes sounded. I didn't bother to react in any way other than automatic motions, standing and deploying my wings. I was too busy sorting through everything in my mind. I didn't even notice the Tribunal enter the box. Usually, I just get lost in the sensation. Right now? I didn't have that luxury.

The door at the back of the court opened. Metatron was the presiding angel. Metatron was a lot like Michael, but without his sense of humor. So however Michael reacted to things, it was a good indicator of how Metatron would view things. He would want to get to the bottom of this, and he would keep the trial running until everything was known. There was no way of knowing how much time that bought me, but if I needed to stall, I could probably get away with it.

Metatron set a record scroll down, off to the side. He didn't even look at it. He surveyed the courtroom, then hit the gavel. He sat and just faced out generally over the court. He didn't look directly at anyone as he asked, "Who is the Petitioner?"

"The Petitioner is Jeanne d'Arc," declared Holman.

"And who are her Advocates?"

"Gideon Forrester, Jack Pidgeon, Steven Green, Hannah Singer, and Noah Holman, acting as lead."

Metatron still didn't turn his head. "And who advocates for the Church?"

"Victor Spire, acting alone," came the response.

"Will the Petitioner please take the stand?"

Jeanne walked out and climbed into the dock. She was determined to face whatever it was head on. The same way she walked when I saw her when she was twelve.

Once Jeanne was installed, I moved to the now empty Petitioner's seat and sat. Forrester and Green took the remaining seats. I turned to look at Michael, and saw St. Margaret and St. Catherine were sitting in those open spots. They were looking at me nervously. They were counting on me to save this woman they loved so much. I turned forward and buried myself in thought, just listening to the trial for any clues and inspiration I could find.

Metatron cast his first look at an actual participant in the courtroom. He looked aloofly at Holman. "Advocate for the Petitioner goes first. Mister Holman, your opening statements, please."

"Jeanne d'Arc was a Messenger Of God. She performed the duties asked of her to the best of her ability, her faith never wavered, there is no good reason to deny her a Heavenly reward. Her petition should be granted. Thank you."

Holman was throwing his turn. Before he could argue, he needed to know what he was arguing against. Every ear turned to Spire, hoping to learn what was going on.

"The purpose of this trial is to address a mistake," Spire began. He sounded very calm and together. That was not like him at all. "d'Arc was charged with an important mission, one that must be completed. God ordained it Himself. The move for reincarnation is the best way to achieve that. The family chosen is close to the French military commanders who admired d'Arc while she was alive. To help expedite things, d'Arc would be born as a man. She won't have to prove herself, and she will return to her female identity when she returns. But she will receive training. The family is already dedicated to the cause. With her new identity, she will rise quickly through the ranks. She will complete the mission God chose for her."

I looked at Jeanne. She was resolute. She was ready for this, even if it meant living in a way completely foreign to her nature, that as a man instead of a woman. She was dedicated. Brave. How could anyone say she was the next Hannah Singer? She was fantastically ahead of me. I could never be her equal.

"She is noble. She is dedicated. Look at her in the dock! She is willing to do this. She WANTS to do this. Her death was a mistake. We owe it to God and His order and His will to redress what happened. She should be reincarnated, not as punishment, but to enable her to complete her charge. Thank you."

I took a quick look at the Tribunal. They were nodding in approval. They were already sold on reincarnation. The trial was literally Spire's to lose. I felt my brain running faster now. The more I thought about it, the more this seemed wrong. But what was it? What was I missing?

Metatron simply resumed looking out generally over the court. He was waiting to see who would make the first move.

Spire was also waiting. The first tactic any Advocate learns is to let the other side advance theories, to bring the fight to them. All you have to do then is react defensively, nullify the points, and you've as good as won. No one likes being forced on the offensive. If you have to be forced, it means you don't have a clear direction, and it makes success with passive arguments that much more certain.

Holman had to try. He carefully stuck his boot in the muck. "Hasn't she suffered enough?"

"A mission from God is suffering?" Spire smiled.

Ooo. Sliced it. "And what would you call being burned at the stake?"

"A mistake. One reincarnation with rectify. Unless you really think her eternal comfort is more important than God's will."

Holman isn't usually on the defensive, and never this early. He was losing. I started focusing more on Spire's motivations. Something had to help. I just hoped it wasn't a blind alley.

Holman tried another track. "Reincarnating her does nothing to continue her mission. Her life is over. Her mission is over. Your recommended fate fixes nothing."

"Sure it does. She is born, and when she reaches age, she can be given her mission again, or even a new mission, if it is necessary at that point."

"It's still not the same mission."

"So?"

"So quit pretending that it is."

"Why? It will work out the same. She wasn't going to quit until she completed her mission, anyway. She wants to go back. She wants to help. It is her will. It is God's will. Those are the most important considerations here."

Spire was on a roll. He continued, "In fact, she will have a better chance of succeeding with her new mission because we can see what went wrong this time and avoid it. We can adapt. And she will finish what she started."

This was bad. This was real bad. I buried my head in my hands. Spire was winning. Whatever his plan was, he was as good as succeeding. If he moved for closing arguments now and Holman couldn't stall, it was over. Come on, Hannah. You need something now. You're out of time.

...time....

Time!

I didn't even realize I'd straightened up and elbowed Holman in the side until I heard his, "Oof!" I looked at him in surprise. He wasn't even looking at me. In fact, if I hadn't heard his reaction, I'm not sure I would have known I'd done something. He simply asked Metatron, "May I have a moment to consult with my junior, please?"

I looked forward. Jeanne looked excited, like her rescuer had just arrived. Metatron, however, continued to look impassive. "You may," was all he said.

Immediately, all the Celestials crowded around me, their backs and wings shielding us from Spire's view. Everyone was looking at me in anticipation. But I felt no pressure. In fact, I felt like I could take on the whole world.

"Please tell me you have good news," Holman said, distant hope in his voice.

"Yes," I said with certainty. "I figured out his plan. I know exactly what he's doing."

I quickly laid it out, and Holman's face darkened. He was enraged. He looked carefully over his shoulder and between the wings. Spire was just standing there, straining for a hint of what we were discussing and looking nervous.

Holman turned back to me. "I'm going to make you lead," he said. In other words, I needed to argue this without going through or around Holman, I had to take Spire head on. "You up to this?" he asked.

"Let me at him," I said without hesitation.

Everyone straightened as I stood up. Holman addressed the bench. "Move for a substitution to be made."

"What substitution do you seek?" Metatron asked.

"Singer to be made lead."

Metatron looked at me. His head angled up slightly. What he was thinking, I didn't want to speculate. He then looked at Spire. "Do you have any objection to the substitution?"

I knew Spire loved to argue with me. He wanted revenge for me foiling his plans almost a hundred years ago. Better safe than sorry. I leaned around Holman, smiled, and waved at Spire.

Spire's smiling teeth remained clenched as his lips said, "None whatsoever."

I moved towards the back so Holman could pass in front of me as we switched places. This brought me right next to Michael, St. Catherine, and St. Margaret as I went. The two ladies looked at me with anticipation. Michael was smiling and whispered as I took up my position, "Give him Hell, Hannah." I gave Michael a thumbs-up and faced forward as Holman, Forrester, and Green sat.

Metatron continued to look at me from up high. I didn't flinch. It wasn't me being brave. I had this in the bag. I knew exactly how to nail Spire without getting on Metatron's bad side. I looked at Jeanne to try and will some confidence to her, and saw I didn't have to. She was leaning on the banisters and had her right leg crossed in front of her left. She was smiling. She was expecting a show, and she had the best seat in the house. I became an Advocate

55

to defend the next Hannah Singer. Time to go to work.

Spire decided to start things off. "So, do you, in fact, have any actual counterarguments to make to my points?"

"No," I said simply without facing him.

The only one who reacted was Spire. No one else thought it was over already. "Glad to hear it. Move for closing arguments."

Without preamble, I declared, "Move to change my recommended fate."

I caught a slight raising of Metatron's eyebrows, but no further reaction than that. "And what do you seek to change it to?"

I kept my smile innocent. It took a lot of work. "Divine Intervention."

Spire. Freaked. OUT! "Motion should be denied!" he screamed.

Before Metatron could address him, I jumped in. "You have no grounds to oppose."

"I have plenty of grounds!"

"Such as?" Come on, Spire. Take the bait....

"This family is part of the military! She will fit in easier!"

"She already has earned the respect and devotion of the military. So you think it just being given to her is better somehow?"

"She will have better training! You know what she did as she is! Imagine what she can do with a proper military background!"

"Therefore, her current work is unacceptable."

"I never said that!"

"You implied it."

"You're putting words in my mouth!"

"Okay. I'll let it drop."

Spire relaxed. "Good."

"After all, we're talking Divine Intervention. God can simply make that part of the package."

"No! You can't go for Divine Intervention!"

I looked at Metatron. "Not your decision, Spire."

Metatron was silent for a few beats, then he raised the gavel and said, "Recommended fate is changed to Divine Intervention. Motion for closing arguments is denied."

The crack of the gavel echoed around the court. Everyone was holding their breath. Divine Intervention was almost impossible to get because the long term effects are unknowable. And that was under the best of circumstances. Did this boisterous Celestial with not even a century under her belt actually think she could pull it off? No one realized it wasn't much of a gamble. By the time I was done, Spire's recommended fate would be a joke. The Tribunal would likely grant Jeanne's petition, but I needed to go for Divine Intervention smash Spire into dust.

I didn't dare look at Michael or at anyone other than Spire. "So, you think reincarnation is better than plopping her back down in France. Why?"

Spire was drowning, and his mind clutched the first twig it found. "You are creating another Jesus."

Whoa! Didn't see that one coming. "Finally! An original argument!" I declared. "And completely wrong."

"Think of what you are suggesting. She has died. She is dead. Cold. Worm food."

"Not exactly. She was burned at the stake."

"My point is," he said with a snarl, "that people will see that she returned from the dead and declare her another Messiah! An entire cult will spring up around d'Arc, and because of a false God we created."

"Jeanne's mission is not to be a Messiah, it's to drive the English out of France."

"People can misinterpret that."

"There are plenty of people that do God's will, and they are not seen as the Messiah. In fact, they are honored, but not worshiped. Moses. Honored as a prophet. Elijah, also a prophet. Saints. They are regarded as saints, not the Messiah. If anything, Jeanne would be seen as a saint. She has all the qualifications."

Spire knew I was setting up my big reveal. What would he do about it? "Saints are acknowledged based on their acts. Coming back from the dead is an act?"

I gave him a smile of pure evil. "Correction: it's based on three miracles. Jeanne turned the tide on the English, coroneted Charles VII, and execution could not stop her. Three miracles. She will be venerated as a saint, whether or not God officially makes her one."

"No!" he screamed. "She can't return!"

"She can't return because, if she does, it will be proof that Bishop Cauchon and the ecclesiastical court murdered a Messenger Of God!"

Spire just stood in shock. He was naked, exposed for the schemer he was. I didn't wait for him to recover his wits, I went right for the throat. "That is why you wanted reincarnation. You know that when all those who tried her come here to stand trial, the Tribunal will never approve their petitions. But, if she reincarnates, she is no longer the person they killed. You can redress their actions as being about attacking a heretic or just doubt because they weren't sure she was a true Messenger Of God or other excuses to create leniency. Doubt. To shield them from paying for their crime.

"If she is dead and born again, her mission from God is over. If she just comes back or gets into Heaven, her mission is ongoing, and your precious bishop and his co-conspirators have defied the will of God. You needed to delay a final judgment on Jeanne d'Arc, so that, as far as the court was concerned, she was just a regular human. Any other option, and Cauchon and the others' murder of a Messenger is still on the books."

"It will still show in court documents!" he countered.

"Not enough to deny their petitions if you argue right. And we know you can," I said. "By the time it is established Jeanne was a true Messenger Of God, your friends will be safely installed in Heaven and there will be no way to hold them accountable!"

Spire went off like a rocket. "How dare you accuse me of gaming the system!"

"Yeah! Shame on me for thinking you would take advantage of a situation for purely personal motives! Where in the world do I get such ideas?!?"

"The English made a mistake. They do not realize what they have done! They deserve a second chance!"

"For someone who constantly tries to Cast people for willful sins, you are being hypocritical."

"I am not!"

"Under ecclesiastical law, Cauchon had NO authority to preside at that trial. None. Zip. Zero. Goose egg."

"Someone claiming they are a Messenger Of God would naturally be heard by the ecclesiastical court. Church courts are within their rights to question and search for conclusions about such claims. After all, d'Arc was vetted at Poitiers at the behest of the Dauphin. Background checks, testimonials, everything."

"She was also vetted by the ecclesiastical court. Nicolas Bailly conducted the inquiry of Jeanne, and he found nothing. Cauchon had no authority, full stop."

"He was still within his rights to examine her."

"If it was an examination, why were there no French ecclesiasticals in attendance?"

"He didn't think to bring French ecclesiasticals."

"Bull. Jeanne herself pointed it out. He stacked the deck. He cheated. His goal was to kill Jeanne d'Arc for the sake of the English crown, and he and his conspirators succeeded."

"There was no conspiracy."

"She sought to appeal to the Council of Basel and the pope. They did not let that happen. It would have stopped the trial."

"She was trying to trick her way out."

I arched my eyebrows. This was going to be good. "And how was she trying to trick her way out?"

Spire glared at her. "By making it seem like she was on trial for being a Messenger Of God. She was on trial as a heretic. She was burned at the stake as a relapsed heretic. For wearing men's clothes."

"Ah, yes. Give her one option, then punish her for that option."

"She could have refused to wear men's clothes."

"It was survival."

"How so?"

"Remember the English lord that tried to rape her in prison?"

"She made that up."

Suddenly, a bolt of lightning streaked through the ceiling and hit Spire square, knocking him on his butt. It's a well-padded butt, so even if he wasn't invulnerable, there wouldn't be any damage. At least, to his butt. The real damage was to his pride. The lightning bolt meant he had just lied to the court.

I reached in front of Holman for a life scroll without a tie holding it shut. Spire had just gotten to his feet when I held it out to him sideways and waggled it. "You've read this scroll. You know who it is and that he did it."

"Men are rulers. It happens."

My jaw dropped. I wanted to make sure I heard him right. "You're saying rape is no big deal?"

A sound made Spire and I look at the Tribunal. The noise came from all the angels shifting in their seats. They were leaning forward and glaring at Spire, like they were ready to vault out of the box and beat him up.

Better cool this situation down before it really gets out of hand. I looked at Metatron. "Move for another bolt of lightning to hit Spire for his statement."

Metatron set the gavel aside and folded his hands together. "If you win this trial, you'll strip away the protection he seeks. All the lightning in the Afterlife won't hurt him as much as that will."

The Tribunal shifted back. They were still upset, but looked less likely to riot. Metatron had done me a favor by bringing us back on topic. I took immediate advantage of it. "Jeanne was supposed to be kept in an ecclesiastical prison, which is guarded by nuns. The English kept her in a regular prison, guarded by men. Her female clothes made her a target. Her choices were to be raped, or be killed as a heretic. How can you honestly defend the choice forced on her?"

"The clothes didn't make her a heretic!" Spire yelled. "Her own admission did! During her trial, she revealed the sign shown to her and Charles VII!"

"She didn't reveal the sign."

Spire grabbed a scroll off the table in front of him. "She swore to St. Catherine she would not reveal the sign. An angel with a crown of pure gold!"

There was a short burst of laughter from one person in the Gallery. Spire turned to glare at who it came from, and found himself staring St. Catherine right in the eyes. He clearly hadn't noticed she'd come in. St. Margaret was looking at Spire like she found a weevil in the flour bag. Michael looked like his angelic strength wouldn't be enough to stop his sides from splitting.

"Didn't read that portion of the trial record?" I asked St. Catherine innocently.

She just shook her head.

Metatron looked out at her. "Your comment on d'Arc's revelation?"

St. Catherine stood and smirked at Jeanne. "She did not break her promise to me. She lied. That was just a vision, not the actual sign shown to them that day."

"Lying to the court! Breaking her vow to tell the truth at the risk of her soul!"

"Be quiet, worm," St. Margaret growled.

Three gavel smashes punched through to us. We all looked at Metatron. He wasn't angry, he was completely calm. He simply stated, "I am ready to consider the motion for closing arguments. Any objection?"

"None from me," I stated with a bow. I had momentum on my side. The Tribunal looked unbelievably angry. Jeanne was safe.

Spire wasn't finished. "Motion should be denied! I have the right to redress her accusations."

Metatron arched his eyebrows. "And when are you going to get around to that?"

Spire tried speaking, but while his mouth moved, no sounds came out.

"Very concise, I must make a notation of this part of the trial," Metatron said dryly. Jeanne laughed out loud. Metatron bowed his head to her, which surprised me. I couldn't remember the last time he showed any kind of reverence to a human. He then looked back out over the court. "Spire? Your closing arguments, please."

Spire forced his mind to focus. This was his last shot to save Cauchon and the rest. "Do not let your desire for vengeance blind you to what needs to be done!" Spire said. "'Vengeance is mine, sayeth the Lord!' That means that it is to be handed out at the proper time. And this is not that time.

"Singer has redressed my recommended fate as an attempt to do an end run around justice. It is not. What good would it do? Cauchon and the rest will be here eventually. We know they did wrong. We can't argue they did wrong. They cannot escape the fate they have created for themselves. We all know that.

"Singer is using d'Arc's trial to put Cauchon on trial. He's not dead yet. There is no way to defend him and his compatriots. This trial has nothing to do with them. It is about Jeanne d'Arc and what should be done. She was charged with a sacred mission. One that simple stupidity ended. No one knew for sure she was a Messenger Of God. They thought she was just some revolutionary. Just like the crowd that chose to free Barabbas instead of Jesus. They did not know the truth. And had they known the truth, they never would have done what they did.

"In the name of justice, of fairness, you must focus on whose trial this really is. That is Jeanne d'Arc. Under other circumstances, I would have filed No Contest. But the fact is, she has a sacred duty to perform. It was not supposed to end. Reincarnation will not only enable her to finish, it will guarantee she finishes it, since adjustments can be made. The people of France are counting on her. They are counting on you. They are counting on us. Jeanne d'Arc should be reincarnated. Thank you."

I looked at Holman. After all, he was originally lead. I was just supposed to argue with Spire, not finish the trial. Holman, though, just looked at me and shook his head. There was no risk to me doing this, the worst thing that could happen was Jeanne's petition would be approved. I was to take this home.

I quickly wrote my closing arguments in my head. Jeanne was as good as saved. But I had a golden opportunity here. I actually had a chance at Divine Intervention. The Tribunal was on my side, and Jeanne would be able to show those who killed her that they made a huge mistake. I was going to go for it.

I looked over the life scrolls on the tabletop in front of me and picked one up from in front of Holman. It didn't have a tie on it. I scrolled through it, cleared my throat, and began reading aloud. "'I greatly fear to be damned.' That is a quote from Geoffroy Therage, who was Jeanne's executioner."

"He has every reason to fear."

I started holding up life scrolls. "These life scrolls chronicle the lives of those involved in the trial of Jeanne d'Arc. All of these people have lied to a court of law, of justice, of God Himself. The greatest heresy is not Jeanne's, but theirs.

"All these people, from Cauchon to Charles VII, will be held accountable for betraying not just a Messenger Of God, but a brave and noble person seeking to restore fairness to the world. That is the central point of this trial. It is to finish up what Cauchon started. It isn't just to deny Jeanne her rightful place in human events, but to get away with it.

"How many times have we seen this? Church officials, both on Earth and here in the Afterlife, consider themselves the ultimate ends of God's work. They hold in their hands the power to forgive sins, to excuse crimes. And they are more willing to guarantee their own salvation than others. In fact, if their salvation comes at the expense of others, well, God can sort that out.

"Not this time. This time, we can sort it out. Jeanne had a mission. One she accepted gladly. The saints did not pressure her to do it. In fact, there were times they tried to get her to pull things back, like when she leapt from her prison tower. No matter what was put to her, she was ready to go above and beyond that. Because she loved her country. She loved her fellow citizens. She loved her family. She loved God.

"Her mission is not completed. It's getting there, but not quite. Divine Intervention, returning her to life despite a body burned at the stake, then burned twice more, is more than justified. It is needed. To show the world that, when people want freedom, no one has the right to deny that. To show the world that, when someone is better than you, you do not resort to trickery and subterfuge to retain your power. To show the world that murder is not acceptable.

"The Ten Commandments state, 'Thou shalt not murder.' Cauchon and the rest have violated this law and killed a Messenger Of God. They knew it. So they have restricted what can be said, what can be known, so that they don't have to think about what they have done. But they aren't just denying themselves, making up excuses that they didn't know. They are restricting others' thoughts, all to protect their delicate sensibilities. That is WRONG.

"Jeanne was chosen for her strength. She was unstoppable. It was only through a quirk that she was captured, only through pure evil that she was stopped. Divine Intervention will change that. It will prove once and for all that her mission was paramount. That it should not have ended when it did. The question is not does she deserve a Heavenly reward. She always has, from the day she was born. The question is, does she deserve an Earthly reward? Knowing peace instead of war. Knowing the love of a good man. The love of children. The respect of history. These were supposed to be hers. They were taken. Give them back to her. Grant Divine Intervention. Let her finish the life God chose for her. Thank you."

Okay. Not my most concise closing argument ever. I was still new at this.

Metatron looked over at the Tribunal and said, "You have heard the Advocates for Jeanne d'Arc state their recommended fates. You may now make your decision. You wish to confer?"

The angels leaned towards each other and whispered. And whispered. And kept whispering. It was going on a lot longer than I had ever known it to. Eventually, the lead Tribunal stood up. "Yes, we do."

"Court is in recess," Metatron said. He banged the gavel, and everyone stood as he and the Tribunal exited from their respective doors.

Once the doors were shut, I let my facade fall away. I could feel the stunned, anticipatory look on my face. They didn't grant petition right away. They were discussing it.

Oh my God! I might actually get Divine Intervention!

I spun around to look at Michael. Everyone else in court had willed their wings away, and most of them were sitting again, but Michael was still standing, and looking at me with a smile that threatened to split his face.

"Can I do it?" I asked.

He knew what I meant. "You just might."

I closed my eyes, put my wings away, and willed myself to calm down. Life conditions certain behaviors, so even though I was a spirit, I felt my breath getting faster, my heart pounding in my ears, and my nerves starting to jangle.

"Boo!"

Reflex made me start to swing my right fist up and to the right to strike whatever had startled me, but I caught the movement and stopped it just as my fist got up by my chest. It was then that I recognized the voice. It was Spire's. He tried to use my instincts to hit him, and maybe get me on attacking an on duty officer of the court. I opened my eyes. I saw the look of disappointment on his face. I also saw that Michael had already moved his left hand to intercept mine and keep me out of trouble.

I looked at the huge, meaty hand and let out a sigh of relief. "Thanks, big brother."

He gave me a warm smile. "Anytime, Hannah." Then, as if prompted, we both turned our heads to glare at Spire.

"You wouldn't have been able to make attacking you stick in court," Michael growled. "And I could have you on Gross Misconduct."

"Don't overestimate your skills," Spire countered.

"Sit down, Michael," I said. "It's another trap."

Michael looked at me. "How so?" He wasn't challenging, he was genuinely curious.

"He's hoping he can keep Cauchon and them out of trouble by saying any prosecution is a vendetta. He's trying to get you to feed him behavior he can depict in a way that will get them out of their fix."

"Liar!" Spire bellowed at me.

"Care to make that accusation when court is back in session?" I asked him.

Spire carefully went back to his position, eying daggers at me the entire time. St. Catherine and St. Margaret came around and pressed down on Michael's shoulders, making him sit down again. All three continued to drill holes through Spire with their gazes.

The scene calmed down enough, I turned to my left to check the dock. Jeanne wasn't there anymore. Before I could register anything, I felt someone tackle me from behind with a hug. Guess who, Hannah?

"Ho ho ho, that was incredible!" Jeanne shouted. There was absolutely no fear or concern in her voice. "Knight in shining armor is right!"

Her grip on me was high enough that I still had movement in my lower arms. With a bit of repositioning at the shoulders, I eventually got my hands in a position to take hold of Jeanne's forearms and release myself. I turned to look at her, a smirk on my face. "It's not over yet."

"Yes, it is," she said. "Whatever fate I get will be a good one, and Cauchon and the others won't get away with their scheme."

"There was no scheme," Spire injected.

Jeanne just looked at him like a kid talking about his imaginary friend. "How can you lie like that?"

"Lying is a serious accusation."

I jumped in. "It's not like she's accusing you of heresy."

"Burn!" Spire screamed, and plopped down on his stool in disgust, looking at nothing.

Everyone on the Celestial side was talking, reviewing what had happened in the trial so far. I noticed Holman and the other Celestials would occasionally look at me with pride. St. Catherine did, too. Even St. Margaret, which really threw me. Once the trial was over, she'd probably be back to referring to me as "little one" again, but for now, I actually felt like one of the group. I focused on that feeling. The Tribunal sure was taking a long time. The waiting was becoming worse than just wondering if I succeeded in getting my recommended fate.

The chimes sounded and everyone went to their positions. Jeanne raced to the dock, jumping the banisters from the front instead of climbing up the stairs on the side. Spire stood up. Our wings came back out, and everyone faced front. The Tribunal entered the box. Metatron came in and sat at the bench. He banged the gavel, and everyone else sat, leaving Spire and I standing.

Every eye was glued to the Tribunal. Metatron looked to them and called, "Have you reached a judgment you are all in agreement on?"

The lead Tribunal stood. "We have."

I took a deep breath.

Metatron asked, "And what is your judgment?"

"Petition is to be granted immediately."

I could feel the joy around me. I acted happy, but inside? I actually felt disappointed. Crushed. I thought I had it. I thought I pulled it off. Not just the fact that I almost had Divine Intervention, but what that would have meant for Jeanne and her legacy. She could have been alive again. Experienced all those wonderful things I never got to. She would have been a true legend and not just some annoyance.

I failed.

Metatron looked at me. I prayed he couldn't tell what I was really feeling. "So be it." He cracked the gavel, adjourning the session. He then walked calmly out of court, the Tribunal exiting at the same time.

I was kind of functioning automatically. Jeanne was still excited. I forced myself to interact with her, unsure if I would see her again. I forced down the feelings churning inside me, expanding like an explosion I wasn't sure I could contain. Eventually, she headed for the Petitioner's exit on the left side of the court, waving to us the entire time, and singling me out for the most praise.

Once the door was shut, Michael looked at Holman. "Would you mind cleaning up? I need to have a little chat with Hannah."

"No problem, Michael," Holman said. I still wasn't quite with it as Michael touched my shoulder. Everything around us shifted, and when it stopped, we were in the French countryside, in the fields of a farm. I recognized the surroundings. It was where I had first seen Jeanne seven years earlier.

I really couldn't do anything more. Numbness hit me. I felt Michael push down on my shoulders, making me sit. He then sat across from me, just looking into my eyes and smiling.

"Should I materialize?" I asked.

"I'm not," he said.

A long beat, then I asked, "Why am I here?"

"To talk privately," he said.

Another long beat. "I miss her."

"Of course you do," he said. We didn't turn up in this exact spot on accident. Michael reached to his side and picked up a pea pod. He then broke it open in the middle, so that each exposed half was showing a pea at the end. He held them so I could see them and just kept smiling.

"Why did I bond with her?"

"You couldn't help it," Michael said. "Friendships still happen. Some will last longer just because it is the Afterlife. Some can be over just as quickly as they would be on Earth. But it's those bonds that make time worthwhile. You shouldn't hide from them."

I let my head sag. "It hurts."

"I know," he said. "I've been doing this since the beginning, when God made us angels, you humans, the Heavens and the Earth. I've had lots of friends come and go in my time. And you know what?"

I looked up at him.

He continued, "As much as saying goodbye hurts, never saying hello hurts more. Those that aren't around anymore, I miss them. But I enjoyed their friendship even more. The pain? The loss? It's completely worth it just to have been with them."

Michael reached out and took my hand. "And I'm going to miss you, too, Hannah. You won't be a Celestial forever."

"You can still visit me in Heaven," I said. Angels can enter and exit Heaven any time they want.

"Sure. Just like I visit everyone else. But it's not the same as actually having you here. And I know I have to prepare for it. Celestials usually only stay on the job for about three hundred years, and then they go on to their Heavenly rewards."

I suddenly straightened. "Holman!"

Michael never stopped smiling. "Yes. He's at about the three hundred year mark, too. I don't know how much longer he has in him. But I'll cling to each experience, each conversation, everything I can for when he's gone."

I thought for a moment as I let my eyes fall. "You think being friends with me is worth the pain."

"If we weren't friends, there wouldn't be any pain. It's how it works. And if the friendship is strong enough, the pain isn't as bad. Because the memories and emotions are that much more powerful."

I just sat for a moment, then put my other hand on his. "I'm such an arrogant fool."

Michael quirked his head to the side. "I'm guessing we're changing topics right now."

I just drooped my head and continued as if he'd said nothing. "I really thought I could do it."

"Divine Intervention?"

"Yes. She deserved to live."

Michael pulled his hand from my grasp, and I fought the urge to reach out for it, to hold on to it longer. I then felt Michael's finger under my chin. He tilted my head up. "You don't have enough experience yet."

"I know. Not even a hundred years, and I thought I could get something even experienced Celestials find hard to get."

"No," he said. "You don't have enough experience to really read the Tribunal." Michael shifted forward, leaning almost right in my face, and whispered, "You almost did it."

My head snapped back. "I did?"

"Yes," he said, leaning back. "If you knew how to read the Tribunal, you'd know how close you came."

I looked to the side in confusion. "What did I do wrong?"

"You did nothing wrong," Michael said. "The Tribunal was just more comfortable letting God decide what happens to Jeanne. God can still send her back, just like if she had gotten Divine Intervention. He can reincarnate her like Spire recommended. Nothing says she's going straight to Heaven. In fact, I can guarantee you she won't."

I suddenly remembered. "God wants to make her a saint."

"That's right," Michael said. "If she is willing to surrender her petition, God will make her a saint. And her work will continue. But that is for the two of them to decide on. Divine Intervention would have forced her back."

I suddenly got it. "And she wouldn't be made a saint until she died again."

"Well, He can make anyone a saint any time He feels it's right, living or dead. But this way, her legacy, her mission, what she is is preserved. She was part of God's plan, He should decide the best way to make that happen."

I winced. "I almost forced God to change His plan."

"Not at all," Michael said. "As powerful as Divine Intervention is, it's still kind of vague. Just granting petition and turning it over to God, though? That lets God be as certain as He needs to be."

I just sort of sagged at that moment. Michael got up and came up to my side. He put his arm on my shoulder and hugged me to him. We just sat, watching the countryside. Being spirits, we could hear what was going on around the country. We heard guns and cannonfire. We heard the sounds of war.

We heard the birth of freedom.

Things after that were a bit calmer. The English who killed Jeanne? Oh, they paid. Michael and Holman decided to chain them, try them in connection to each other. It's a very risky ploy to score victories in court, because you are building a chain, and if one loss occurs, the chain not only won't reach the others, but a retrial can be called for. Nowadays, we call this "pulling the train." This meant they couldn't go for Casting Down for Cauchon and the more egregious members of the trial, but Michael and Holman are ingenious, Michael leading the trials himself. Holman juniored. So did I. I didn't have to say anything, just enjoy the show of Michael facing Spire and winning.

Jeanne went through the Petitioner's exit and came face to face with God. She didn't even think about being made a saint, she jumped at it. She wouldn't be recognized by the Earthly churches for centuries, but that didn't make her any less a saint. She immediately got to work, and I didn't see her for a long time.

I didn't ask about her. It was like I didn't want to admit her friendship to myself. In fact, I wondered if maybe she had simply gone to Heaven instead of taking sainthood. I couldn't imagine it, but I forced myself into the dark, so it was as good a guess as any.

I was at my usual spot in the Water Gardens, going over some scrolls. It was 1452. The Hundred Years War that Jeanne had fought in was almost over. I was wrapped up in my reading when I smelled something.

It was wine. And not the kind they have up here.

My nose lead my head up and around. My eyes shifted so I could see just behind me. Holding a wine bottle in one hand, the cork in the other, and standing on the other side of the trough that I was sitting against, was Jeanne. "Long time, no see, Hannah."

I stood up. All my reservations were gone. It was just great to see her again, to see that she was all right. I couldn't stop the smile that burst on my face. Jeanne simply leapt onto the far wall of the trough, jumped the water, and landed on the ground next to me. She then wrapped me in a huge hug.

I was still processing everything. "What...what are you doing here?"

"I have some free time," she said, pulling away and holding up the bottle. "Feel like celebrating?"

"What are we celebrating?"

"Pope Callixtus III. He has just authorized an inquiry into Cauchon's trial. St. Michael made sure the truth wasn't really lost. My name is going to be cleared."

"Will the pope really do that?"

"Hannah," she chided me. "You know not all people with the church are like Cauchon."

I looked aside. "It's a lesson I keep forgetting."

"It's okay," she smiled. "It's an easier lesson for me to remember. After all, I've known nothing but bad about the English, but I have one of the best examples of them right here."

We went off to my quarters. I grabbed a pair of pints and we sat at my table. She poured some wine and we started catching up as if no time had passed. I told her about some of my cases, and she told me about the events she was helping shape back in France. I actually had to keep track of time because I had trials coming up.

"Go ahead, we can talk more later," she said. "The war is almost over. I'll have some time now."

Jeanne has been a great friend since then. She was one of the patron saints of France, so she kept busy, but never too busy to be with others. It was actually strange to find out how she viewed me. First, she was actually jealous of the bond between Michael and I. She felt she could never be as close as that. I couldn't explain it, and felt she could easily have him as a big brother, too. But they never really got as close as that. I guess it's true -- you can't pick how friendships go.

The other thing she mentioned to me, around the start of the 18th Century, was that she was going to miss hanging around with me.

"What?" I said, looking up from the billiard table.

We were in a pub in England. I became friends with the family there, and it was now a place where angels and Advocates could hang out on Earth. Great food, great drink, and plenty to do, from darts to billiards. Billiards was Jeanne's favorite, I think mostly because she could brag about its rich French history. King Louis XI had the first indoor table. "Billiard" came from a French word for "stick", and the cue came from the French word for "tail"....oy, gevalt! You see how much I've listened to that?!?

"I said, I'm going to miss you," she said, holding the stick and looking forlorn. A lot more forlorn than I'd ever known her.

I straightened up. "I'm not going anywhere."

She started speaking perfect French. I'd have no trouble understanding her, but the other Brits here wouldn't know what we were saying. "How long have you been an Advocate?"

"A little over three and a half centuries," I answered in French.

She didn't say anything. She didn't have to. I just shook my head. "I'm not burning out."

"You will one day. All Advocates do."

"Jacob Abramson has been Advocating almost twice as long as I have."

"The odds are against it."

I let out a hearty laugh and returned my attention to the table. "That's rich, a woman who wound up commanding the French army talking about likely odds."

"Burn," she sniffed.

I looked up at her again. She looked really upset. This wasn't the time to make light. When I crossed over, I'd still see Michael once in a while. But Jeanne was a saint. She had surrendered her petition in devotion and service to God, and would never enter Heaven. I straightened up, set the cue on the table, and walked over to her. I touched her hand, and she looked at me. I saw the exact same fear that I felt all those years ago after her trial.

"We still have plenty of time to be friends," I told her. "You don't want to feel pain when I'm gone?"

She nodded.

"Then let's do more. So that, when you think of me, you don't think that I'm gone. You remember when I was there."

She dropped the cue and wrapped me in a hug. I returned it happily. One of the guys in the pub apparently thought this was sexy. There's at least one in every crowd.

"Hey, you two! You want people getting the wrong idea about you?"

We looked at him as we separated. I smiled, "No sex for me, thanks. I'm British."

Jeanne jerked her thumb at me and said, "No sex with her, thanks. She's British."

He was dumbfounded, and we erupted into hysterics. We resumed our game. When we tallied everything up, it actually ended in a tie.

Just like me. Two peas in a pod.

DAY OF JUDGMENT

The 18th Century was a very interesting time to be around. Upheaval everywhere as power structures were challenged and defied. Led by people who felt the system was unfair. Revolution was the word of the day.

And that was just among the living.

In the Afterlife, similar ill winds were blowing. They had been going for a while, long before my own death. While the Reformation was still centuries away, a split was already occurring between the Churches in the Celestial Courts and the religious leaders of the time on Earth. The Catholic Church had not been as concerned with literal translations of the Bible and did not have that "circle the wagons" mentality that gave us Celestials fits. Good thing, too. Some individuals like Saint Thomas Aquinas (an amazingly clever guy – I have yet to win a single mock trial against him) never would have become what they did if it had. But other religious leaders who died and became Church Advocates were becoming resentful. Heaven was a reward and there was lots of leeway, with spirits that hadn't been particularly religious getting in. After all, God wanted everyone to have a Heavenly reward. The Churches started feeling these people hadn't done enough. A Heavenly reward was something to earn, not lose.

The Churches felt the system was flawed, and they'd been trying to stop the flow of nonbelievers and those they just didn't think were good enough for a long time. So when unrepentant Atheist Hannah Singer popped up around the middle of the 14th Century, they quickly hatched a plan, using me to exploit the covenant God made with His people and dismantle the Celestial Courts. And had they tried it on someone else, it might have worked. I represented myself and won, alone and without a leader. My arguments were quickly adopted as precedents, making it easier for others to claim their Heavenly reward. That was bad enough for them. When they found out I decided to postpone my Heavenly reward to become a Celestial, they were livid. They did everything they could to frustrate me so I would quit. I refused to break, and after I led the opposition of Torquemada's petition and won, they accepted I wasn't going anywhere until I was good and ready and eased up the pressure a little bit.

Part of the reason they gave up trying to force me out was they couldn't do it. The other part was that it took them away from their plotting to dismantle the Celestial Courts. Bubbling up to the top of this group of conspirators was Thomas Calvary. About one hundred years earlier, I had squared off with him in a special court over a mermaid's soul. He tried to make her vanish into nothingness, and thanks to me, he failed spectacularly. He had been very nice to Celestials, but at that point, I became his archenemy. He swiftly pushed his way through the ranks to become senior Church and went out of his way to face me in as many trials as he could, no matter how trivial. The courtesy he extended to others was gone for me. The only bright side is that he continued to argue for his usual fates of penance and guardian angel duty. He knew asking for Casting was almost a sure loser against me.

That was just one of several turning points from that trial. Another was my junior in the case, Joshua Hunter. He became my assistant because he wanted to learn how I approached cases and figured it would make him a better Advocate. The kid was a really fast learner. I watched a few of his trials as time went on and he just advanced by leaps and bounds. Another was St. Michael, my boss and surrogate big brother. He had always been impressed with my mind and my assertiveness. But there was this uncertainty as well. It's like having a horse that looks like a great runner, but you aren't sure it can really go the distance and win. After that trial, my grey area cases went up in number, and Michael's attitude made a subtle switch from, "Can she pull it off?" to "How will she pull it off?" It's almost my proudest day, life or afterlife.

So, I had gotten to a point where I could actually settle in. I had routine. This was my job, I was good at it, I knew what to do and when to do it. The only problem with routine is that you miss things. Little details whose significance escapes you.

It was the later part of the 18th Century when Michael came by my quarters with another batch of scrolls for me. They were cases he wanted me to advocate. He set them on my table. I reached for one to read when Michal cleared his throat.

I stopped and raised my eyes to him. He simply shook his head.

I looked back at the scrolls and moved my hand over to another. I looked him. He shook his head again.

I kept my eyes on him as I moved my hand around. When it got to a certain scroll, Michael started nodding. Apparently, this was where I was supposed to start.

I opened the scroll to start reading, but I got hung up on the name at the top. "'Andrew Adams.' Really?"

"Yep."

Adams was a Church. He'd been around for a little over a hundred years. Protestant background, Calvinism and predestination were his stock in trade. Not a bad guy. I mean, he was a pain to argue against in court, but outside of it, he was okay if you ran with that sort of crowd. "When did he vacate? Or has he vacated yet?"

"Short time ago. Resigned, filed his petition, marched straight to Penance Hall, very efficient."

Something about that struck me as odd. It was too efficient. "Resigning under protest?"

"Sure seems like it. I mean, he wasn't rising through the ranks quickly, but he was going up. He seemed fine with it. No one was really expecting it."

I skimmed over the scroll. "Nothing to it. Is there some reason I'm getting this case?"

"He requested you."

"Well, that's flattering. Odd, but flattering."

"He also requested protective guard."

That was surprising. "Getting a little paranoid, is he?"

"Maybe. Maybe not. Lots of Churches are hovering around him."

"Trial been requested yet?"

"Churches have, we haven't. I wanted to see how tough you thought it was."

"Their Recommended Fate?"

"Cast Down."

I gave the scroll a good read. Not a lot to it, no potential problems I could see. I was smelling an ambush. And I was the best at shutting those down.

"Request a trial. I got this in the bag."

We left my quarters and headed for the Celestial Courts. Michael was going to put in his trial request for Adams, I had a couple of cases to hear. Those Petitioners had been soldiers for a British colony fighting for independence, a place that would come to be known as the United States. I don't spend much time on Earth, so hearing about such massive changes, history being written as it happened, was amazing to me.

The trials were over quickly. Soldiers and warriors have some differences from regular trials, but nothing special. I was coming out of court when I ran into Warren Stratford, another Celestial. He was carrying a scroll. "Adams trial is set to begin as soon as council for both sides gets there."

"Are you my junior?"

"If you need me to."

No point in getting careless. "Sure. Lead on."

We started walking to the courtroom. "Anything special I should know?" I asked.

"Nothing anyone can see."

"Who's the opposition?"

"Dale Virtue."

"Hmph," I said. "This should be quick." Virtue was a very easygoing, non-confrontational Church. I got along well with him, but I wasn't going to let my guard down.

Trial started, and I got my first hint that something was really wrong. Adams had nothing in his record. Nothing. Virtue's case turned on what we call "interpreted" sins – that is, they weren't sins because they violated the universal sense of Right and Wrong. Murder is an absolute sin. Rape is an absolute sin. Enjoying an alcoholic drink is interpreted, because whether or not it qualifies as a sin depends on the individual church the person belongs to.

Virtue was arguing that a lot of things Adams did while alive were sins. And he was really stretching. And he knew it. A lot of these things, the Churches didn't contest under normal circumstances. The Tribunal didn't deliberate at all, immediate approval of petition. As soon as the gavel came down to end the session, Adams stalked out of the dock and through the

Petitioner's exit, not even looking at anything else.

"Well, that was rude," Warren said.

"Don't let it get to you," I said. "I'd bolt, too, if I was subjected to a payback trial."

He looked at me. "What do you mean, 'payback?'"

I looked at Virtue. He was just picking up his scrolls. "The Churches were just trying to put Adams through the wringer," I said as I watched. "No real case, but they couldn't just say, 'No contest.'"

"So, they deliberately wasted Adams' time."

"Yup," I said. Virtue was getting ready leave when I waved him over.

Virtue came up, still seeming calm and clueless. "Look, don't get mad at me."

"I'm not mad at you. You were handed the case, weren't you?"

"How could you tell?"

"I can tell when an Advocate has a personal stake in a case."

Virtue looked at the Petitioner's exit. "I have no idea why this case was even contested in the first place."

We chatted casually for a moment more, then set off. Virtue went his way, towards the Church Campus, Warren and I were heading for the Office Of Records to return all my scrolls. When had gotten around a couple of corners when I felt it.

Deep inside me. By my heart. A pull.

It meant only one thing.

I politely asked Warren to take the scrolls back for me, I had something to do. No problem, he took them without question, and we went our separate ways. I got around a corner and just kept going. I needed an isolated place. There clearly weren't supposed to be any witnesses, and given how busy the courts were right now, there were too many casual walkers going by. I started going up to courtroom doors and listening in. After a few tries, I found a court that didn't seem to be in use. I went inside. No one around. I shut the door, then gasped as the feeling in my heart burst and enveloped my body in motion and light.

When the light faded out, I was standing outside the Gates Of Heaven. St. Peter was standing there, along with Jesus.

And a third person. Adams.

They had been waiting for me, they were watching where I would materialize. I strode up to the trio, and promptly dropped to one knee in front of Jesus and Peter. "Yes, what is your will?"

"Well, Hannah," Jesus said. "Adams has something to tell you."

I rose up, looking at Adams in confusion. "What is it?"

Adams looked infuriated. More than I'd ever seen him. "You probably are wondering what my trial was all about."

"I will admit, it did seem unusual."

"You figured it was a payback trial, right?"

"Yeah. If I ask what you did, would you tell me?"

"The Churches are going to dismantle the Celestial Courts."

My jaw dropped. "Are you serious?"

"Completely. I was involved in some general brainstorming until I figured out what they were up to. I wanted out. They kept an eye on me. Wanted to make sure I wouldn't ruin their element of surprise. So I petitioned."

"Are you going to wait to go back, or just go to Heaven?" He could delay going to Heaven so he could still Advocate. That was my situation.

"I'm going in."

I felt it then. Fear. Real and unmistakable fear. Whatever was going on, there was a good chance of success. "What are they planning?"

"They are going to say the Celestial Courts violate God's covenant."

"On what grounds?"

"Because the covenant was supposed to give man dominion over the fates of their souls. The Celestial Courts change that. Therefore, it must not be allowed to exist."

My mind was already sorting through pieces. "This will have to be heard by God."

"Yes. Angels can be argued to have a conflict of interest."

"Not only that, but God's will cannot be overrode. They can get a retrial with angels. They can't with God."

"This is why I'm telling you this, Singer," Adams said. He walked up to me, looking me square in the eyes. "Michael needs to know this. Forewarned is forearmed. They are waiting for the right time to move and will ask for an immediate trial. They want to catch the Celestials unaware. Michael will need the absolute best there. He has to stop them."

"Why are you telling me this? You don't like the Celestial Courts, either." He was very vocal in his opposition to the Courts. He was the last one I expected to try and preserve them.

"Yes, I think the Celestial Courts are wrong and should be gone. But not like this. I want them replaced with something better, not destroyed by trickery. Whatever my feelings, this just isn't right."

My mind reeled. I didn't know what to think. I needed more information. But I couldn't leave just yet. Once Adams crossed over into Heaven, he would never be back. I had to make sure there was nothing else he could tell me before he was lost to me forever. "Is there anything else that will help?"

"The whole thing is Calvary's idea. And he's specifically planning on you being at the trial."

I felt a queasy feeling in my stomach. Calvary went out of his way to make me miserable, to make my cases harder. And the more I refused to break, the harder he tried.

Adams noticed my unease. "Listen, you're smart, Singer. So do the smart thing. Once you tell Michael about this, claim your reward. Get into Heaven as soon as you can. Once the Courts are gone, your approved petition will be worthless. You will either need to stand trial again with the Churches, or you might be Cast Down without a trial."

In a flash, I banished the feelings from my body. I felt my expression change. It was now the one that appears when the trial is hard, the odds are long, and the Churches are almost guaranteed to win. "No! Michael is going to need me! The Celestials are going to need me! And if my only chance of Eternal Life is something the Churches are offering, I'd rather be in Hell!"

Adams blinked. "You don't really mean that."

"Wrong. I know about Hell. All about it. This isn't hyperbole, I know exactly what I'm saying."

Adams looked afraid for me. "You don't know what you're losing."

"I'm not losing anything. Because the Churches won't win."

"You're a fool, Singer."

"No. Calvary is the fool. And I'm going to expose him for it once and for all. When this is over, one of us will no longer be an Advocate. And I'm going to make it him!"

This would be a good time to explain something about God and how He handles His creation. The question most people have at this point is, "If He's God, why doesn't He just say to the Churches, 'The Celestial Courts are staying, so suck it up?'"

The simple answer is, He can.

And no one wants Him to.

God specifically engineered the world for souls to learn and forge their own identities with. That means people have to be allowed to do their own thing, for better or for worse. God can get involved and will do some miracles here and there. But He's very limited in what He can do. If He overrides how His own creation works too much, it is no longer our own lives and our own world, it is His, and we are just cogs in the machine. We lose our rights to have lives. Choices. A soul.

If God were to take charge of the world and our lives, it would be over. Reality itself would unravel. That includes the Earth, Heaven, everything. It would reset existence itself. That means the rewards people earned would be gone. Heaven would be gone. Hell would be gone, and Lucifer and his minions would be free of the consequences of their choices.

This is why we Celestials fight so hard for the Celestial Courts. People have a tendency to think that living for others and living for God are two separate things. They are not. In fact, living for others is our primary responsibility to God. He made us many to live with and be there for each other, not to take advantage of each other. It is the whole reason the covenant is honored so highly. It enables us to exist and live. To be who we are instead of God's puppets. We are not assigned our roles, and it makes us and our lives and our afterlives better.

So, God telling everyone what to do, to use a modern expression, is the nuclear option. And everyone does what they can to keep that button from being pushed.

I watched Adams go through the Gates Of Heaven. Sometimes, you can catch a glimpse of what is on the other side. I didn't even try this time.

I turned to Jesus and Peter. "Please, I need to talk to Michael."

"Done," Jesus said. I felt the energy swell and the light brightened. When they faded, I was in Michael's chambers.

Michael was alone, sitting at his desk and going over some paperwork. When I appeared without notice, he jumped from his chair, willed his flaming sword to appear, and took up a battle stance. He quickly realized who I was. As he willed his sword away, he looked off to the side. "Oh. So, THAT'S what that feels like."

I quickly moved for one of the chairs in front of his desk. "We've got a huge problem."

Michael's hand shot out. "There's a tack there!"

Conflicting actions in my brain made me stop dead as I sorted through everything. It took a moment for me to realize what he meant. I picked up the tack on the chair and set it on the end of Michael's desk. Michael flicked his hand at his door, vanishing it into the wall and locking everyone else out. The two of us sat at the same time.

I got right to the point. "The Churches are going to try to dismantle the Celestial Courts."

Michael looked off to the side. "Well, it's been a few hundred years. I guess we were due. How do you know this?"

I recounted the discussion I had with Adams before he crossed over. By the time I was done, Michael had folded his hands and was propping them under his chin. He was deeply in thought. "I have to admit, that's pretty sharp."

"We can't let them do it, Michael."

"You're right, Hannah," he said, standing up and walking around to me. "We need a consultation."

"With who?"

"With my boss." And Michael snapped his fingers.

A shaft of light angled into Michael's chambers, coming from beyond the ceiling corner at the back. It started to swell, flooding out everything as it went. It reached my chair, and I felt it start to vanish beneath me. I jumped to my feet, staring at the source as it continued to expand. Soon, everything else about the room was gone.

Eventually, the middle of the light started to open, like the middle of a tornado. As it extended, a crystal staircase became visible. It stretched up towards the light source. The stairs themselves eventually stopped – you couldn't see the landing, but you knew it was there. And I felt that presence. God Himself. I was just a few dozen yards from standing before Him.

No matter how many times I stand before and talk with God, I always hesitate before meeting Him each time. My first reaction is always that I'm unworthy, even though I never would have made it through the light if I wasn't. I looked at Michael. He looked at me with complete pride. I swallowed and nodded my head. Side by side, the two of us climbed the staircase.

Once we got to the top, we were in the presence of God Himself. If you limit yourself to your eyes, your ears, your immediate senses, God is just a white glow with a gentle voice. But I can't really describe the rest of Him. There's just no frame of reference.

Michael dropped to one knee, bowing deeply. "Thank you for granting us audience, my Lord."

I snapped out of it and probably set some sort of speed record, dropping to one knee and bowing. I heard Michael chuckle a little. And I sensed God's good-natured amusement. Quickly, I felt Him calming me, reassuring me that I had done nothing wrong and to be at peace.

"What troubles you?" God asked.

Michael started speaking a strange sort of whisper that sounded like several voices saying different things at the same time, but I could comprehend everything he said. From facts to his suspicions, all streamed out in communication with God.

The voice of God drifted through our minds. "The Churches will not succeed. The Celestial Courts will emerge from this stronger than ever."

"How do we make that happen, sir?" Michael asked.

"Hannah must lead."

I couldn't have been more shocked if God had simply dropped me into Hell right then and there. "Sir, no! Michael should lead!"

"An angel cannot lead this time."

Michael spoke gently. "There would be no conflict of interest if I led. Angel or no, I am in charge of the Celestial Courts. My responsibilities outweigh my origin."

God's voice drifted through us again. "The Courts were created for the benefit of humans. It is through a human that the Courts will be protected. It is through a human that the Courts will continue. It is through a human that this will happen."

There's no arguing with God, but my mind was racing like squirrel in a barn fire. Me?!? Save the entire Celestial Court system?!? How?!? I'm not omnipotent! I'm just human! God said the lowliest angel is greater than the highest human! How could I ever do this?!?

I forgot God could read my thoughts. I felt His peace encircling me, calming me, reassuring me. And His words echoing around my head -- "It is through you that the Courts will be protected. It is through you that the Courts will continue. It is through you that this will happen."

I forced my fear from my head. "I will not fail you."

Suddenly, the light of God grew brighter, bleaching out everything around Michael and I. When it faded, we were no longer on bended knee. We were standing in Michael's chambers, everything where it was before.

Michael looked at me and his eyebrows flew up. "Hannah? You okay?"

"Fine. Why?"

"You look really pale."

I tried being flip. "Well, I am dead, remember?"

I didn't fool Michael in the least. Never kid a kidder. Suddenly, Michael's chambers shifted and swirled. When everything settled, we were in my quarters and Michael was offering me a giant, steaming mug. I recognized the scent right way. Jasmine tea. My favorite.

I gently took the mug from him. "Show off."

I took a careful sip as Michael guided me to my couch. I took the corner by my reading lamp, Michael took the middle. I was grateful that my big brother was there for me right then.

I swallowed some more tea and inhaled deeply. "Why does God believe in me so much?"

"Why wouldn't He?"

"He thinks I can defend the Celestial Courts from the Churches."

"He KNOWS you can defend the Celestial Courts from the Churches."

"How can he know that?"

"Well, it's not like this would be the first time for you."

I just swiveled my head to him. "That was luck."

"A fluke?"

"Yeah. An accident."

"It was none of those things, Hannah. It was skill. It was determination. It was intelligence. You were thrown into the worst possible scenario. Everything you thought and knew was wrong, and you were terrified. And yet, you saw through it all. You knew what was happening and what to do.

"Think about this...He's God. He's smarter and more aware than anyone anywhere. There are probably dozens of ways to stop this. He could simply appeal to Calvary, talk with him one on one. He can refuse the trial. And yet He's not. He's going to let the trial happen, and you will lead the defense. You know why?"

I shook my head. "No. Tell me. Please tell me."

Michael smiled. "Because this is the best solution. Not only to affirm the Courts, but also to take the Churches down a few pegs."

"Blind faith is the strongest faith of all."

"God doesn't have faith, Hannah. He has patience. Our question is, what will happen? His question is, when will it happen? And for this, you are the one He knows will make it happen fastest and in a way that can't be undone."

I took another long drink. "What if I fail?"

"That's not going to happen, Hannah."

"There's always a chance."

"There is no element of chance here. God knows how this has to end, and He knows what it will take for that end to come. He doesn't think you can pull it off, He KNOWS you will pull it off. You winning this is as sure as the sun rising."

"What about humans being too unpredictable?"

Michael just looked at me. He stood up and leaned close to my face, touching my nose with his finger. "I'll give you a hint -- God knows all of us better than we know ourselves. He even knows me better, and I'm an archangel. Do you really know yourself well enough to be that certain that you'll fail?"

Michael then turned and walked out of my quarters. I kept drinking my tea, trying to figure out how to spin mental straw into courtroom gold.

Michael and I spent every spare moment we could brainstorming. He brought in other angels and trusted Advocates for mock trials. St. Thomas Aquinas even sat in. I watched him defend a mock trial against me, seven angels, and four Advocates. He won before anyone knew it was over, and his expression didn't even change. The guy is a rock.

I asked him if he would lead.

"No," he said. "I heard about what God wants. You're to lead this."

I stepped on his last couple of words as my next question rushed from my lips. "How about junioring? Will you junior for me?"

"You would defer too much to me. I would only technically be a junior. In reality, I'd be lead. That is not how it's to be." He noticed my expression. "Brave heart, Singer. The trial is in expert hands."

Greeeeeeeeeeeeeat….

A trial by God works a bit differently. As soon as trial was ready to begin, God would draw the representatives. Usually, Michael would choose the lead at that moment, but thanks to advance notice, I was already set. The next question was who would be my juniors. I had to think quickly. There was no telling when the trial would start, and I didn't want my delay to cost me.

The first junior I chose was Joshua Hunter. He became my assistant for a while so he could learn more about how to handle cases. He was now a top notch Advocate, recently leading his first trial in the shadow court and demolishing the Church case.

The second junior I selected was Galileo Galilei. Galileo was a firebrand who enjoyed honking off the religious types. He was good at distracting religious bodies, taking advantage of their assumptions and not giving anything he didn't have to. He was a natural.

"Anyone else you can think of?" I asked Michael.

"I wasn't really thinking," Michael said.

"Thanks for having my back," I sneered at him.

"You could have every Celestial there as a junior and it won't make any difference. It all comes down to you, Hannah."

Hunter and Galileo had the same mindset. While they were taking it seriously, they both explicitly stated that they doubted they would get to say anything. "After all, you are lead," said Hunter.

I looked at Galileo. He just nodded.

The amount of faith everyone was placing in me boggled my mind. To keep myself calm, I took extra trials. Calvary wondered what was going on that my case load was suddenly so high. He continued to pull rank and face off against me. He was clearly hoping to burn me out. But even if he was getting to me, I would have forced it from my head. I had been made the focal point of this trial. I refused to let everyone down.

There were no new trials to hear. Literally. Between my handling of cases and the sheer number I was taking on, the backlog of petitions was actually cleared. I had nothing to do now but keep my thoughts focused. I went to the Water Gardens, my favorite place to think. The sound of the flowing water, controlled and gentle, was a great model.

As I walked around, my mind drifted to the upcoming trial. I was still working on further twists when Harold Davis, one of the good Churches, called out from behind me, "Hey, Hannah! You might want to...."

I turned to look at him, wondering what he would say. And my eyes went wide. Harold was just standing there, frozen in place like a statue. His eyes had a faraway look. Like a trance.

I felt it faintly then. A buildup from deep inside my heart.

The time of trial was upon me.

I started walking towards the Celestial Courts. I had to talk to Michael. Just a little reassurance from my big brother that everything would be fine. The buildup was becoming noticeable. I started jogging. Others around the grounds would see me and wave as I went past. Then they would trance out as well. It was like I was leaving paralysis in my wake. The distance between myself and the outer rim of the trancing effect was getting smaller. It was catching up to me. I couldn't let that happen yet. I needed a little more time. I broke into a full sprint.

I tore through the Celestial Courts, racing for Michael's chambers. Down the halls, I could hear footsteps stopping and voices silencing. Some people couldn't even finish saying, "What's going on?", before going quiet. The wake was closing in on me. I could hear the silence getting closer. I could feel it pouring in, like waters through a trough. My heart was vibrating with energies. It was almost time.

I saw the door for Michael's chambers ahead. I prayed it was unlocked, I wasn't sure what a delay would cost me. I got to the door and twisted the handle. It was unlocked. I dashed in and slammed the door shut behind me.

Once the door clicked closed, I saw Michael's chambers. There were several Advocates and angels in here, all turning to look at me. Banners were everywhere, proclaiming, "Congratulations, Hannah!" and "You did it, Hannah!" Streamers stretched across the room. Michael was standing behind his desk, wearing a very formal suit and a silly commodore's hat. A variety of sweets were on his desk, along with bags of confetti, waiting to be torn open and thrown around. Michael had his hands wrapped around the neck of one of several champagne bottles sitting in a tub of ice, twirling it back and forth. He looked up, saw me, and smiled. "See you on the other side, Hannah."

I felt myself smile as confidence flowed into me like warm honey. Then I froze. I felt the effect take hold. Suddenly, bright light flooded my vision and I felt weightless. Then, as quickly as it began, it ended. I was standing in a great courtroom. Everything was crystal. Unlike a regular

Celestial courtroom, this one was shaped like a half-circle, with the two sides against the curve on the far end, and a grand open space in the middle of the flat end. There was no Gallery, but I felt everyone watching. The paralysis effect was God taking everyone out of time -- the trial would be over in an instant, but the events would still play out. Every consciousness in the Valley Of Death, the Celestial Courts, everywhere here, could see and hear the trial. No one would miss a detail.

I looked at the table in front of me. It followed the curve of the wall. My juniors were already here. The scrolls and other files that I wanted for the trial were here as well.

I looked quickly to the Church table. Calvary was in the lead position. He took one look at the scrolls on my table and realized what it meant. "NO!"

I held a scroll like a miniature long rifle and pretended to shoot him with it, yanking it up like it recoiled.

Calvary was enraged. "I hate how smart you are."

"Burn!" I told him. I faced the front where God would be and deployed my wings. The time for being uncertain and afraid was over.

It's star time.

God suddenly appeared in the grand open space in front of us. Calvary and his team of five juniors deployed their wings. Hunter and Galileo were a beat behind. They leaned over to me. "Instructions?" Hunter asked.

"No prisoners," I stated simply. They nodded and went back to their positions.

There was no real procedure to follow at this level. Still, I waited for Calvary to start. Just to make sure what I was reacting to.

God spoke. "You have requested this hearing because you feel the Celestial Courts should be disbanded."

Everyone reacts to God's voice differently. What you hear in it depends on what your character is like and how you view Him. If you believe He is merciless and vengeful, the voice is booming and terrifying. If you believe He is loving and merciful, the voice is calm and reassuring. You can't fake your reaction. As the anxiety left me, I looked at the Churches. They stood ramrod straight, some eyes wide with fear. Was that a sheen a sweat forming on Calvary's forehead?

Calvary swallowed, then spoke. His voice was far more timid than I had ever known. "Yes, sir. The Courts violate the covenant."

Steady on, Hannah....

"How do the Courts violate the covenant?" To me, God was asking. To Calvary, God was demanding.

Calvary was silent for another moment before he spoke again. "You established churches on Earth. Religious leaders who know your will and do you bidding. They were charged with helping developing your people and teaching your Word. And yet, our works are for naught. Because the Celestial Courts get in the way. They can change the outcome that is sought of our work. There are simply too many who do not deserve the rewards they receive. They don't deserve souls. They don't deserve Heavenly rewards. The Celestials themselves defy your will. You have stated what is needed to be in your company for all eternity. Most of those who are being granted eternal life have not followed those instructions. If we are truly responsible for your people, we should determine who is worthy and who isn't, not a group of Celestials who do not live among them or teach anything, just reward their ignorance."

In order to win this, in order to preserve the Courts, I couldn't argue my points to God. This wasn't about getting a decision from God. That would be the first step towards undoing reality. I had to destroy Calvary's points, or at least enough of them that his request was just a dream, not a practical way to address the fates of souls. If Calvary had nothing to argue, God had nothing to listen to, and everything would go back as it was.

Usually, I try to finesse my opponents, move in carefully while watching for traps and counters. Not this time. I had a boulder on the hill, and yanked the chock out. "You want to make yourselves into gods."

Calvary looked like I just accused him of dining on slow roasted babies. He faced God and panicked. "Absolutely not! We just want the duties that go with our responsibilities! We teach that devotion to God is the only way to get into Heaven! Celestials undermine that! What good is it to teach something that is disregarded?"

The boulder was picking up speed. "You cannot guarantee salvation with your teaching. Your teachings are ignored when convenient."

"People know God created them and they are to serve Him. We teach that very well. Our lessons last from the cradle to the grave."

The boulder was right on top of him. "You also teach that extramarital sex is a sin, and that hasn't stopped."

SQUISH!

Calvary staggered up and started up the hill again. "We do not teach that, people choose to do that."

"Which is what we Celestials argue. So your alternative is the same as the system you wish to replace."

"You excuse frailty and reward weakness with salvation. We would not."

I pulled the chocks from another boulder. "Pope Innocent VIII."

"Who?"

"Pope Innocent VIII had two kids, and they lived with him in the Vatican."

Calvary looked at me and smiled. "That all you got, Singer?"

He wasn't trying to stop me, he wanted me to continue. Big, BIG mistake. I obliged. "Paul III made two of his grandsons cardinals while they were teens."

"Anything else?"

"Pope Sergius III ordered the deaths of Christophorus, his predecessor, and Leo V, the next predecessor, so he could be pope. Leo was caught because Christophorus imprisoned him so he could install himself as pope. From 882 to

1046, there were thirty-seven different popes."

"Aw, all that research and fire, and your ad hominem attack is for nothing."

"And what flaws can my argument possibly have?"

He didn't see the avalanche coming at him. "That is about the papacy. It has nothing to do with the Celestial Courts."

"Humans reward themselves for their bad behavior and punish others for the same sins. And you are saying you can be trusted to pass judgment on yourselves?"

Calvary's expression was a thing of beauty and a joy forever. It was like he finally noticed my vast well of resentment, and that I was drinking deep. I looked at him, pure fury radiating from me. "You're not playing with kids anymore, Calvary," I snarled at him.

He was panicked. He was desperate. He tried to stall for time. "Well, it's not like the alternative is better."

I immediately knew where he was going. I readied to hit him as soon as he said it. "Oh, dry up. What can possibly be wrong with the set up for the Celestial Courts?"

"Because most Celestials are human. Some angels argue, but not many and not often. The will of God and the faith He puts in us to govern ourselves is overridden by flawed humans. You just don't want to let go of the leash."

Cute. Trying to paint my arguments with the same brush I used on his. "Wow. And you said my ad hominem attack was a waste of effort."

"It is not a waste. It cuts to the very heart of your statements about humans being fit to judge other humans."

"We don't judge," I told him. "The Tribunal does. They can and do override our recommendations. They are made of angels, and the lowliest angel is superior to the greatest human. Who would you rather have deciding your fate?"

"You influence the angels," he shot back. "We have a say because this is our fate on the line. Celestials interfere with that."

"So, angels are actually inferior to humans."

"I didn't say that!"

"You implied it. That we Celestials of human origin are such expert manipulators that angels can be swayed by us."

"You yourself have gotten many undeserving individuals in, so I would say that is true."

I did a quick adjustment. My first impulse was to argue about who was deserving and who wasn't. But I thought better of it. That would just distract from the main point. We weren't putting past Petitioners on trial, we were putting the Celestial Courts on trial. Besides, Calvary's statement opened him up to attack, and I went for it.

I shot him a condescending smile. "And you want to manipulate the angels instead of us."

"We don't manipulate."

"If we Celestials are capable of it, so are you. You're as human as we are. So the angels could have ideas about who does or does not deserve Heaven and you could override it. In which case, a counterargument is necessary to make sure your statement isn't flawed. That's what we Celestials do. The Celestial Courts are necessary to mercy, fairness, and justice. QED."

Calvary blanched. Once again, I'd seized control of his argument and twisted it against him. The high ground he had perched on was quickly crumbling away under my pick axe. He knew the best he could do now was lose with some ambiguity, so that the Churches could hatch another plan and try again later. But he also knew my MO for big cases. I had a surprise waiting for him, and I was going to hammer him with it sooner or later. If he used up his arguments and I countered them all first, there'd be no revisiting later.

He looked at me. I knew what it meant. He was going to try and make me play my ace and pray that he could trump it. It was the worst move he could make. I just stood and waited.

"The Celestial Courts themselves are a good idea. But the Celestials are putting themselves ahead of the covenant."

My ears perked at this. I couldn't believe it. He was positioning himself right where my ultimate argument would do the most damage. Merry Christmas, Hannah! Here's a gift for you!

Calvary hesitated a moment. I guess he saw my smile. But he soldiered on. "The covenant you made with man is sacred. It is important. It must be upheld. It is what protects us from error, knowing that our mistakes will be excused, not held against us...."

I looked to God and stated, "Move to strike the covenant from consideration."

Calvary just looked at me. His eyes had the look of the damned. All his anger, all his fear, all gone. There was nothing left but acceptance that this was how things were, like an animal cornered by a hungry predator. His voice barely a whisper, he asked, "...on what grounds?"

"The covenant applies to those living on earth. This is the Afterlife. The covenant does not apply here."

I stepped out from behind the table, walking up to Calvary. He watched, hypnotized, as I slowly closed the space between us. "God made the covenant with the living. When you die, you become a spirit as God made you. Your time on Earth is over, as is the protection of the covenant."

I paused for a moment, then lunged for the throat. "You are not seeking to scale back the Celestial Courts! You are looking to expand the covenant, applying it to areas and things it was never meant to cover!"

"It is supposed to grant us control over our destinies!"

He was struggling, but my jaws had locked. "You don't want it to control your destinies, you want it to control others' destinies! The covenant is supposed to grant mercy! That mistakes will be understood and forgiven! You want to use it to eliminate that mercy, so that rigid laws that punish those you disagree with will be upheld! You want to use the Lord God Almighty! You want to place your own values and judgment ahead of His! You want to usurp God!"

Calvary was leaning against the wall. I was right on top of him, my face barely an inch from his. His eyes darted to God. "No! We are your agents on Earth! We are your chosen! We're supposed to win!"

Listening closely, I heard the collective gasp of everyone in the afterlife hearing this. My voice lowered. No need to overdo it, I had this in the bag. "You're supposed to win? Is this why you are challenging the Courts? Because you're tired of losing?"

Calvary closed his eyes. He wasn't looking at anyone. His lower lip was starting to quiver.

I smirked. "You aren't winning, so you're going to change the rules to favor you." I leaned close to his ear and whispered, but I know everyone heard me say, "You're cheating."

Calvary snapped his head to his juniors. They looked at him, completely lost. They even started moving down. They wanted nothing to do with him now.

Calvary looked back at me, pleading in his eyes. "We're supposed to win. We state the facts. You find exceptions. What's the point of rules with so many exceptions?"

"You are not worthy of God."

Calvary gasped like I'd struck him in the stomach. In a way, I did. In a flash, he broke from me and raced up to God, falling on his knees and bowing before Him. "I want to be worthy. Forgive me! Please! I'm begging you!"

I watched Calvary with cold detachment. It was over. All that was left was for God to make His formal pronouncement.

Eventually, the voice came. "You were asked to explain why the Courts violate the covenant. You have not done so. The Courts shall remain."

Suddenly, light started streaming from God. Shards of light, millions of them, each with a different color of the rainbow, racing out and through us all. More appeared, moving faster. They quickly became so numerous that the courtroom itself could no longer be seen. Then a burst of white light pushed out from the center. When it faded, I was back in Michael's chambers. The judgment had been made.

Michael bounced up to me. "And you thought you couldn't do it!"

He slammed his commodore's hat on my head, and we hugged each other tight as his chambers erupted into noise and confetti.

Michael likes to talk about the unpredictability of humans. The fallout from the trial was a textbook example of it.

The party in Michael's chambers finally died out. What a relief. Everyone with champagne bottles aimed them like rifles and popped the corks at each other. Thank God I'm invulnerable now, or I just know I'd have a mouse above my right eyebrow.

Hunter and Galileo were a little late to the party, but still showed up.

They looked at me smugly, joining everyone else, especially Michael, in thinking the same thing – I told you so.

After the party, I left and checked my caseload. A couple of really simple cases, nothing to them. I took the scrolls and headed for the Water Gardens. No time to rest, I was needed. I sat and started reviewing, planning my defenses, when I heard someone politely clear his throat behind me.

I turned and saw Henry Gallows standing there. If there was anyone more misnamed than him in the afterlife, I had yet to meet them. Gallows was late fifties without a speck of grey in the hair on his head or the thick mustache on his upper lip. His long, bushy eyebrows that met above his nose. A little overweight, which fit his rounded face and nose. You just wanted to cuddle him like a pillow or teddy bear. He was one of the friendliest Churches and a great guy. Almost never asked for Casting. Calvary was friendly, and it made me suspicious. This guy, I had to remind myself to be suspicious.

"Hello, Gallows," I said. "What brings you around?"

He walked up and extended his hand to me. "Just trying to get off on the right foot."

"What are talking about?"

He lowered his hand. "You didn't hear? Calvary vacated."

My eyes popped and I sprang up. "You're kidding!"

Gallows tilted his head to the side. "Okay, fire away."

He knew I'd have questions. "When did this happen?"

"Just after the trial by God."

I grabbed the scrolls and looked through them. "Figures I wouldn't get his case. No way he'd let me be his Advocate."

"He didn't petition."

"What?!?"

"He didn't petition. He just vacated."

"Where is he?"

"He walked out to the Valley Of Death. That's all anyone knows."

I actually felt a twinge of sympathy for Calvary. He was broken. But that was as far as it went. For everything he said and did, I felt nothing but grim satisfaction.

"All his juniors from the hearing vacated, as well. As well as those who helped formulate the plan to destroy the Courts."

"Will they petition?"

"They will eventually. They're a little afraid. They're hoping the fact that Calvary was the mastermind and they were just helpers will work in their favor."

"Calvary thinks he's going to Hell."

"In a handbasket."

"One that I wove."

"No. Calvary wove it. His arrogance and intolerance bound the whole thing together. It's a lesson I try to keep in mind."

I smiled at him. "You're one of the good ones, Gallows. I don't think you have anything to worry about."

"I'm not just one of the good ones, Singer. The number of vacancies left a vacuum at the top. Guess who's the new senior Church?"

I tilted my head. I tried not to smile. "Interesting."

"Isn't it?" he said. He extended his hand to me again. "Here's hoping I can present mercy as expertly as you do."

Fine, I'll be nice. I took his hand and shook it. There was determination in his grip.

He was actually serious.

He walked away, my mind awash in questions. What was Calvary going to do now? Was Gallows as decent as he acted, or was he like Calvary, a dark heart exposed in certain circumstances?

The only way to answer these questions was time. And in Eternity, there's plenty of it.

DEVIL MAY CARE

A frequent philosophical question is, if you could teach one lesson to all people and they would heed it, what would it be? The most frequent answer is God loves you, no matter who you are and what you have done, and if you seek forgiveness, He will never ever deny you. The second most frequent is the Golden Rule – do unto others as you would have them do unto you. Me? I have a different answer. The lesson Hannah Singer would teach all Christians and want them to remember is this:

The devil is real. He exists. And no one is safe from his influence. Not the living. Not the dead. Not angels. And definitely not humans. If he decides he wants you, fear for your immortal soul.

It was early in my Celestial Advocate career. I was leading regular trials and starting to junior on grey area cases. Everyone was impressed with how quickly I was advancing, especially St. Michael. He figured from how I handled my own trial that I would be a perfect grey Celestial, basic cases were beneath my skill. I sat on some interesting trials, but nothing all that tricky. Juniors are there for backup, they don't usually get involved. I kept my mouth shut out of respect and only jumped in if the momentum of the trial was getting away from the lead. It didn't take long for me to start dealing aces, and everyone was wondering when I'd be leading my first grey case.

I was wondering the same thing. Noah Holman was the senior grey Celestial and my teacher. I asked him, "When will I lead my first grey case?"

"I don't know yet," he shrugged. "You haven't had The Talk yet."

"What's 'The Talk?'"

"I think you'll find out before too long," he said, looking at me cryptically.

I probably could have found out what The Talk was on my own. But Holman's statement implied all greys who lead had had it. If I was continuing to improve, then I'd find out what it was soon enough.

I was leading the opposition to a Petitioner who had killed and robbed a toll taker. During arguments, a putto entered the court and flew right to me. Generally speaking, once trial begins, no one can enter or leave except for these child angels. He clearly had a message for me. "St. Michael wants to see you in his chambers as soon as possible."

The Tribunal ruled, I won, and I stepped out of the courtroom. I started walking to Michael's chambers, not even bothering to return my scrolls. Strictly speaking, I could have called a putto to do it for me, but I never liked the thought of treating them as my servants.

I got to Michael's chambers and rapped on the door. "Come in," he called. There was a strange distance in his voice, nothing I could put my finger on. I opened the door and entered.

There was no one else in there. The lights had been dimmed. Michael has two highback wooden chairs in front of his desk. The farthest one in, he had turned it so it was facing a tapestry hanging on the wall across from the door. I couldn't really see him, but what I could see suggested he was sort of sprawled in the chair, like a rag doll.

I took a quick look at Michael's desk. No scrolls. No petitions. It was unusually clear. This is it, I thought to myself. I'm going to have The Talk.

I closed the door and heard it latch quietly, like it was afraid of drawing attention to itself. Michael's right hand came off the armrest and flicked at the door, vanishing it. "Please sit next to me, Hannah."

I came up carefully. I mean, I knew I was in no danger. But I knew this was something of great import. I wanted to be as reverend as possible. I came on Michael's right and knelt on the floor next to him, facing the tapestry. I stayed silent for a few moments. When Michael didn't speak, I turned to look at him. He was smirking at me. "I said, 'sit next to me.'"

I blushed and stood. I dragged the other chair over and sat down in it, Michael and I facing the tapestry. I sat at attention, back straight, feet together, hands clasped in my lap. I couldn't see what was so important about the tapestry, but I knew that had to be it.

Michael let out a soft sigh, and said, "You've examined this before, haven't you, Hannah?"

"Yes." The tapestry seemed completely random. Lines curved, weaved, and squiggled this way and that, no real rhyme or reason, other than some general colors in three layers.

"Focus on it. Meditate. What do you see?"

I did as he said, feeling the flow of my consciousness. I thought I saw something, part of the wall hanging coming into sharper relief. I sensed its flow and followed what I felt. It was like my mind and the wall hanging were talking to each other. I saw order to it. Lines were actually like shadows. Contours were like walls. While still a two dimensional image, it started looking three dimensional. I started seeing what it was. I whispered, "It's a map...."

"Yes, Hannah."

I continued to build the right frame of mind. I couldn't will the image to appear, I had no control over it. I had to catch up with it. Eventually, the top layer clarified. I recognized the structures and my jaw fell open. "It's the Afterlife."

"Yes, Hannah."

I saw the Valley Of Death in its entirety. When I first arrived here, my friend Artie and I spent time exploring it. And yet, despite how much we traveled, we'd barely scratched the surface. I saw the Celestial Courts. And I got my best view of what was on the other side of the gates of Heaven. My God, it was beautiful. For a brief moment, I was tempted to pray to Jesus and claim my Heavenly reward right then and there. But I remembered my duties, how I wanted to advocate and help those in deep trouble like I had been. I pushed myself back. Heaven could wait. It had to wait.

"Still with me, Hannah?" Michael asked. I heard the nervousness in his voice.

"Yeah. I'm not going anywhere," I said, forcing the disappointment from my mind.

Did I just hear Michael sigh with relief? I ignored it and kept looking. I saw the Earth itself. I only knew a tiny sliver of it when I was alive. I knew it was much bigger, with more people and places than I could imagine. Now, I saw it all. The people. The cities. The frontiers soon to be conquered. I saw the planets of the solar system, I saw how the galaxies moved. It was mind boggling.

A thought occurred to me. This was a map of the Afterlife. I saw Heaven and I saw Earth. I took a fortifying breath and looked to the bottom.

And I caught my first glimpse of Hell.

Hell is simply an abstract concept. People can't imagine it. Just as they can't conceive of the perfect paradise that is Heaven, they can't conceive of the horrors of Hell. It's worse than any nightmare, worse than any curse. Because of that, it's easy to simply overlook Hell, to not dwell on it, to act like it isn't there. Especially because so many people either don't believe they'll go there or don't believe it exists.

I felt it. Fear. It was unimaginable, worse than anything when I was alive, worse than my appearance in the Valley Of Death. Looking over the map, it was a horrible land. Lakes and rivers of fire everywhere. Rocky terrain. Areas that looked like nesting places, from which angels with blackened wings – demons – resided. And a section of opulence and luxury. It was beautiful. Even more so than the Celestial Courts. Amazing designs, fantastic materials. Areas for activities of all kinds, from pits that seemed to be for gladiatorial combat to rooms filled with soft fabrics and cushions for sex, individually or en mass. Within this area, anything human desire could conceive of could happen.

"Yes, Hannah. That is where Lucifer is."

"The devil?"

"If you want to think of him as such," Michael said. There was no mistaking the sadness in his voice.

"What was he like? I mean, before the Fall?"

Michael's eyes looked distant. "He was the most beautiful angel. Still is. Being the leader means he gets the best of everything. He feels it befits him. That he's entitled to it."

I kept studying the landscape. I felt confused.

"Ask, Hannah," came Michael's uncharacteristically quiet voice.

"What does he want from humans? Why does he tempt humans? How can he even be a threat? He has nothing to offer."

Michael reached out and patted my hand. He took it back, and I felt the urge to grab onto it, for contact with my big brother as I viewed this. But I forced it down. I had to be strong. I had to be worthy of this.

When Michael spoke, his voice was distant, like it was reaching out to me from the past. "To answer that, you need to understand what the Fall was. The Fall was the end of an event. A rebellion. One that Lucifer led.

"When God created us angels, he gave each of us certain characteristics. Lucifer was the embodiment of everything human. It's why he was so close to God. God so admired these traits that he created an entire race of beings based on them, you humans. We angels were simply made to exist and serve. You were created to advance, to start special and become great."

"And that's Lucifer's problem with humans? He's jealous?"

"He does get jealous, but that's not why he started the rebellion. He was never jealous of humans. He just views you differently. Remember, he is every human characteristic, gathered into a single entity."

I gulped. "He sees himself as one of us."

"And you as just like him," Michael said sadly. "Remember the Book of Genesis?"

I nodded.

"Did you ever wonder what that part early on was about? About 'the sons of God?'"

"I...tried not to think about it."

"And that's your first mistake, willfully ignoring something important and dangerous," Michael said. "Can you guess what they were?"

I just sat silent, trying not to panic.

I heard the smile in Michael's voice. "You know what they were. But you don't want to say."

"...I don't want to insult you angels."

"You won't be insulting us. The ones we are discussing? They were the ones who insulted us. Tell me who they were."

A long beat, then I spoke. "They were angels."

"Yes, Hannah. In the early days of Creation, some angels did not honor the separation God created. Humans were another part of the world, just like the rocks, the sky, everything. Angels are superior to humans, so you existed for their whim. Most of us felt that was wrong. God created you, and we were to help nurture you, make you the best you could be. Lucifer and the others saw no reason to make you more than what you were."

"So they rebelled."

"Yes. And this is the reason for his interest. He isn't simply tempting humanity. He is trying to convert them. Make them embrace their baser natures. To celebrate what they are instead of what they can be."

I felt my eyebrows knit as a thought struck me. "So he's not after worship?"

"In a way, he is. After all, Lucifer shows them an easy to attain truth, one that requires no effort, no sacrifice, no discipline. He becomes like a god. And the fact that he's proving God wrong about his own creations? That's his ultimate happiness."

"He's like a god."

"In his mind."

"Because he surrounds himself with followers who can never be superior to him."

There was a pause. I looked at Michael and saw the first genuine smile on his face since the discussion started. "That's exactly it. Once again, humans are not superior to angels. He gets his amusement and use and never has to worry that he'll be overthrown."

"And any angels on his side aren't strong enough to do it. Or they'd be in charge now."

"Exactly," he said. "Some agreed with his philosophy. Others were conned into it. He's a gifted speaker, a smooth talker. The rebellion was an attempt to assert themselves, establish themselves as separate. God granted this, and consigned them to Hell."

"What is Lucifer's philosophy? It can't be that being evil is how it is supposed to be."

"You are correct, that isn't it. Good versus evil is a dangerous oversimplification. Lots of people think all they have to do is be good and not do evil, and there are no further factors than that. By considering nothing more, by not seeing the bigger picture or how things really work, it enables Lucifer to operate unhindered. His philosophy is very simple. The strong rule, the weak serve the strong. Get yours, and take his. God teaches to look out for each other, that the weak have just as much right to live as the strong, that we are diverse to help protect each other's shortcomings. It's not that taking what isn't yours is good, it's that, if you can, why shouldn't you?"

"Because it's wrong."

"Among the living, that can be easy to ignore. Life is hard. Life is full of opportunists. And seeing someone constantly getting their way, having everything handed to them, it breeds resentment. And in some of those cases, when the realization hits that the only thing stopping them from taking what they feel they should have is themselves...."

"That's when Lucifer's influence is strongest," I finished.

"Yes. Violence. Sex. Defiance of authority. Once again, it's not the what of your actions, it's the why. When the why becomes, 'Well, why not?', that is when Lucifer gets what he wants."

"What becomes of the souls who go to Hell?"

"The majority of them? Words can't describe how terrible it is. Strength survives there. Just to end the pain and suffering, those Cast must reject their humanity. Their emotions. Their compassion. They must become strong and start taking without hesitation."

"'The majority of them?' What else is there?"

"Depends on what you offer. Weakness is allowed if Lucifer or his subordinates can get something from you. Some humans become their pets. It's humiliating, but it saves them from the pain. Others? Lucifer and the others can absorb the souls into them, experiencing their lives and feelings for themselves. Living vicariously."

"What happens to the soul?"

"It still exists. And when they are done, whatever happens next happens. There are sections of Hell that are like a library of humans, where

Lucifer and the others can take and live what they want."

"What if the human is strong enough to survive?"

"If you can impress Lucifer, you can live with him and his main subordinates. They have fashioned a paradise of their own down there. Opulence, luxury…just as there is pain beyond all understanding, there is pleasure beyond all understanding. And if you can prove yourself to be just like Lucifer, he will give it to you."

I shivered. I felt horribly cold. It was a paradox. The more I could imagine being offered, the more afraid I was. Anything that I wanted and could have could be mine. And I knew my strength. My determination. My ingenuity. My will. I would never suffer there.

Because I could be just like Lucifer.

I forced myself to breathe deeply. To focus on myself instead of Hell. I refused to be swayed. I fought the temptation. I felt disappointment. It was understandable. A fantastic gift could be offered, one I would never have to give up. But how much I wanted it made me not want it. I closed my eyes, and with one last push, I felt the desire that was reaching out to me falling away. Vanishing. Becoming almost nothing. Not gone, it was still there, but as close to gone as it could get.

When I opened my eyes, the tapestry was flat again, just a random jumble on the wall. I breathed a sigh of relief, then turned to look at Michael. Michael was just staring at me, his face registering shock. When he finally spoke, he was so quiet, I could barely hear. "…you fought it."

"Yes," I said, nodding my head. "I did."

Michael started smiling. "No, you aren't getting this. Most people, the way they handle temptation is to ignore it. To resist. You fought it."

I blinked a couple of times. "Is that unusual?"

"It's very rare, Hannah," he said. It was kind of shocking to hear an angel talking so reverently about a human. It was even more shocking that it was Michael talking about me. "We are to use our strengths to protect others. Few have the strength that you have."

Michael got up from his chair and stood in front of me. He reached down. I took his hand, and he pulled me up into his embrace. "Thank you, Hannah. Thank you for using your strength to help others. Thank you for becoming a Celestial."

I didn't know what to say. I just hugged him back, my actions expressing what words could not. I felt Michael rub the back of my head before he spoke again.

"You needed to know this," Michael said. "You'll be leading grey area cases before long. Those cases have a high risk of someone getting Cast. Sooner or later, you're going to come face to face with Lucifer. We have lost some Advocates to him, Church and Celestial. They are drawn to what he can offer, what he represents. Usually, The Talk is to see who can be strong, if they can withstand him." He took a deep breath. "You won't just withstand him. You can fight him. You can beat him. Keep that strength. You're going to need it."

    I knew I couldn't avoid confronting Lucifer forever. But I knew I face him. That I could emerge on top. Michael had faith in me. God had faith in me.

    But most importantly, I had faith in me.

Shortly after I had The Talk, I started leading grey cases. And started winning. Or, if not winning, getting some other fate other than Casting Down. Eventually, this registered with everyone. Churches, Celestials, angels, everyone. I had not had to face the devil yet.

    It was truly remarkable how long my streak lasted. Others had seen Petitioners Cast, I hadn't. Part of it was shrewd strategy. The really reprehensible people, like Tomas de Torquemada, I would frequently pick some other fate than Casting. I'm a big fan of poetic justice. The few times I had gone for Casting, the Churches managed to dig them out and get them some other fate. But the other part was simply skill, the skill that served me so well defending. I thought fast, I was smart, and I knew how to throw the Churches off their game.

    Despite that, I would occasionally go into Michael's office and look at that tapestry. I kept reminding myself what was down there. Michael would also give me The Talk again every once in a while. It was to keep myself ready, because I knew it couldn't last. I couldn't avoid facing Lucifer forever.

    And in 1814, my luck ran out.

James Brock was not his original name, just his most recent one. Brock's first life was as a privateer, running down pirates for fun and profit. He really loved his work. There was what he would describe as an "unfortunate" incident where he raided another privateer's ship. Official records? Brock's ship got the goods from pirates, and the other privateer's ship was lost at sea. He had been planning another such raid, focusing on covering his tracks, when two pirate ships came up on him. A firefight ensued, with Brock getting a cannonball in the gut. Or, more accurately, through the gut.

    Brock's first trial was a bit odd. The Churches opposed his petition just because of the incident where he raided another privateer. The Celestials opposed because he was more interested in picking fights and satisfying his greed. With no option of Heavenly reward, the question was what else would he get? Both sides expressed uncertainty that Casting was the appropriate response, maybe he was just misguided. Brock was given reincarnation to try and get it right.

    Well, he didn't. He wound up becoming an actual pirate that time. His ambition got the better of him. He attempted a mutiny and he got run through. Returning to the Valley Of Death, he suddenly remembered he wasn't supposed to live life quite like that. He cooled his heels for a long time. Meanwhile, Churches and Celestials wondered what exactly to do with him. By now, Calvary had vacated as senior Church and Henry Gallows took over. Gallows didn't like Casting if it could be avoided, and in Brock, he saw someone that needed a hand, not eternal torment.

Gallows asked for a consultation with Michael. They discussed what it would take to get Brock on the right path. Eventually, they settled on reincarnation in a new country, the United States of America. When Brock petitioned and both sides opposed, their recommended fates were for him to live in frontier country. Without the distractions of competing in a social order, he could focus on himself and develop as he needed to. That was the plan, anyway.

The Tribunal agreed with both sides' recommended fates and Brock was on his way to be born again. He was actually doing really well. Then, the War Of 1812 broke out. Brock wasn't part of the armed forces, but sort of tagged along for the Battle Of York in 1813. When Americans took over the city, they spent a few days at the end of April looting buildings or burning them. Brock was in his element, but got caught in a burning building. Smoke inhalation got him before the fire did.

Brock returned, and remembered everything, and petitioned again almost immediately. He figured, nothing to it, he'll get another go around. Michael wasn't happy. Neither was Gallows. Bad enough he was anxious to start fighting, killing, and just acting evil. The disregard he was exhibiting towards the whole court process irked them as well.

By this point, I had become the most senior Celestial. I was reviewing cases when a putto came up to me and said I was needed for a consultation in Michael's chambers. I trust Michael blindly, so I didn't ask any questions. So I was a little surprised to enter and find Michael, Gallows, three angels, and two Advocates from each side in there.

I immediately got into the right frame of mind. Meetings like this, you have to speak a certain way to keep anyone from accusing you of Collusion. Trying to prearrange the outcome of any case at any time for any reason was grounds to automatically Cast Down. Collusion is odd. Making the charges stick could be nullified by asking for a trial by God. But the precedents aside from clear cut cases were vague, and there was always the fear of your actions being twisted. Not only that, but being accused of it made other Advocates avoid you for fear of tainting their case. Everyone takes extra steps to keep themselves in the clear.

I stood in front of Michael's desk. "What am I facing?"

"We don't know if you'll get the case yet, Hannah," Michael said, gesturing to one of the chairs in front of his desk. "We first want to see what we are looking at, and we'll decide based on how this unfolds."

I took the chair. I didn't bother to check for a tack. I never have to when Michael is really on the clock. Gallows took the other chair.

Michael looked at one of the angels and gestured to me. The angel produced a life scroll and handed it to me. I took it, untied it, and started reading. "Three bites at the apple, huh?"

"That's the reason for this consultation," Michael responded. "It's going to be hard to convince the Tribunal to give him another chance. I mean, the guy has potential…."

"Not necessarily."

I could hear in Michael's voice that I had his attention. "What do you mean?"

"Think about it. You've been trying to shield him from temptation. And it's obviously not working."

"Forbidden fruit?"

"No," I said, diving back into the scroll. "It's the rush. The power. If you keep him isolated, he wouldn't get Heaven because he's lived, but hasn't shown he understands why those behaviors are wrong. Living a clean life wouldn't get him in."

"We wouldn't oppose," Gallows stated.

"Sure, you would," I said, looking at him. "Just as sure as Michael would. And you already know the Tribunal would never allow it."

Gallows and Michael looked at each other. They knew I was speaking the truth. Michael broke the silence. "Well, you're clever about thinking of recommended fates, Hannah. Any ideas what the Tribunal would go for that might actually help Brock?"

I rolled up the scroll and tied it absently. The details of Brock's lives were immaterial. It was a matter of finding the right situation where he could learn his lesson. "I don't know. I'm trying not to think about Mark Of Cain."

Michael and Gallows blanched. Mark Of Cain is a very radical move. A lot of people think the Mark Of Cain is a curse. It's actually the opposite. When Cain was exiled for killing his brother, he was afraid of being attacked and killed by others. God gave him the mark to warn others not to harm him. It's protection, not a curse. It's basically God saying, "Leave him alone, I'll deal with him Myself." He could do just about anything he wanted and he couldn't be excommunicated, he couldn't be condemned, and Advocates on either side had to keep their hands off. Mark Of Cain is basically an all or nothing move. The person would be born one last time, and afterwards, would be judged by God. If they pulled it off, they get Heavenly admission. If they failed, they get Cast Down. No other options, no other chances. It was the endgame for the soul.

Mark Of Cain was usually extended to certain people. Everyone chosen in the Book Of Judges got it, for example. Not every warrior or soldier or person living in danger does, but they are the most likely to, because how they are forced to live can never equate to what the Bible teaches is proper. Those that are given it are people that won't abuse the privilege while alive. And no one had faith that Brock would do that.

After some back and forth between the three of us, I eventually suggested, "How about making him part of the ruling class during a revolution?"

"Make him a soldier?" Gallows sounded like he thought I lost my mind.

"Ruling classes don't usually fight in revolutions, they have others do it for them. Instead of Brock starting off with nothing, we start him off with everything and he sees it get taken away. From there, he starts making choices based on what is important and what isn't. At the very least, he should show some progress if reincarnation comes up again."

Gallows was unconvinced. "Where would we even send him? France's revolution is already over. Although there's likely another one right around the corner."

I thought over some of my recent cases. "How about Mexico? They're hip deep in trying to break away from Spain."

"Remember time, Hannah," Michael said gently. "Right now, forces are dwindling. All that will be left soon will be guerrilla bands. It will end one way or the other before he's old enough to realize what is happening around him."

"Any other places that fit the bill?"

Michael put his finger under his chin and thought. "Well, America is starting to have some real problems due to using slavery as an economic model. He'd have to stay here for a while so that we can have him born at the right time."

"He'd be an adult when the situation became bigger than him."

"Exactly," Michael nodded. "I think a life where things can't revolve around him might be what it takes."

Gallows shrugged. "I'm more partial to France, myself. And based on the turmoil, Brock wouldn't be waiting as long as he would be in America."

I arched my eyebrows diplomatically. "That is for you to decide. We have our conclusion, you have yours."

Gallows smiled at me. "Agreed."

As Gallows and I stood, Michael pulled over a petition. I figured it was Brock's. I saw him write that he was contesting it. Gallows interrupted my thoughts. "I need to get back to my chambers so I can file my contest. Michael? Who am I facing?"

Michael had pulled out a request for trial. He looked at me, then extended the document to me. "Hannah? You want to fill this out?"

I smiled and took the document. "Yes, sir."

Gallows extended his hand to me. "See you in court, Singer."

I shook Gallows' hand, oblivious to what was coming.

It literally was the calm before the storm. Build up to trial was uneventful. Nothing special happening. Brock was interviewed by both sides, our individual recommended fates were filed, pretty straightforward.

I will say this much for Brock – he was…well, let's be polite and say abundantly self-confident. He didn't really say more than single syllable responses in the interviews. While he was condescending, he wasn't insulting. I faced enough of those that someone like Brock who was simply disinterested didn't bother me.

Eventually, the time of trial approached. I marched through the Celestial Courts for the appointed trial room, not even blinking. Gallows and I stuck with the recommended fates we settled on in Michael's chambers. Not a lot of surprises here, so neither of us had any juniors. We weren't even carrying scrolls. We'd stand, make our arguments, and see what the Tribunal thought.

Gallows came around a corner I was walking past and fell into step with me. "Greetings, Miss Singer. It's going to be an interesting trial."

"How do you think the Tribunal is going to lean?"

"You don't think they'll take one of our recommendations?"

"Brock makes them a tough sell. We're basically trying to win despite him."

Gallows sighed. "Sometimes, this whole 'love the sinner' thing is problematic."

I just grunted in agreement.

We got to the courtroom. Gallows held one of the doors for me. I gave him a quick curtsey and said, "Thank you, m'lord."

We got to our respective tables and sat patiently. Gallows was softly whistling a piece by Beethoven. I let my mind wander, thinking about what was coming up next. After this, I had a few reviews to do. Nothing too tough, though. I started working on what my defenses would be.

I heard the footsteps of the two Guardians and another set of steps. They were bringing the Petitioner in. As both sides were contesting, Brock would not be sitting with either Advocate. The Guardians took him to the middle of the courtroom, facing the judge's bench. They then went and stood in front of the judge's bench, facing out to the court. Brock just stood there, sagging a little, like he just wanted this over with so he could get back to life.

A few more had filled in the Gallery when the chimes sounded. Everyone stood, and Gallows and I deployed our wings. As we weren't real angels, we each had ceremonial wings. They weren't attached to our backs, but they floated behind us and moved like they were. Mine are very simple, each looking like an upside down teardrop with a smaller upside down teardrop on the outside and a flat top. Gallows' wings were a little more ornate than mine, but not by much. They suggested wings without drawing undue attention to themselves. He was as respectful of the angels with his choice as I was.

The door on the right by the Tribunal box opened and twelve angels, wings already out, marched in. I wanted to close my eyes, losing myself in the wonder of the sensation, but I didn't. I like looking at the angels every chance I get.

The door at the back opened and the presiding angel entered. It was Muriel. Muriel is a bit smaller than any other angel and a bit droopy. If it weren't impossible, you'd swear he was narcoleptic. He walked like he was plodding to the kitchen in the middle of the night for some water and seemed to drift up the steps. He sat and was dwarfed by the bench – you could barely see his head. He lightly tapped the gavel, and the Gallery and Tribunal sat.

Muriel's voice drifted out, like he was talking in his sleep. "Who is the Petitioner?"

Gallows spoke out. "The Petitioner is James Madison Brock."

"And who advocates for the Church?"

"Henry Gallows, acting alone."

Muriel didn't seem to change position. In fact, I don't think he even moved his eyes. "And who advocates for the Celestials?"

"Hannah Singer, acting alone," I responded.

"Will the Petitioner please take the stand?"

Brock sauntered over and climbed into the dock. He bent at the waist, leaning his elbows on the banister and looking out at us. I think. His eyes seemed kind of far away. I briefly wondered if whatever Muriel had was contagious.

I almost missed Muriel's next question. "Who has Privilege?" That meant, who had first and last word at trial? Gallows and I looked at each other. He gestured to me, I held up my hand and shook my head. We looked to the bench. "I do," Gallows stated.

"Your opening statements, please," Muriel said.

Before anyone could say anything, I smelled something. It was faint, but there. I kept facing front, but shifted my eyes, wondering where it was coming from. Sulfur? Up here?

Suddenly, I felt dread wrap around my heart like a boa constrictor. I hoped that I was wrong, but when I looked at the Tribunal, I saw their faces had become strong. Threatening. Ready for battle. The Guardians had their hands on the hilts of their swords, ready to draw. I looked at Muriel. He looked wide awake and ready to fight.

Oh, no. It can't be.

Gallows noticed the smell. He had stopped talking. He was looking around, holding out hope that it was his imagination. No point in that at all. I dashed from my table up to the Guardians. They were so baffled by my actions, they didn't even move as I grabbed one of their swords and held it in front of me, battle ready and facing the center of the court floor.

Before the Guardian could try to take the sword back, things shifted into high speed. A plume of flame appeared in the center of the court floor, sparks and ashes geysering out of the top and landing on the stone. The piles rose quickly, forming perfectly shined shoes and starting to form the pant legs above them. The Guardian whose sword I took stood right next to me, fists clenched and ready to attack. The other Guardian drew his sword and took up a battle stance.

Gallows was starting to move back along to dividing wall between his table and the Gallery.

Every angel in the Gallery was ready to fight. The figure was now complete up to about his chest area, the high quality suit he was wearing being obvious now. From my vantage point, I could see the entrance to the courtroom. The doors don't usually open while court is in session. A vertical crack of bright light appeared over the center of the doors. It then split in two, joined at the very top. The cracks swung up like the edges of a curtain, revealing a blindingly bright white light on the other side. Standing in front of the light was a shape I would know anywhere. St. Michael's wings were out dramatically, flexed and ready. He held his flaming sword in his left hand and had twisted his body so that he was shoving his right hand towards the wall. He was entering the court with a show of force. The energy radiating from him and surrounding him made everything shimmer and shake, like looking at something beneath the surface of a roiling sea.

The figure finished forming. He was beautiful. Absolutely beautiful. I could feel the power. The strength. The control. The desire. He materialized facing Brock in the dock. Lucifer, the most beautiful angel, the ultimate traitor, looked the Petitioner over, sizing him up.

I readjusted my stance and bellowed, "He's not yours yet!"

Lucifer turned to look at me, as if deigning to acknowledge my presence. I immediately wished he hadn't. His face lit up. He was impressed with me. He was enamored with me. I felt his emotions reaching out to me.

Dear God. He wanted me.

I dug in my heels. He wasn't getting me.

I could see Michael past Lucifer. Lucifer wasn't paying him the slightest bit of attention. Michael was looking into the courtroom at the Celestial table. He was looking for me. His eyes shifted to the Guardians. He saw me with the sword at ready. Michael then did something I never expected.

Michael smiled and willed his flaming sword away.

Michael walked down the aisle that split the Gallery in half. Once he was past the courtroom wall, it poured back into place like a waterfall, shimmering for a moment before returning to normal. His wings remained out. "Hello, Lucifer. What brings you around?"

Lucifer didn't take his eyes off of me. "Wow. You're getting faster, Michael."

"Look at me when I'm talking to you, runt."

Whatever spell Lucifer was under, that snapped him out of it. He spun to glare at Michael. "You will not call me that!"

By now, Michael was standing right next to Lucifer. Michael towered over him by more than a head. Lucifer was lean and wiry while Michael was covered with muscle. While Lucifer was beauty and grace and elegance, Michael was almost pure power and strength. No wonder the prophecies said Michael would ultimately destroy Lucifer in the Apocalypse. It had nothing to do with Michael being an archangel and Lucifer just a basic angel.

Michael bent so his eyes were a little below Lucifer's. It was like a grown-up trying to be sociable with a child. It didn't improve Lucifer's mood in the least. "How you going to stop me, squirt?"

Lucifer looked at Muriel. "Move to Silence Is Golden Michael."

Michael laughed. "You're not an officer of the court, shrimpy."

Muriel glared at Lucifer. "Shut up, shrimpy."

I was momentarily thrown by Muriel calling anyone "shrimpy," but recovered when Lucifer gave Michael an evil smile. "Still think I can't hurt you, Michael?"

"I know you can't."

Lucifer twisted a little to look at me. "So, you're his little sister. The infamous Hannah Singer."

He was turning up the charm. The better he made me feel, the more I fought it. I noticed Michael simply straightened and looked at me. He was smiling, like there was some great joke he knew and Lucifer didn't. That was when it hit me. Michael wasn't afraid for me. There are few endorsements better than St. Michael saying you can handle the devil.

I had been willing the sword I held to stay still, to keep my hands from shaking. I let that go. Sure enough, I was steady as a rock. "Look what crawled out of the thunder mug."

He didn't even flinch. "Hatred is bad and unchristian, Singer."

"You would know."

"You don't have to be adversarial. Give me time. I'll grow on you."

"Just like the Black Death did."

Lucifer started approaching me, like the greatest salesman in the world. I quickly lowered the sword so the point was aiming for his abdomen. He kept walking until he felt the sword tip poking his stomach.

Lucifer's face changed. He was no longer showing what he wanted, he was showing his inner thoughts. "You aren't afraid of me."

I didn't say anything. I didn't trust him not to twist it somehow. I let the sword do the talking, giving him a sharp poke. He yelped and jumped back. As he recovered, I saw his face change again. If I thought he was enraptured by me before, it was even stronger now. "Come on, be nice."

"I don't make deals with the devil," I responded.

"I'm not offering a deal, I'm offering a truce."

"We each behave in a way to get what we want. Sounds like a deal to me."

"And how else am I supposed to represent myself in this court?"

"You aren't a part of the Celestial Courts."

"Due to my involvement in this case, I am."

I didn't think I could feel any worse. Suddenly, I did. "What do you mean, 'your involvement?'"

Lucifer turned and walked up to the dock. Brock was transfixed. He couldn't look away from the most beautiful angel. "I've been watching this one. Helping him along. He's perfect."

Michael laughed. "He's not yours."

"He's been becoming mine," Lucifer countered, turning to Michael. "He understands. He gets it. No one gives you what you want, you have to take it."

"Wow," I piped up. "So you wanted and took Hell instead of being given Heaven."

Lucifer looked at me. By now, I was used to his presence, so his focus didn't phase me. "You have fire, Singer. I like fire."

"Yeah, I can tell by your neighborhood."

"My neighborhood doesn't have fire," Lucifer said, smiling at Brock. "That's for the losers."

"By definition, that's everybody," Muriel stated.

"No, it isn't," Lucifer said, still dazzling Brock. "Those are the ones that won't take anything."

"You mean, 'can't'," I stated.

Lucifer smiled at me. I felt his pull again. "I mean, 'won't.' They could join us. But they won't. They act like being good and conscientious will make any difference. There is no leaving. They have nothing to live for. Nothing to prove. And yet, they hold themselves back." He looked at Brock. "You went past that long ago. You have no hesitation. You don't want to suffer. You want what you deserve. And that is the difference between you and the losers. You can have it. They can't. Because they won't. And you will."

Brock was smiling. He was as good as sold. He looked at me, and I recognized the mindset. He was ready to rush me. Attacking an on duty officer of the court is grounds to automatically Cast Down.

I looked at Muriel. "Move for emergency consultation!"

Muriel slammed the gavel. "Granted!"

I smiled at Lucifer. "Off duty 'til further notice. And you won't be recognized as an officer of the court until we're ready."

Lucifer smiled back at me. "No wonder God is so impressed with you, Singer. You are something very rare."

I stalked up to him, pointing the tip of the sword right between his eyes. "You're not an officer of the court," I hissed. "I will attack."

"The lowliest angel is superior to the mightiest human," he stated. "Fallen or no, I'm still an angel. You really think you can defeat me, human?"

Suddenly, one of Michael's meaty hands wrapped around Lucifer's neck from the back and gripped hard. Although Lucifer wasn't choking, he was really really uncomfortable as Michael hosted him in the air and turned him like he was examining a kitten. "She just has to keep you away until I get in there." My big brother always has my back.

Only now did I return the sword to the Guardian. "I say we consult here off to the side."

Everyone looked at me in surprise. Only Michael didn't look like he was going to argue. "Sure."

Michael and I walked over to the Gallery. Everyone on the Celestial side moved to the Church side to give us some privacy. Michael and I put our heads together, facing the wall and with his wings shielding us from view. We knew Lucifer wouldn't try anything. Too many other angels had our backs.

"What are you thinking, Hannah?" I did notice the undercurrent of worry in Michael's voice.

"This trial has to proceed. Like this, right now."

"What about juniors?"

"I don't trust them. This isn't like other trials, where Lucifer turns up after judgment is made. He wants to be an active participant. You know what Lucifer is doing. He's using his sway to disorient and confuse. Even if he can't corrupt my juniors, I don't trust them to stay focused enough not to sink the case."

"We can always deny him," Michael pointed out. "Keep him from acting at trial. He is not a member of the Celestial Court."

"Brock is looking at Hell one way or another. Not only does he want it, but what if Lucifer goes for trial by God? God will have no choice but to Cast. The only hope of keeping Brock out of Hell is to do this here and now."

"God doesn't have to grant Lucifer a trial."

"Don't be so sure. Lucifer could argue the covenant. Someone willing to go to Hell and living as evilly as Brock did? No one on Earth would consider anything other than Casting. This trial is Brock's only chance."

Michael looked at me levelly. "Look, you know I have faith in you. But are you sure you're up to this?"

I thought everything over. My odds were astronomical. I already had to convince the Tribunal to give Brock one more chance. Michael would have to act as a Guardian due to Lucifer's presence, so he wouldn't be able to help. Gallows was in over his head, and might even be used by Lucifer to trip up my arguments. Brock was going to do what he could to get Cast. Lucifer was going to work me over to throw me off my game. And, of course, he was a gifted speaker. A con artist. The most beautiful angel with a golden tongue.

I looked at Michael levelly. "I will be up to it."

Michael just nodded at me. "Please be careful."

We came out of our huddle and stalked out of the Gallery to the court area. Everyone in the Gallery resumed their original positions.

Michael took his spot in front of the judge's bench. He folded his arms across his chest and looked levelly at Lucifer. He was daring him to give him an excuse to go after him. Lucifer wasn't the least bit phased, his arrogance acting as his shield.

I looked at the bench and said, "Move for trial to resume with conditions."

Muriel simply tilted his head. "What conditions do you seek?"

"The Celestials have no objection to Lucifer acting as his own council. However, I also move for Ties That Bind on Brock."

"On what grounds?" He was asking purely as a formality.

"Threat To Self."

I looked at Gallows. He was cringing a little. He was having a lot of trouble keeping it together. I barely heard him say, "I concur."

"I object," Lucifer said, calmly and easily. "People are not usually confined in the dock unless they demonstrate harmful potential. He hasn't done anything yet."

I didn't waste any time. "Move to strike Lucifer's argument."

Muriel looked very interested. "On what grounds?"

"Trial has not reconvened. He is not an officer of the court and has no standing."

"You are advancing proposals for how a trial should go," he responded. "Sounds like court is in session to me."

"It is not," I stated back. "Muriel has not reconvened, we are discussing procedures just like we would during a consultation."

"If court is not convened, then you are off duty, too. Therefore, you shouldn't be able to make motions," Lucifer smiled at me.

"I'm already recognized as an officer of the court, you aren't."

"She's right," Muriel said, demonstrating a strength I never suspected he had. "So shut up. Motion carried." And he slammed the gavel.

The smile momentarily vanished from Lucifer's face. He had been using charm and attitude, and he just got his first hint that this might not be as easy as he thought. He looked at me strangely.

I didn't even blink. "You want Brock? You got to get through me first."

He smiled. "I accept your challenge."

Muriel looked at me, like he was trying to will extra strength to me. "You ready, Singer?"

"Yes," I said.

"Ties That Bind on Brock, and court is reconvened." And he struck the gavel.

Brock was suddenly straight as a board and wasn't moving an inch. Muriel then declared, "For the purposes of this trial, Lucifer is recognized as a temporary officer of the court. He is to be extended the same courtesy and exhibit the same behavior," and Muriel glared at Lucifer as he said that, "as all other officers present. This is only for while the case is being heard. If court is in recess or the session is ended, Lucifer is not an officer of the court." And he struck the gavel.

Muriel then looked at Gallows. "Mister Gallows? Your opening statements, please."

Lucifer politely raised his hand. "I would like first Privilege."

I immediately said, "Move for the bench to determine Privilege."

Gallows croaked, "Seconded."

Lucifer glared at Gallows, making him cower. "Motion should be denied."

"Angels always have the right to reassign Privilege when no one supports petition," I responded.

Muriel glared at Lucifer. "Singer has first Privilege, Gallows has second, you're third."

Lucifer clearly wasn't used to being denied what he wanted. He looked at me again, and I could see the wheels turning in his head. He had ambitions for me. And I didn't trust them. I had to keep Lucifer from getting to me and throwing me off my case. I had to keep him from swaying me, tempting me to fall with him. I had to keep the Tribunal from giving up on Brock. I had to keep Brock from giving up on himself. And I had to do it with no help. Not from Gallows. Not from Muriel. Not from Michael. Just me against the devil himself. I clasped my hands and said a quick prayer to God.

My eyes sprang open.

I slapped my hands together.

It's star time.

"The eternal debate, the one that explores the concept of evil. Is someone really evil, or are they simply misguided? It is vital to consider, because no one wants to give up on someone who just needs a hand. Likewise, no one wants to waste time and tears on someone who doesn't deserve it.

"The question is, where does Brock fall on this scale? There is true evil," I said as I jerked my thumb to Lucifer, who didn't seem to appreciate the gesture, "no one is denying that. But after three goes, we are no closer to knowing the truth about Brock's nature than we were before.

"Rather than deciding his final fate here and now, my recommended fate is a proposal. The main goal has been to isolate Brock from temptation. My proposal will isolate him, but in a different way. He will have his desires taken care of, then see them removed, one by one. It will force him to confront his motivations. To consider what is important. That he can't have it all back...."

At this point, Lucifer let out a loud, wet cough. He patted his chest and said, "Pardon me." Naturally, he was playing dirty. Opening and closing arguments are the only times Advocates are allowed to speak uninterrupted. Lucifer was trying to disrupt my momentum, minimize the impact of my words on the Tribunal. He would use trickery to keep me from gaining any ground.

Muriel raised the gavel, ready to censure Lucifer for talking out of turn. I had to move fast to shut Lucifer down for good right now. "Is Brock as bad as Lucifer?" Muriel had just started to drop the gavel when he stopped cold. He gave me a smile, he knew what I was doing. "Brock has done some terrible things. But can you compare him to our special guest today and say they are the same?"

Lucifer's smile dropped and he looked at me in shock. He knew I'd just backed him into a corner. The more Lucifer flaunted rules and concerns, the better Brock looked in comparison, and the better my chances of getting leniency from the Tribunal.

I heard Lucifer quietly whisper to me, "You are good."

I gave him a sneer. "Don't play slick with me, chummy. I'm better at it." I returned to the Tribunal. "What if Brock cannot do it? We have one more trial and he likely will be Cast. But this one lifetime could make those concerns unnecessary. It is the only option that hasn't been tried, and it promises to show the true measure of Brock. Can he learn? Does he have compassion? Will he forever be a law unto himself? We cannot, in good conscience, Cast anyone unless we know for sure there is no hope for them. Brock isn't hopeless yet. Give him one more lifetime to prove us right or wrong. Thank you."

Everyone looked at Gallows. Gallows was completely overwhelmed. No wonder Muriel gave me first Privilege -- I had the better chance of standing up to Lucifer, so I got the first and last word. Gallows mumbled a few things, about the grace of God and forgiveness, and closed his arguments.

That left Lucifer. He was calm and collected as he spoke. "I am aware of the families being recommended for Brock's reincarnation. They are good families that are about to have tragedy run them over.

"And your idea of mercy is to compound that suffering?

"Just to prove how right you might or might not be about Brock?

"Remember, this is no sure thing being proposed. Brock could go back and be just as ruthless as he is now. He likely will be, given that war is about to sweep through the areas the Celestials and the Churches are proposing he be born into. And he likely will. He hasn't been improving in his lifetimes. The only way to keep him pure is to box him away, isolate him from everybody. And not only is that not possible, he won't learn any different that way.

"Ultimately, he can't learn any different. He is what he is.

"Hell is largely empty, due to God's mercy and the skill of the Advocates in the Celestial Courts. But aside from the clear cut cases, God does allow people to choose to go to Hell, just as he allowed me and my followers to go there. It is a question of their will. Brock wants to go. To a place where his talents, his mentality, his basic nature, are allowed to be as they are instead of hidden away behind rules he cannot conform to. He would never fit in in Heaven. You know that. Too much anger. Too much anarchy. If it is truly not a sin to be who we are, why force him into a place where he won't be happy?

"This is very simple -- angels don't want to see anyone suffer for all eternity. God doesn't want to see anyone suffer for all eternity. But what is being proposed will do just that. A lifetime that will never feel right to him, and an eternal reward that will drive him insane. This is one time a man can be Cast and everyone will have a clean conscience. Hell is where he belongs. It's where he will thrive. It's where he can be happy. The Petitioner's will must be taken into account in your decision. His will is to be happy. There's only one place that can happen. And it's not the place you can allow him into. Cast him. It's what he wants, it's what is right. Thank you."

I pulled through the haze that settled over me as Lucifer spoke. He truly was a gifted speaker. And he was well aware of the rules of the court. He was trying to back the Tribunal into a corner, so that they would defy both Gallows' and my recommended fates. I didn't know why Lucifer wanted Brock so bad, but I didn't care. I had a duty to defend him, to keep him from getting Cast. And I was going to do it.

I quickly went through my thoughts. I needed a plan of attack. Lucifer's opening statements were full of fallacies and twisted logic. But I couldn't just go after them. I didn't trust him not to lead me in the wrong direction and then spring a trap when I wasn't expecting it. I needed a golden thread that I could run through my arguments, reinforcing them, and binding Lucifer up with them. Muriel waited patiently as I searched.

I found it.

I had to play my cards close to my vest. Any slip up would clue Lucifer in to what I was doing, and I needed the element of surprise. That was when I realized I could easily distract Lucifer just like he was trying to distract me. I had to play up my confidence. Lucifer liked what he was seeing in me. He was almost transfixed by it. And he knew that, if he could tempt me to fall, it would be a great triumph over Michael. I prayed Michael would see through my act, and I began.

"Hell is for the weak," I stated simply and with confidence.

Lucifer looked confused. "Hell is for the strong. The deserving."

"Then why is it that, in order to gain entry, you have to surrender to all your baser desires? Strength comes from overcoming them. From controlling them, not letting them control you."

"An environment as harsh as that? And you think weakness can survive?"

"So you admit Hell is no picnic."

Lucifer blinked. Brock didn't even react. Good. Just what I wanted.

Lucifer smiled at me, as if realizing he needed to step up his game and he was up to it. "Hell is indeed a picnic, if you are human enough."

"Kind of a contradiction, that humanity earns you an inhuman environment."

"There is nothing inhuman about Hell," Lucifer said. "Heaven is inhuman. In order to enter Heaven, you can't be human, you have to be better than human."

"For such a gifted speaker, you don't lie very well."

"It's not a lie. Humans are a certain way. It's how they were created. And yet, just being human, flaws and all, being how God created them, isn't good enough. Heaven is a punishment. You denied your very nature, and you are now rewarded with something unnatural to you."

"The nature of man is to be savage?"

"The nature of man is to be strong. God created man to experience pleasures. To achieve legends. And most people don't have it in them to rise above the rest. So they live miserably and spend eternity miserable."

I saw an opening. I had to be careful it wasn't a trap, so I approached cautiously. "So Hell is just as difficult to attain as Heaven is."

Lucifer looked at me like I was nuts. "Not at all. Anyone can go to Hell. We'll take anyone. All they have to do is want to go."

"But in that environment? How can anyone find happiness and fulfillment there?"

"They do what comes naturally. They take what rightfully belongs to them instead of waiting for it to be given to them."

I moved. "'Take what belongs to them.' That's interesting. Why do they have to take it in the first place? If it rightfully belongs to them, why does someone else have it?"

"Because they took it first, and if someone wants it, they must take it back."

"If they take what rightfully belongs to them, then they have every right to have it, do they not?"

"Yes."

"So why does someone who has already taken it not deserve it? What makes those without more worthy of possession than those with?"

Lucifer looked a little thrown. "Worthiness is determined by strength.

The ability to take."

"So not everyone in Hell has what they truly deserve."

"Sure, they do."

"Conceivably, a single person who is strong enough can take everything from everyone else down there. He can have it all. And those people are left with nothing but a harsh environment."

"Then they need to learn to be tougher and hold onto what they want."

"But that's not possible. Not everyone has the same strength. There will always be those weaker. And they deserve the pain and torture?"

"Yes."

"And where does Brock stand on that scale? Is he truly strong enough not to suffer like the others? Will he truly be the strongest there and able to avoid their fate?"

"Sure, he will be."

I looked at Brock and saw it. A glimmer of doubt. I shifted my attention to the dock. "Brock? Think about who you think goes to Hell. Do you really think you can compete with them?"

Lucifer saw he was losing ground fast. "Not everyone people think goes to Hell actually does."

I returned my attention to the figure at my left shoulder. "You mean like Attila The Hun? Gehngis Kahn?"

"They aren't in Hell," Lucifer said. "They reincarnated and are now in Heaven. Brock won't have to fight anyone like them."

I looked back at Brock. "What do you know? Two people with the strength and will to take what they want and live comfortably in Hell, and they opted to go around until they could get into Heaven. Why do you suppose that is?"

Brock blinked. If he could have shaken his head, he would have, like someone trying to wake up but still dozing off. I was weakening Lucifer's grip on him, but it wasn't completely removed. I looked at Michael. He wasn't looking at me. He was smirking at Lucifer.

Lucifer really wanted Brock. It was like he was looking in the window of a bakery he would never be able to afford to buy from. He stated, "Brock would never suffer in Hell."

I snapped my head around just in time to see a lightning bolt shoot through the ceiling and hit Lucifer square. He sizzled for a few seconds before the char marks vanished. Brock would have jumped if he could. I smiled at Brock. "Lying to the court is not advised."

I was pretty sure Lucifer was getting careless. He wants to be trusted, and being caught lying to the court doesn't help that image. Which meant I was winning. If Lucifer wanted to win, he'd have to back up his statement that Brock wouldn't suffer.

"Brock would reside in that Palace. I would give him a place there."

Yes! Lucifer just went out on a limb. I readied my saw so I could cut it off when the time was right. "In what capacity?" I asked.

"What?" Lucifer asked, feigning innocence.

"In what capacity? You are just giving to him instead of him taking what is rightfully his, right? So what are you giving him that he won't have to take?"

"Isn't living in the Palace good enough?"

I smiled at Brock. "Good point. I mean, if you can't trust the devil, who can you trust, right?"

Brock looked ill. I decided to gamble. Without taking my eyes off him, I said, "Move for Ties That Bind to be rescinded."

Lucifer kept quiet. I think he was holding his breath. Muriel said, "Lifted," and struck the gavel. Brock was now free to move. But he didn't rush me to attack me. He stood there, carefully moving back to the far end of the dock, leaning against the rail and back to the wall. If he could have gotten any further away, he would have.

I smiled at Lucifer. "You still want to sell him on going to Hell? You better put something up."

Lucifer smiled back at me. It was a charming smile. "I could really use someone like you."

It didn't affect me. I felt silent relief that it didn't. "Quit stalling or I move for closing arguments. Offer Brock his deal with the devil."

I looked at Brock as I waited. He was getting desperate. He was looking at me in outright fear. Wide eyes pleading with me to get him out of this. He mumbled, "...I don't want to go...."

Lucifer pounced. "Petitioners do not speak unless addressed."

Reversal. I asked, "What did you just say, Brock?"

Brock looked shaken. I stated, "I can compel you to talk if you refuse."

Brock looked at Muriel. Muriel had the gavel up, ready to give the order. Brock gulped audibly and said, "I don't want to go."

There was a subtle but distinct change in Lucifer's vibe at that moment. Underneath the sleek presentation was anger. Outrage. Fury. He was going to be denied what he wanted. He had to be hating me at that moment. This lowly human was actually besting an angel. That could not stand. Scary as the thought was, it was exactly what I wanted and needed to win the case. I didn't need to toughen up, but I did it anyway just to be sure.

Lucifer said with a smile and a cheery tone, "He can stay in the Archives."

I hated that. Naming portions of Hell the same as portions of the Celestial Courts. I kept my calm, though, as I asked, "And what, exactly, does that entail?"

"I'm not the one on trial," Lucifer countered.

"Very well, I'll explain it."

"There's no one to explain it to. The Tribunal understands, the presiding angel understands, we understand."

"Brock doesn't understand."

"He's just a Petitioner. He doesn't need to understand. He's just to answer any relevant questions as we decide his fate."

Opportunity knocked. I opened the door. I asked Brock, "Do you know what happens in Hell's Archives?"

Lucifer wasted no time. "Move to strike Singer's question."

Muriel looked at him. "On what grounds?"

"Relevancy."

Muriel looked at me. "Objection, Singer?"

I smiled. "No objection."

Lucifer's jaw dropped. I wasn't wasting time arguing, I was simply maneuvering around any blockades he set up. I didn't need to argue relevancy of my question to make my point. I just started speaking. "The Archives in Hell are like a library, but instead of case histories, they hold," and I leered at Brock, "you."

The ramifications were hitting him. I continued. "Hell has Archives, just like the Celestial Courts. But that is in name only. Their function is completely different. Demons can take you, absorb you into themselves, and relive your life. Everything you felt, everything you thought, everything you did. And when they are done, they put you back in your box until they feel like using you again."

"We aren't using them," Lucifer said.

I pointed to Lucifer just as another lightning bolt hit him. It took longer for the char marks to vanish this time. Not only that, but Lucifer was wincing a bit. He was in pain. The bolts were getting stronger, and would keep getting stronger each time he lied until he was vaporized from the court.

Me? I was actually easing up the pressure on myself a little bit. Brock was no longer swayed by Lucifer's words. The first part of my battle was over. Brock's will was no longer an issue. He wanted to live again instead of being Cast. Now, I just had to work on the Tribunal. And if Lucifer did what I suspected he would, I would have the whole case in the bag.

Lucifer had to come up with something else fast if he wanted Brock. There was no lying in front of God. He couldn't guarantee Brock's happiness in his Archives. He had only one card left, and he had to hope I couldn't trump it. And he clearly knew the chances of that weren't good. Come on, Lucifer, you know what you have to do....

Lucifer finally spoke. "He would stay in the Palace with me."

Brock didn't look reassured. Good.

Lucifer smiled at me. He was trying to be smooth. "Let me describe what the Palace is like. There is no suffering there. Every pleasure you could want is there. You want a good scrap? We can give you anyone from a challenge to a pushover. Either way, you'll never lose. I know you like your drink. Plenty of that. And that's just for the flavor. The feeling is always good, that buzz you get when the alcohol is just right. You can drink all you want and it will never get worse and it will never go away. How about sex? Everyone loves sex. Anyone you want, you can have."

"Are your comments for me, or for Brock?" I asked. I was still resolute, nothing about me had changed.

Lucifer smiled at Brock. "For Brock, of course. You're getting paranoid, Singer."

Trying to cast doubt on my faculties, eh? Better fix that. "So, he can take whatever he wants. How is that possible?"

"It's my world. All he has to do is will it, it will appear, and he can take it."

"So, he's still taking what is his, he's just not taking it from anyone else."

"Essentially. The best shouldn't have to fight for what is theirs."

I looked at Brock. "You're fighting over trash."

I looked at Lucifer. He wasn't hiding his anger now. "How dare you suggest that."

"All you have is what God isn't bothering to give anyone else. Table scraps. Cast offs. Garbage."

"Not at all," Lucifer countered, recovering most of his charm. "God made certain things so that everyone could enjoy them. You could be an Atheist and still appreciate good food or a sunset."

Nice try. "All the things you can produce are immaterial. They are things that can be acquired, not earned."

"It's God's arrogance that makes it so that people cannot have what gives them true joy and comfort. Earning is overrated."

"If they are all things that humans can appreciate, why not let him live again and experience them? Why does he have to go to Hell?"

"In Hell, he can enjoy them for all eternity."

As soon as he finished his last sentence, yet another lightning bolt hit Lucifer. This time, he actually doubled over in pain and the char marks were taking longer to vanish.

I moved to take advantage of Lucifer hurting too much to interrupt. I looked at Brock and the Tribunal as I spoke. I jerked my thumb towards Lucifer and said, "Look at him! Is that who you want to be like, Brock? Members of the Tribunal, is that what you want Brock to become? Brock has the ability to earn his place, just like every other human on Earth. Those more evil than him have done it. It's not that difficult, it just takes the right mindset. All Brock has to do is learn it. And you can see from his behavior in the dock, he's already learning!"

Lucifer finally recovered. "Move to strike Singer's last statements from consideration!"

I was already working on counterarguments when Muriel simply looked at him and smirked. "Denied," he said, striking the gavel.

I felt the Tribunal on my side and I had Lucifer on the run. "Move for closing arguments," I stated.

"Motion should be denied!" Lucifer was panicking now. The situation was completely beyond his influence and he knew it.

I gave Muriel some ammunition. I looked at Lucifer and said, "What, you want to tell us about what a paradise Hell is?"

"My palace is a paradise."

"So is Heaven. What can you offer better than Heaven?"

Lucifer was dead silent. He knew that anything he said would be asking for another lightning bolt. Muriel waited patiently, then said, "Closing arguments may begin."

Lucifer pulled himself together. He was smooth again. "Singer is good," he said. He looked at me with longing. "She's really good. She has actually convinced you all that Brock shouldn't go with me.

"That's talent.

"She has shown herself to a gifted speaker. A smooth talker. Someone with the intelligence and skill to manipulate the angels themselves.

"She's practically another me."

I bit my tongue and kept my mind running. Insulting? Oh, God, yes. But I couldn't let that distract me from my goal. I scanned every statement for things I could use once I started my closing arguments. I'd deal with Lucifer's comparison later.

"You have the Morning Star and the shining star standing here before you. What are the differences between us? Well, our genders. I'm an angel, she's human. But the biggest difference is that, in this case, I am actually speaking the truth. We all know what is to become of Brock. Before my appearance, Singer and Gallows were hoping desperately to change your minds, so you would go along with reincarnation instead of the fate you were ready to give, Casting Down. You know how this is to go. The right thing is to send Brock to me. Any other choice is not your own, it is given to you by her, a lowly human. She is not the authority, you are. You know what you are to do. Cast Brock, as his crimes and inhumanity are exactly what you are supposed to Cast. Thank you."

I kept at ready. Gallows had to speak next. But he was silent. Everyone looked at him. He was huddled against the wall, facing away from Lucifer and eyes squeezed closed.

Muriel made the obvious decision. "Singer? Your closing arguments, please."

I went right for the throat. "I am a gifted speaker. I am a smooth talker.

"I am not on trial. Brock is.

"There is no manipulation going on here."

Lucifer let out a snort.

"Well, there is on his part," I said while pointing to Lucifer. I looked at Michael, and he mouthed to me, "Good recovery." I continued. "The Celestial Courts are not about reviewing a person's life. Angels already know everything about the Petitioner. What they are about is establishing mercy. Showing that people deserve understanding, forgiveness, and a Heavenly reward. Mankind, by its very nature, makes mistakes. Sins. Hurts. And those factors are weighed by you, the Tribunal.

"The tendency of the Court is towards mercy. Always has been, always will be. It's why so few are ever Cast. You look at Petitioners and want to see them gain a Heavenly reward, either by their immediate lifetime or through some sort of atonement. How is agreeing with the Tribunal manipulating them?

"It isn't. Angels want humans to learn. Brock wants to learn. He's doing it already, his behavior changing before your eyes! That is with the short exposure of this trial. Imagine what another lifetime can do! You know what you are to do. You are to help humanity become great. Here is a chance to do so. One more lifetime. If he blows it again, he gets Cast next time. But can you honestly say he is beyond hope? That one more lifetime won't do it? You know the answer. Grant him reincarnation. Thank you."

Muriel looked at the Tribunal. "You have heard the Advocates state their recommended fates. You may now make your decision. You wish to confer?"

The angels on the Tribunal whispered to each other for a few moments. It seemed to take longer than usual. Finally, the lead Tribunal stood and said, "We are ready to rule."

"And what is your decision?"

"Petitioner is to be reincarnated in accordance with Singer's suggestion."

Muriel declared, "So be it!" and slammed the gavel, ending the session.

In a flash, Lucifer moved. He still had the speed of angels. He was up to me before I knew what was happening. He grabbed my breast with one hand and my crotch with the other. He pressed against me, flooding my body with sensations. Wondrous sensations. Orgasmic sensations. It didn't matter that I was a spirit instead of a physical body, he knew exactly how to get my reactions. He was trying to take what he wanted. He was raping me.

The feelings were like cloth bandages, mummifying me and cutting me off from the outside world. Somehow, I saw Michael's flaming sword appear and heard him scream, "Hannah!"

I immediately forced up my right hand in a stop gesture to Michael. "No!" I ordered.

I felt my mind slipping under the torrents of euphoria. Nothing ever felt this good. Nothing would ever feel this good. Not Heaven. Not becoming an angel. Nothing. And it could never be taken away from me. I wouldn't let it. And if I somehow lost it, I would do anything to get it back.

My will, my self-control, could not stop my mind from spiraling away. I focused on moving, stepping slowly, carefully, deliberately to Michael and the Guardians. As I did, Lucifer kept his grips and continued fondling me. He would get his lips on mine and give me a kiss that shook me to my foundations. I let the sensations happen, forcing myself not to accept this. I pulled my mouth away, and disappointment descended on me like an avalanche. The only respite from it was another kiss, filling me with bliss.

I finally made it to Michael and the Guardians. I reached with my right hand and felt the hilt of the Guardian's sword. I twisted my wrist, getting a grip on the handle.

And I attacked.

In one motion, I drew the sword and swung it onto Lucifer's back. It wasn't enough to chop into him, but it put me into position to pull it across him, like carving a goose. Lucifer knew what was about to happen. He released me and spun out from the blade.

I forced my mind to ignore my emotions. Strong though they were, they were manageable, just like my rage and fear. As the shock and disappointment processed themselves, I gripped the sword in both hands and took up a stance, ready to lunge at Lucifer. I sneered, "Now I'm going to take what I want....

"Your head!"

Lucifer produced a sword and took up a defensive position. But he had heightened me so much, I disarmed him with one swing. His sword slid across the floor of the court as I pressed, taking advantage of his shock. He spun and scrambled, running into the Celestial table. He turned to see me raise the sword above my head. He dashed aside as the sword clanged against the table.

Lucifer quickly reached out and grabbed my breast again. I elbowed him in the face. It was enough to make him break contact and fall back. He held up his hands. "Stop! A human cannot defeat an angel!"

"Then you don't have to worry!" I swept in with an arcing motion. I heard Lucifer cry out. I repositioned the sword and my stance and went defensive so I could see what happened.

My last swing had cut a good gash in Lucifer's left forearm. A thick, black substance, thicker than blood, was starting to come out of it. It didn't pour, but stretched, like molasses on a cold day.

Lucifer raced over to his sword, grabbing it with his right hand. He held it out to me, and I could see it wavering a little. He was scared. "I'm not going to hurt you!" he cried. "I love you!"

Lucifer was focused on me, and didn't notice Michael come up casually behind him. Michael had already willed his flaming sword away. Michael extended his left arm and put his left fist on top of Lucifer's head. Then he windmilled his right fist up, around, and smacked it on top of his left fist like a pile driver. Lucifer dropped through the floor so fast, I almost missed the movement.

Michael looked at me. There was concern on his face, but it was nothing compared to the pride. It was that smile, the one I always missed and never got tired of. The kindred spirit smile. "You okay, Hannah?"

I took quick stock of myself. Only now did I notice that I wasn't panicked. Infuriated, sure, but not panicked. A solid core of strength and faith, permeating every part of me. I didn't feel like smiling. I just nodded and said, "Yeah. I'm okay."

I shifted into a regular stance, and only now got a good look at the blade. There was some black ooze on it from when I cut Lucifer. I laid the sword flat, my right hand holding the hilt and my left hand supporting the blade, being careful not to touch the ooze. I walked up to the Guardian I took it from and presented it to him. "Your sword, sir. Thank you."

The Guardians smiled at me. Was it the same smile Michael had? The Guardian placed his hands against mine and pushed the sword back. "No. The sword is yours now."

I blinked in confusion. "But it's a Guardian's sword."

He pointed to the ooze. "You did this. You have earned this."

I felt tears welling up in my eyes over this honor and gift I was being given. "But what will you do?"

"I will get another from the armorer, Singer."

I choked out, "...I'm not an angel. I'm a human."

I suddenly heard Michael whispering in my ear. "That's right. So quit arguing with the angel, human!"

I turned to look at Michael. As he beamed at me, he said, "Let me just make sure this is safe for you. Please present your sword."

I did everything automatically. I stood proud and held the sword straight up, like a knight saluting his lord.

Michael willed his flaming sword to appear. First, he touched the ooze with it. I heard the sizzle as the angel fire seared the ooze. The scent of sulfur erupted, then quickly drained away.

Michael then touched his sword to mine. The flames engulfed the blade, their lights merging and reinforcing each other. When Michael removed his sword, the flames on mine vanished. But instead of glowing red like heated metal, it glowed a brilliant white before the light poured inside the blade.

I was just staring for a moment, then I remembered. I looked to the dock. Brock was still in there, crouching down a little, like the banisters would actually provide him some protection. I glared at him and stuck my arm straight out, pointing to the Petitioner's exit. "Get moving!"

He scrambled out of the dock, actually tripping a couple of times as he raced to the door, opened it, and vanished through it. Once the door closed and the latch echoed around, I looked at all the angels. Muriel was smiling. The Tribunal was smiling. The angels in the Gallery were smiling. I felt their admiration. Their respect. Their love.

And in that moment, nothing Lucifer did to me felt better.

My cases after that were simple stuff, so Michael reassigned them so I could catch my breath. I wanted to take them, but he insisted.

Michael then raced off to talk to God. That figured, given Lucifer had been in our midst. When Michael returned, he took me to Earth, to a great place in Germany. Great beer. Being spirits, Michael and I can drink as much of it as we want and never get hammered, so it really was the taste that kept us coming back.

We turned up on the streets away from the place. We needed to get some cash first. There are bank accounts set up around the world with very trusted people where extra money angels find or earn is deposited for any of us to use. Michael kept his arm around my shoulder, like the big brother he is to me, hugging me to him and laughing heartily. I love Michael and love being around him, but I was looking forward to the restaraunt, when I'd finally have a little personal space.

We finally got there. We took seats (across from each other, my insistence) and ordered. As the giant mugs of beer were set at our table, I looked at Michael odd. "This is quite a celebration."

"It's a big day for you, Hannah."

I picked up my mug. "Well, okay, I beat the devil. I guess it is a big deal."

I started drinking, and soon got far enough that I could see Michael through the glass of the mug over the beer. I stopped drinking and lowered the mug so I could get a better look. He was looking at me...strange. It was the kindred spirit smile, but there was more to it. "What?" I asked him.

He picked up his mug and held it out to me in toast. "Just celebrating a great spirit."

I let out a snort. "You had to be worried back there."

"Not really," he said. "I mean, you were resisting Lucifer. Even I never expected what he tried, and you still fought it off. And the trial? Never a moment's doubt in my mind."

"Bull," I told him.

"I'm serious, Hannah," Michael said with a smile. "The devil can't win. He's not allowed to."

I looked at Michael strange. "Then how does he succeed in his evil?"

"Well, in those instances, he's allowed to win by someone. But anyone that defies him? He can never defeat them."

"That's kind of a mind boggling concept," I told him. "I mean, fallen or no, he's still an angel. And the lowliest angel is greater than the greatest human."

"He makes himself lower," Michael explained. "In order for him to do what he does, he has to reject being an angel."

"Just like people in Hell reject their humanity."

"Exactly. In those moments, what he was falls away. Angels don't do those things, so in those moments, he's not an angel. QED."

"So, in those moments, he's actually inferior to those he tempts."

"Yes. And it is why he will never win." Michael leaned close and whispered, "It's God's perfect revenge, because Lucifer can never have what he truly wants. And he knows it. And it drives him crazy."

I shivered a little as I said, "He wants me."

"That he does," Michael said.

"He said he loves me."

"Well, he sort of does."

I knew what Michael meant. Lucifer loved me the way he loved a trophy -- something to show off, something to horde. Not something to appreciate, something to let be.

I finished off my beer. Michael downed his entire mug in record time and looked at me. "Feel any different?"

"Yeah," I said. "Much better."

Michael just kept looking at me, then signaled for refills. We were part way through when the food arrived. Great stuff. Being human instead of a spirit does have certain perks. It truly was the greatest day of my afterlife.

LIVE TO SERVE YOU

The downside of Advocating is that you experience several lifetimes, both your own and others. You get a great overview of what makes humanity so wonderful and what makes humanity so frustrating.

Humans started of as a very savage race, struggling for survival in a harsh world. It was in this world that the Old Testament was written. Before that, rule of law came from a king or ruler and what he (it WAS a male dominated society) thought was right and fair. The Old Testament was the birth of democracy, where people sought mutual laws that enabled them to live without interference, for themselves or from themselves. Adherence was crucial and defiance was severely punished. It was an era when dissension could expose entire societies to destruction. Things improved quite a bit by the time of the New Testament. Before, God was seen as powerful and angry and continually disappointed in His creation. Jesus showed up to correct that erroneous belief. God was wonderful and good and benevolent. He also taught the simplest lesson – be good to each other.

Needless to say, lots of people don't want to hear that. They didn't want to hear it back then, when becoming powerful and great was the most important thing. No one wanted to be told that their quest for power and greatness was ultimately not what they were supposed to do (this is partly what got Jesus in so much trouble with the Pharisees). And even when they embraced The Way, as Christianity was called in the early days, they still were after power and greatness. God's glory came from bringing people into the church, not living in harmony with those who thought or were different. It's an element of human nature that, sadly, doesn't go away.

Now, there are parts of humanity that are pleasantly surprising. Exhibit A – Henry Gallows. The Church hierarchy hadn't just been shaken up, it was a tectonic shift. Several Churches had vacated their posts due to a collective act of hubris. Nature and power abhor a vacuum, and when this one finally filled, Gallows was standing on top of the pile, the new senior Church.

It was supposedly a quirk and dumb luck that saw Gallows rise to power. I eventually started wondering if it was actually Divine Intervention. I mean, God would never interfere with the Churches' business. But at the same time, there was no way in the world Gallows would have ever become senior Church under normal circumstances. It's possible the Churches were trying to distance themselves from the stink of Thomas Calvary and chose someone as unlike him as possible. All I knew was I liked Gallows as senior Church.

Okay, that last sentence is a bit loaded, so I better clarify. See, I liked Victor Spire as lead Church, because every win against him was personal. He had tried using me to destroy the Celestial Courts, and I enjoyed every bit of his anger when I bested him. I like Jeff Fairchild as lead Church, because he's fun to antagonize and can be easy to beat when he puts too much confidence in the hand he holds. But I loved Henry Gallows as lead Church because he was understanding of people and was far more compassionate. Spire and Fairchild are the toughest senior Churches I've ever had the displeasure to deal with. In my nearly seven hundred years experience, I would say Gallows is the best senior Church I ever had the pleasure to deal with.

Gallows' forgiving nature didn't go over to well with certain underlings. In particular, one named John Fulton, the number three Church. There are those who simply do what they are supposed to. Ethics or philosophy or whatever keep them from reaching beyond their limits. They see no reason to. But all it takes is one person who sees no reason they shouldn't reach beyond, to push those limits, to do things no one bothers to forbid because it never occurred to them that someone would try, and it creates a crisis. Like a tidal wave, it starts out small, and by the time it reaches its full height, the only question is, how do you survive it?

As much as I liked Gallows, Fulton hated him. The number of petitions the Churches contested had dropped dramatically. There were more than enough Celestials to handle the basic ones that went to trial, meaning my case load was almost exclusively grey area cases, which were my specialty anyway, and even those were fewer. In fact, most of my trials against Gallows were ones where both sides contested. I actually had time to catch up on my reading. It was great.

Frankly, the light work load concerned me. Gallows couldn't be a Church forever. Sooner or later, he'd vacate, and I'd likely be facing another fire and brimstone type. After all, that was just about everyone rising through the ranks behind him. I wanted to know I still had my talent, that Hannah Singer could take on the really hopeless cases, and protect some soul who was in serious danger of being Cast Down but didn't deserve it. And in 1855, I got my wish. And then some.

Hal Douglas was a slave from the southern United States, just before a horrible event called the American Civil War or War Between The States began. The sides were divided by attitude. One side of the country felt the need to regulate and tell others what to do, the other wanted to be left alone. There were several places where the conflict played out, but the biggest stage was the subject of slavery. The southern states had an economy that hinged on it, the northern states had been moving away from it. Environment was the deciding factor. Weather patterns in the southern states were ideal for plantations. Not so in the northern states with their unpredictable weather, harsh winters, and rocky regions. The north adapted to become more business and manufacturing based. Since these things were fixed as far as supply and demand went, they were able to excel. Not so farming, where natural disasters, bad crops, or harsh luck could still sink an entire family fortune.

The debate about slavery and whether it was wrong or not was divisive. New states brought into the union had to maintain a legislative balance. Shortly before it happened, St. Michael was telling me about the upcoming secession of the southern states into the Confederacy and the war that would follow. It would be the bloodiest war ever fought on American soil.

"That's a frightening prophecy," I told him.

"It's not prophecy," he responded.

"Logic and reason?"

"Sometimes, that's all prophecy is."

It was horrifying. The Battle of Gettysburg was about to happen, everyone here knew it and how it would play out. I went to talk with God and we watched it all begin.

"I wish I could make it stop," I told Him.

"I wish I could, too," He said sadly.

And the worst thing was, as deadly and horrible as that war was, it was just a warm-up for a couple that would be starting the following century.

No one realized the future bearing down on them like a runaway train. Least of all Hal. Hal was a good Christian. At least, he thought so. He wasn't entirely sure what being a Christian meant. See, slaves weren't allowed to learn to read or write. This created a problem, because Christianity was used to control the slaves and keep them in line. Southern Christians used the Bible as justification for slavery, and told slaves that, if they did as the Good Book told them, they'd have no trouble getting into Heaven. But since they couldn't read themselves, there was considerable doubt that the Bible really said that, and meant that a lot of questions were unanswered (how many people who champion the Bible actually know its contents in depth?). This stirred feelings of rebellion that the slave owners had to deal with.

The Douglas plantation had a slave uprising. Hal wasn't entirely sure how he got swept up in it. All he knew was he was tired of the life he was living. He didn't have a plan, he didn't have an objective, he didn't even really try for escape. He was just lashing out, and he got caught. In order to teach a lesson to the other slaves, the master of the Douglas plantation brought everybody around the tallest tree on the property. Everyone watched in horror but were helpless to do anything as Hal was put on a horseback with a noose around his neck. The horse took off, the weight of the knot did its job, and Hal was on his way to the Afterlife.

Angels found Hal. He was too panicked to try hiding. It was then that he got the best news he'd ever heard. Everything he'd been told about slaves getting into Heaven was true. Slaves fell under Automatic Entry. They were slaves. They had a harsh life with no love, liberty, or compassion. It wasn't Divine Rule so much as simple consideration – you've suffered enough.

With a couple of angels talking and keeping him happy, he went to the Clerks office and filed his petition. He then went right to Penance Hall and took care of his sins. Nothing he had to stand trial for. He wasn't even taken to the Interim with the other Petitioners, everyone figured he'd be on his way to Heaven shortly. No one expected any problems. No one expected a trial. No one expected me to even learn of Hal's existence, let alone defend him. And no one was expecting a crisis that could have destroyed the Celestial Courts.

And it was all thanks to John Fulton.

As I mentioned, I was not initially involved in any of this. However, both Michael and Gallows told me about it later, and I know them (and Fulton) well enough to fill in any gaps.

The first stop for Hal's petition was Michael's office. He didn't even look as he signed, "No contest". This is actually where things went wrong. Had the petition gone to Gallows first and he entered "No contest," none of this would have happened. Hal's petition was left on Gallows' desk while he was handling a trial. Fulton had come in to look over the newest batch. His timing couldn't have been better. He looked over the petitions, and when he got to Hal's, his eyes shot wide. He raced to the Archives and requested Hal's scroll. Reading it, a sinister plan grew in his head.

He summoned a couple of Putti and asked them to simply locate St. Michael. Michael was in a perfect spot, talking with a couple of Celestials and giving them pointers on their cases. Fulton put on his game face and walked up.

"So, Michael, are you ready for Douglas' trial?"

Michael looked at him strange. "'Trial?' Gallows is contesting?"

"Well, yeah. I mean, he was part of a slave uprising. Nearly killed a couple of his masters."

Michael knew Gallows better than to think he would actually contest. And yet, Gallows was supposedly going to contest. The cognitive dissonance was strong enough to confuse Michael, which doesn't usually happen. He sent the Celestials on their way. "Where is Gallows?"

"Finishing up a trial in the Celestial Courts."

Michael walked to the courts, not realizing Fulton had fallen into step behind him. Fulton motioned a couple of other Churches he was tight with to follow. The moment he waiting for was at hand.

Michael had just gotten to the courtroom when the doors opened and Gallows came out, a junior Church and a couple of Celestials in tow. "Hello, St. Michael. How are you doing today?"

"Why are you contesting Hal Douglas' petition?"

Gallows tilted his head in confusion. "I'm not contesting it."

"I thought you were."

"Not at all. You already filed 'no contest', right?"

"That's right."

"I was going to decline contest, as well. Douglas is going to Heaven."

As soon as Gallows said he would decline contest, Michael freaked. Too late, he knew what was happening.

Fulton stepped deftly around everyone and said. "You will oppose petition on the grounds of Biblical violation. And I'll lead the case."

Gallows looked at Fulton like he lost his mind. "I'm senior Church. That is my decision to make, not yours."

"Collusion."

Gallows paled. Collusion is the greatest crime that can be committed in

120

the Celestial Courts. Cutting a deal with anyone anytime for any outcome was grounds to automatically Cast Down. Fulton had just set Gallows up. Michael was safe, it is nearly impossible to make Collusion charges stick to an angel. Gallows, though, was on very thin ice.

Michael thought quickly. Could he defend Gallows against Collusion? Very likely. But even if Gallows pulled through, the accusation would not only affect his decision making, but it would increase the chances of an insurrection among the Churches. Their last senior had tried to boss God around. Now, another bad apple in the barrel. They'd be concerned they'd never be taken seriously by the Tribunals ever again and would try to force him out.

Faith is hard. A belief in the face of all evidence to the contrary that things will work out the way they are supposed to. It makes everyone nervous, humans and angels.

"Contest it," Michael said.

Gallows and Fulton looked at Michael in surprise. Gallows looked scared. Fulton looked like a kid with a lifetime of Christmas presented to him at once. Gallows choked out, "I can't...it's not right...."

Michael put his hand on Gallows' shoulder and smiled. "Contest it, and let Fulton lead. Don't put yourself at risk here."

"What about Douglas? What about you?"

"Those are my problems anyway. Do what you have to do."

Gallows was now facing the faith conundrum. All he could do was nod. He shuffled off, his shoulders drooping, his spirit battered. The Churches followed behind, talking excitedly amongst themselves and celebrating. As they walked, Fulton turned around. Walking backwards, he said, "You might want to stay away from this case yourself, Michael. You know, just in case." Fulton might not get Collusion to stick to Michael, but he could make a mistrial if he lost a very good possibility.

Michael stood in numb silence. He and the Celestials just watched in shock as Fulton and his crew went around the corner. Once they were gone, Michael's face darkened with fury. He shot his hand into the air, one finger extended. A putto zipped up. Before the child angel could even salute, Michael grumbled without looking at him, "Have a guardian bring Hannah Singer to my chambers NOW!"

The putto practically vanished. Asking a Guardian to bring someone meant time and speed were of the essence. Michael was equally fast, and went straight to his chambers to wait for me.

There was no need to substitute me at trial. I had finished up a case and returned my scrolls. My copy of "Eugene Onegin" was with me. I was heading for the steps by the Eternal Sunrise to get some reading in before returning to my quarters. A guardian zipped up directly in front of me. I almost ran into him. I didn't even have time to register anything as he touched my shoulder and we wound up in Michael's chambers. I knew my surroundings, so I recovered. A guardian? No explanation? Something very very bad was happening. Michael needed his best Celestial.

When we arrived, I was facing the back of Michael's chambers and the guardian faced the front. I turned around, and saw Michael and seven other angels. All had their wings out. Official business. The angels stood and looked stoic. They weren't here to consult, they were witnesses. Michael was seated and looked ready to spit nails. Every other thought vanished from my head. I strode forward, standing between the two highback chairs in front of his desk.

Michael didn't bother with preamble. "You are to lead the defense of Hal Douglas."

"Background?"

"Slave. Southern United States. Killed for his part in an uprising."

"Grounds for contest?"

"Unknown. Gallows isn't handling it."

"What happened?"

"Fulton set him up. Tried to frame him for Collusion."

"He's leading the opposition?"

"Yes."

"Douglas' scroll?"

"Was in Gallows' possession. Fulton likely has it now."

"Fulton's playing dirty?"

"This is beyond playing dirty."

"Casting Down?"

"Yes."

"Instructions?"

"Two items – first, you must uphold the Bible. Fulton's case will likely hinge on how slaves are their masters' property. The Bible is still the foundation the Courts are built on. You can examine, you can explain, you can interpret, but you cannot undermine it."

"Second instruction?"

"Do not do this pretty. Nail Fulton to the wall."

"Already working on it."

"Good."

And I walked purposefully out of Michael's chambers.

The Churches had filed their opposition to Hal's petition and requested trial. Because Michael didn't contest, he never requested a trial. As I was lead, it was up to me to do it when I was ready. That gave me time to figure out how I was going to handle this.

I had squared off with Fulton a couple of times, but they were low risk cases. He was bound and determined to win this one by any means he could. I started working and examining as much as I could without Hal's life scroll.

I started by pulling the life scrolls of his family, his masters, everyone that I could think of in his life. It would help me figure out the hole at the center of the puzzle and make it easier to fit the piece when I got it. Then, I talked with Hal for a while. He was a good guy. Fulton was way out of line.

Even after all this, Fulton still hadn't returned the scroll. I decided it was time for a show of force. Fulton enjoyed rumors and being sneaky, so I wagered that he would react to it. I let word get around that I was going to the Water Garders to consult with Gallows about Fulton and how he argued. I then went to the Water Gardens, by myself, and waited.

I was lying back on one of the walls, reading the Bible to get an overview of how slaves were regarded in its pages. Eventually, I heard footsteps approach. The section I was in was relatively isolated. The stride and direction said whoever it was wasn't wandering around, they were looking for someone. I carefully closed the Bible and set it aside, looking up at the sky. "Hello, Fulton. Fancy running into you here."

Fulton stood next to me, looking down into my face. "Hello, Singer."

I extended both of my arms towards the sky, sticking out my index finger on each hand and crossing them into an "X". Suddenly, five guardians appeared out of nowhere, glaring at Fulton. Calling guardians is not something generally done, there has to be a threat of some kind. Word had gotten around about what Fulton had pulled. The guardians weren't about to let Fulton rook over the greatest threat to his plan.

Fulton smirked. He knew I called the guardians to act as witnesses against his manipulations. "Good talk, Singer." He turned to start walking away.

"Ah, ah. Not so fast," I said.

He turned to look at me. "What is it?"

"Douglas' scroll."

He knew he could never get away with keeping it from me, but he wasn't going to just give it to me. "When do you need it by?"

"You want to risk a mistrial on grounds of interference?"

I saw Fulton suddenly straighten up. Gallows would be able to decline to contest a second time. Fulton could be replaced as lead. And he could be hit with Gross Misconduct charges.

"I'll get the scroll."

"Would you like some help?" I gestured to the guardians around me. When someone won't give up a scroll, guardians can force its surrender. With the scroll no longer in his possession, the risk of a mistrial went way down. But I wanted to make sure he knew he wasn't playing with kids here.

"I'll be right back," he growled. Fulton left, and eventually returned with the scroll. I hadn't changed position. He thrust it at me. I sat up, lightly plucked from his grasp, and gave him a sunbright smile. "Thaaaaaanks."

"You're going to need more than your cute little tricks to beat me in court, Singer."

"You think I don't have a winning strategy?"

"You haven't requested trial yet. Admit it, you're stumped."

"I am never stumped for long. Hal will be on his way to Heaven, and you'll be wiping egg off your face."

"We'll see, Singer. We'll see." And he walked away.

123

Once he was gone, the guardians bowed respectfully to me and went on their way. Only when I was alone did I let my mask fall away. I had been hoping the scroll was unnecessary. But all the information I was getting gave me nothing. The Bible said that, for a slave to earn a Heavenly reward, they needed to faithfully serve their master. Hal defied his. No one had really argued like this, so there was no way to tell how the Tribunal would rule. In order to get Hal into Heaven, I had to create an exception to Biblical law. Establishing that the Bible was wrong would create a dangerous precedent that would either eliminate all Biblical law, or dismantle the Celestial Courts. That wasn't an exaggerated fear. Celestials had a duty to uphold the Bible. Doing otherwise was a violation of that duty.

You have to keep in mind that we Celestials know the true history of the Bible. We know who really wrote it, we know what parts of it are true, what parts are fiction, what parts are embellished or rewritten, what was excluded, and the reasons for it. We have to keep it secret, because we are still arguing against laws built on what it is. It is still the foundation. Exposing true Christian history and the actual history of the Bible itself could plunge a lot of soul's fates into chaos.

I skimmed Hal's scroll. There was literally nothing in there I didn't already know by now. It was a dry hole. I was up against the brick wall of what the Bible says about slaves and how they are to behave. It would have been easy to simply toss aside, but that would mean invalidating the Bible.

I kept up my workload. Everybody was avoiding me for fear of giving Fulton ammunition to use for a mistrial. Michael couldn't help me. I couldn't even visit him. I missed my big brother. I would have even been happy with some sort of prank. Other Advocates couldn't offer anything more than a sympathetic ear. Even the other greys weren't sure what they could say or do to help me.

It was after a case wrapped that I came out of court and saw St. Thomas Aquinas. He was leaning against the wall, waiting for me. There was a picnic basket by his side. "Hello, child. I was making myself some sandwiches, and I appear to have made too many. I don't want them to go to waste. Would you care to join me?"

I smiled, the first real joy I felt since this whole thing began. Aquinas was a legend. I personally regarded him as the sharpest mind that ever lived since the time of Jesus. The only reason he wasn't considered a prophet like Moses or Jesus was he refused the label. Being a saint was enough for him. Exceptional insight, great humor, and lightning quick, he was someone I admired, despite some of his ideas.

Aquinas wrote on the subject of gender roles and women's places in the world. His views were very traditional. Needless to say, a woman like me would regard his summations as bunk. To be fair, his stances weren't as annoying and offensive as Timothy's from the Bible. I was pretty much the only who called him on it. We would debate back and forth quite frequently. I did notice he debated with me differently from others on the subject. It wasn't because I was a woman, but because he was exploring my ideas and considering what I had to say. I did likewise with him. Despite our disagreement, we still liked and respected each other.

When the subject was something other than gender roles, Aquinas was wise and his council was incredible. I had yet to win a single mock trial against him, the guy is just too good. We weren't exactly friends, certainly not on the level that Michael and I were, but we got along well. And just having a friendly person to be with that understood what I was going through was a big relief.

We strolled to the Blooming Meadow. Aquinas chose a spot next to a duck pond. The spot had a shade tree with a couple of rocks perfect for lounging. We sat down, Aquinas keeping the basket close to him. He first produced a large canteen. He uncorked it, and I recognized the scent right away – jasmine tea, my favorite. He gave me a pint glass, held one for himself, and filled them both up. He then produced a sandwich for each of us. We ate and drank in silence, watching the ducks paddle along the surface.

After a little while, I said, "Thank you."

"Well, I heard what a hard time you were having in court."

"I'm not having a hard time in court."

"I sat in on your last trial," he said with a smile. "Your closing arguments are usually far more succinct."

I winced. I was become wordy and verbose. I tried to get myself on track so that I wouldn't lose the Tribunal when I spoke, but I was distracted. I just couldn't keep focused.

"Hal Douglas' case is that hard, huh?"

"Yeah," I said, leaning my head back against the rock. "It's the whole thing about how slaves are to be to their masters."

"Ah," he said, topping off our glasses. "The ancient ways applied to the wrong times."

"The problem is convincing them that ancient ways don't apply anymore."

"I'm not sure that should be such a problem."

"What makes you say that?"

"Well, child, the ancient ways you are arguing are just that – ancient. Times have changed. Otherwise, there wouldn't be debate about whether or not slavery is wrong anymore, would there?"

I smirked at him. "Are you saying, had you been born today, your philosophies about gender roles would be different?"

"Maybe a little, but not much. I still believe the differences in the genders are assigned by God. Women are the life bringers, the nuturers, and the men provide for them so they can do so. I might have clarified my stances more, but I don't think they'd be all that different."

I looked at him levelly. "So how do you even put up with me? I should be an affront to your beliefs."

"Living in a way that works for you is not an affront to me. If I rejected you for living as you see fit, THAT would be an affront to me. Remember, I was addressing generalities, not specific people. I mean, have I ever denied the import of Deborah?"

Deborah was a prophetess and a warrior. She was selected by God to be a Judge, saving the Israelites from the Canaanites. She pulled together an army and created the plan of attack. With the help of another woman, Jael, she soundly defeated the Canaanites. When I was alive, those reading from the Bible did not mention her. She's one of the few Biblical people I'm sorry I never met.

"No," I admitted. "You haven't."

"My beliefs are not centered on what people do when they are needed. They are centered on how mankind developed with the traits they possessed. The world is changing. It is getting to a point where the individual talents of the gender groups can be applied in new ways. Women will eventually become more self-sufficient and able to handle duties that used to be left for men. Men will eventually have the opportunity to appreciate the experiences of women. And all because society has evolved to a point that will enable that to happen.

"Look at history. Farming? Science? Manufacturing? The arts? None of these things existed until basic survival needs were no longer an issue, when people were able to think about more than where the next meal could be found or where they could hide from the weather. As more survival concerns are handled, more human concerns can be addressed. I wouldn't be surprised if mankind develops to a point where almost all gender roles have to be reconsidered."

"Lots of people on Earth will have problems with that."

"They might. Or they might not. Many will be open to the possibilities, of seeing what the changes enable mankind to do. Of the new horizons of life that can be reached. And those that don't? Well, if they hold back human development too much, God will simply select another prophet and charge them with a whole new Testament. And the Word and Wisdom Of God will be taught and people will see the light."

I felt like I'd been drenched with a bucket of ice water. Something about what he said hit a nerve with me. "Wait a minute...let me get this straight. You are saying that mankind will have a new prophet and a new Testament if they refuse to advance as they are supposed to. But if they keep advancing, no new Testament is made, because it won't be needed."

"Yes," he said with a nod. "That is exactly what I'm saying. Such a Testament would be redundant."

Aquinas was looking at me strangely. He didn't see the import of his statement that I did. I shot from my rock and wrapped him in a big hug, kissing his cheek. "St. Thomas, you have no idea how much you just helped me!" I pulled back. "I need to get back to the Archives!"

"Then, go, child! Go! Your duties come first!"

I raced away from the Blooming Meadow. I looked behind me as I went, and saw Aquinas simply shaking his head. I felt quiet pride. After all, confusing Aquinas didn't just happen, and I did it.

My first stop was Ernie Haley's desk at the Clerks' offices. He was in charge of setting up trials. I got a document from him and filled it out, requesting a trial and stating my Recommended Fate, immediate approval of petition.

I knew things would happen quickly after that. But prep time would do me no good. There were no previous rulings I could use, and no juniors I could select. Before, I was handling the case alone because everyone was too afraid of charges resulting from their involvement. Now, I was going to handle it alone because I had to. For example, Aquinas couldn't junior for me. I was going to turn on philosophical points. Fulton would have a field day with Aquinas' beliefs about gender roles and would take over all the attention. Michael couldn't help because of mistrial fears.

But I wasn't that worried. I had a plan of attack, one that Fulton wasn't anticipating. I kept going over my arguments, what he would argue back, and any twists I could think of. This case could result in a precedent, one that would prevent people like Fulton from trying things like this again. And I wanted this precedent.

Trial was set up quickly. I had a suspicion that, given the unusual circumstances, from Fulton cheating his way to trial to me going solo, that the curiosity value would be high. Sure enough, Hal's trial was assigned to the Grand Courtroom. It was the biggest courtroom, with a Gallery that occupied two floors. Lots of people were expecting a real show, from the arguments presented to the inevitable me getting in the face of my opponent.

I strode down the corridors of the Celestial Courts, carrying a couple dozen case file scrolls. Fierce determination was etched on my face, and my bare feet slapped on the stone floor as I went. I was moving briskly enough, my robes billowed slightly in my wake. I have no doubt I looked very dramatic.

I kept the vibe going when I got to the entrance to the Grand Courtroom. Before the guardians on either side could move for them, I pushed the double doors open from the center, flinging them in without breaking my stride. The entire lower Gallery and the Churches at their table turned to look, and they got the full effect. Silence descended on them, and it eventually drifted up to the second floor. Everyone was watching Hannah Singer take her place at the Celestial table.

I began organizing the scrolls. You can tell how tough I think a trial will be by how I place them. If I keep them close to me, I want to keep the facts they contain within immediate reach. If they aren't that important, I leave them more scattered. I knew the trial would hinge mostly on arguments I made at the spur of the moment, they were relatively isolated. Still there, but not right on top of me. I know the Churches saw.

Conversation had more or less resumed in the Gallery. It was packed. I sat and twisted in my seat, taking a quick scan, and saw only two seats left open. One was directly behind me, and the other was directly behind Fulton. Eventually, Michael and Gallows entered. They were side by side. But their faces showed the difference between them. Gallows was hoping I could pull this off, but he wasn't sure how. Michael knew I could pull it off, but he wasn't sure how. Each of them sat on their respective sides and waited for trial to start.

Eventually, the two Guardians entered, escorting Hal Douglas. As I was his defender, they dropped him off with me. Douglas took the seat to my right. He looked scared. He had every right to be. I fed off it, steeling my resolve to end this farce once and for all.

I reviewed some of the scrolls, keeping my mind sharp. I could no longer hear the Gallery or anything else. When I'm that focused, only one sound will penetrate the fog. I heard the chimes that signaled court was convening. Everyone shot to their feet and those with wings deployed them. Hal got a look at my simple ceremonial wings. Each was shaped like a giant, upside down teardrop, with a small teardrop on the outside and a flat top. Even after five hundred years, I hadn't changed them. Everyone else's ceremonial wings were more detailed, more ornate, more accurate, more angel-like. Hal didn't ask questions, but I know he was wondering.

The door on the right by the Tribunal box opened. Twelve angels, wings already out, marched in. I took a deep breath as I lost myself in their presence. Angels are so incredible. It makes me feel a little sad, knowing I'm only human and can't be one of them. But I can always dream.

The door at the back of the court opened, and the presiding angel entered. I got my first real ray of hope. Barachiel would be running the show. Barachiel was an expert hand. He kept things going smoothly and any attempts to derail things were handled immediately. Barachiel would force Fulton to stick to my points. If I created an exception and Fulton couldn't dance around it, this whole case was in the bag.

Barachiel banged the gavel and sat down along with the Tribunal and the Gallery. He checked over a record scroll, making sure it was ready. He didn't usually do that, so he was clearly expecting this to get loud. He then called, "Who is the Petitioner?"

"The Petitioner is Hal Douglas," I answered with confidence.

"And who are his Advocates?"

"Hannah Singer, acting alone."

"And who Advocates for the Church?"

"Jeff Fairchild, Mortimer Erlfog, and John Fulton, acting as lead," came the equally confident response from my left.

"Will the Petitioner please take the stand?" Barachiel asked.

Hal crept out to the dock and went inside. He looked at me. He had no idea how to get out of this. I was literally his only hope, and his fate hinged on a crazy scheme that had never been tried before and I had to not only sell the Tribunal on, but hope that Fulton and his juniors couldn't shut it down.

It's star time.

"This is very simple. Douglas was a slave who lived a good life and deserves a Heavenly reward. He has done nothing to warrant being blocked from it. His petition should be granted. Thank you." I threw my turn with my opening statements. I wanted Fulton to advance his Bible idea first, and I didn't want it to sound like I was trying to reinterpret anything. I was letting him bring the fight to me.

Fulton was unconvinced. "The Bible states that, for a slave to gain automatic admission, they are to serve their masters. Douglas defied his masters by participating in that uprising. That is not how slaves are supposed to act, and it bars him from automatic admission. His petition should be denied. Thank you."

Fulton advanced a little of his argument, but nothing I could really use. Barachiel decided to break up the log jam. "Miss Singer, the Bible does unfortunately state that slaves are to serve their masters. How does rebellion constitute serving his master?"

Here we go. "Master/slave relationships are now beyond the purview of the Bible."

Fulton wasted no time. "They are explicitly governed by the Bible."

"The society Douglas was a part of no longer sees slavery as acceptable."

"The American South absolutely sees slavery as acceptable."

"Then why are they trying so hard to justify it? They are searching for Scripture and reason to support their stances. If they really thought slavery was okay, they would simply say, 'We have slaves, and that's that.'"

"They are facing pressure from others to eliminate slavery. This isn't their choice."

"Then why are these others trying to eliminate slavery? The movement is relatively recent, starting about the 17th Century with the Quakers. Surely, if it was acceptable, all the other groups would have united to stop the spread while it was small. There are groups arriving at the conclusion on their own, so the problem isn't pressure, it's resistance to change."

"A resistance the Bible says is acceptable. Slaves exist within the society Douglas lived in. Even with outside pressure, the Douglas plantation was Biblically correct to own slaves, the rules apply, and Douglas violated the laws of God."

Fulton wasn't sweating. Time to turn up the heat. "But that society already disregards Biblical laws it either has no use for or disagrees with."

Fulton's face said he had a sinking feeling. "Such as?"

"'If someone has a stubborn or rebellious son who will not obey his father and mother, who does not heed them when they discipline him, then his father and his mother shall take hold of him and bring him out to the elders of his town. They shall say to the elders of his town, "This son of ours is stubborn and rebellious. He will not obey us. He is a glutton and a drunkard." Then all the men of the town shall stone him to death.' Deuteronomy 21, verses 18 to 21. A decree from God about how people are supposed to behave and serve, completely disregarded now because it is now considered morally reprehensible. Same principle applies to slavery."

"Not bad, Singer, but your argument has a critical flaw."

"Please enlighten me."

"Gladly. The context of the passage you quote has ceased to exist. The context of slavery still exists. Slavery is valid, stoning a disobedient son is not."

"So, God's law have an expiry date?"

That caught him off guard. "No, they do not. God's laws are absolute."

"Then people are choosing to nullify God's laws that no longer apply, they have the right to do so, and slavery is one such situation that no longer applies."

"They are violating God's will by disregarding what he says."

"They why haven't you contested any parents' petition on those grounds? Any opposition is already based on violating the Bible. Clearly, you do not have a problem with people disregarding absolute laws. Good enough for them, good enough for Douglas."

Fulton tried to redo his argument. "Some of God's laws do have an 'expiry date,' as you put it. But slavery is not one of them."

"Okay. What is the qualification?"

"What?"

"What determines if God's governing rules have expired? And if you have a way of determining what is disallowed, what all mentioned in the Bible no longer applies? Just the rebellious son thing? If a woman is not a virgin when she marries? Lepers declaring themselves unclean? Let's see the list."

Fulton stood there in stunned silence. I took advantage of it. "So, God's laws can expire, but you don't know for sure if the one you are prosecuting Douglas for has expired. How can you say your recommended fate is not unduly harsh?"

"Slavery is still okay."

"On what grounds? You haven't produced anything to back up your assertion, and I'm doing pretty well defending mine. I am establishing grounds for petition to be granted, you have done nothing to establish it should not."

Fulton and I stole a look at the Tribunal. They were nodding and smiling at me. Fulton's arguments were in serious trouble.

Fulton tried a different route. "If it's wrong, why doesn't God send a prophet to establish a new Testament?"

I made a note to bake St. Thomas Aquinas a cake when this was over. "God only does that when his people need to be corrected. That is why there is only an Old Testament and a New Testament."

"The New Testament was to absolve us of our sins through Jesus Christ."

"Then why did Jesus bring new laws? Why did He bring a new understanding of God? Those operating under the Old Testament had an angry, wrathful God, despite their later prophets saying God was love and understanding. Their understanding of God and humanity had stagnated, so Jesus came to show everyone the right direction. There has been no further Testament since then. Mankind has continued to develop, leaving behind things that served them in a brutal society for rules that serve them in an enlightened age. Rules they create themselves. Rules they agree to themselves. Rules either absent God's involvement or nullifying it. The laws of God are intended to be reconsidered as mankind advances, as they don't need certain things anymore."

"Not quite. We are talking about servitude. Servitude, to God, to each other, is required. It is involuntary, because it is part of dedication."

"If involuntary servitude is okay, why do the Americans specifically ban impressment into the armed services?"

"That's among humans, not in relation to God's laws."

"Slavery is among humans, not in relation to God's laws. We are God's children, not his slaves."

"We volunteer to be his servants."

"That's volunteering. We can quit any time. Slaves can't do that."

"We shouldn't quit serving God."

"But we can. We can be Atheists or not do certain things or help only certain people. And God allows us to. Ergo, we are not his slaves. And if treating people as people instead of slaves is good enough for God, it should be good enough for us."

Fulton tried getting slick. "So you are saying the Bible should be disregarded."

"Oh, no, you don't. I have said nothing saying the Bible should be disregarded, only its approval of slavery."

"You are suggesting changing fundamental laws of the Bible so this one individual can be spared the fate they have earned. Sounds like you are undermining the Bible to me."

With that one statement, Fulton put me on trial instead of Hal. I had to advance my arguments carefully and eliminate his assertions without giving him anything he could use. My mind sped up. I needed something fast. And I found it. "Others undermine the Bible, I'm simply pointing it out."

"Blaming others?"

"When it's their actions doing it? You bet."

"Like when? How do others undermine the Bible?"

"They are the ones ignoring the decrees. They aren't paying for doing so. Saying Douglas should pay while others get away with it is selective enforcement. It's unfair, it's excessive, and it should not be allowed."

Fulton was back on the defensive. "He was part of a revolt."

"A revolt against an unfair system that exploited him. Revolts and uprising exist all through history, often encouraged by Christian leaders. Remember the Crusades?"

Fulton had a choice to make. If he continued to advance slavery as okay, I could paint the circumstances as a social revolution for positive change. With my earlier assertions and the Tribunal already leaning my way, he'd be finished. If he wanted to Cast Douglas, he couldn't do that with slavery still on the table, it validated too much. But he would be risking he could still sway the Tribunal with what was essentially a new argument he had no preparation for. And against a Celestial who specialized in handling spur of the moment and ambush tactics.

"He fought in an uprising. Slavery has nothing to do with it."

"Did you read his role in the uprising? I don't see anything that constitutes Casting Down. He certainly didn't kill anyone."

"He punched a couple of people out. He trashed one of the houses."

"I believe the Irish call that 'Saturday night.'"

"It's not the same thing."

"Right. The Irish are also drunk and do far more damage. They still get into Heaven."

There was a pause, then Fulton said, "The damage he did was to the social order. No matter what you say, he was a slave."

I genuinely smiled. The precedent was as good as set. "Move for closing arguments."

Fulton looked shocked. "I object."

Barachiel looked at him. "All right. Say what else you wish to say."

Fulton just stood there, mouth moving but no words coming out. Barachiel just watched him and said, "Begin closing arguments."

Fulton tried to readjust. "This...this case...this case is about defying God's will. Douglas was a slave. Everything he was to do, everything expected of him, was presented to him. And he ignored it. Just because we don't like slavery doesn't excuse defying God's will. Douglas should be Cast Down. Thank you."

I really had Fulton shaken up. Now, my only concern was the Tribunal. They didn't have to rule according to the Advocates' Recommended Fates, they could come up with their own ideas. I had to make sure they had a good reason to rule the way they wished, and also sell them on my Recommended Fate.

"God created us. He gave us many different gifts. He gave us life. His love. His liberty. But He also gave us His trust. He gave us minds that think and reason and hearts that feel and strengthen. He gave us general, simple rules, to guide us in how we relate to the world, the times, and the societies around us.

"Had the rules been intended to be immutable, we would not need any of these faculties God gave us. We wouldn't even be part of a world beyond control. We'd still be in the Garden Of Eden, the Trees of Life and Knowledge removed so we could stay there forever, safe from the consequences of our choices.

"God guides us, but He doesn't advance us. We do that. Part of our responsibility to God is to advance. To understand things that are right and wrong and build on them. To live up to the potential God instilled in us. God did not set down His laws, from the Commandments to the teachings of Jesus, until mankind stagnated, staying where it was, advancing no further. Family relations, how to worship, these things constantly shift and change in ways we determine. God is not threatened by them, and only gets involved if we are wandering off the correct path.

"The world is changing. Ideas that, years ago, would have seemed unbelievable are happening every day. New frontiers in science. Schools for girls. The end of slavery. All these events are covered by the basic laws of the

Bible, but not the minutiae. It is why it is minutiae. When it is no longer needed, it can be disregarded, while the fundamental laws, of love, honor, and respect, still stand.

"The Bible is under no threat from this. It is why it is as it is. Mankind does not need another Testament yet. It is moving just fine, and any laws another Testament would cover are already being figured out, understood, and accepted. Slavery was part of an ancient world, where societies were harsh, survival was nearly impossible, and love was metered out only to those approved of, no one else deserved it.

"Those days are OVER.

"Slavery is being thrown away. Remove it from Douglas' sins, and what do you have left? A hard life with no real harm done, certainly less than many others who see their petitions approved. He does not deserve Heaven because he served as a slave his whole life. He deserves Heaven because he lived a good life, doing what he was supposed to. Anyone else living as he did without the canopy of slavery would see their petition approved. He should, too. Grant him the Heavenly reward that isn't promised to slaves, but earned by good men. Thank you."

Barachiel looked to the Tribunal. "You have heard the Advocates for Hal Douglas state their recommended fates. You may now make your decision. You wish to confer?"

I steeled myself, hoping that I had done right. I fought the nervousness as I watched the Tribunal whisper amongst themselves for a few moments. Then, the lead Tribunal stood up. "We are ready to rule."

"And what is your verdict?" Barachiel asked.

"Petition is to be approved immediately."

"So be it," Barachiel said. He struck the gavel.

"Call for a mistrial!" Fulton yelled.

I cringed. The trial had just been handed off to God Himself. Fulton was wagering that I was twisting the Bible and God's intent too much. And the worst part was, I could see how God might see it that way. Fulton had a valid case, and which way God would go, I had no idea.

Shafts of light streaked through the ceiling of the courtroom, illuminating Barachiel, Douglas, Fulton, the juniors, the Tribunal, and me. It was God, looking into our minds and our hearts, deciding who had erred. I felt my consciousness shifting and bending from the examination. There are no secrets from God.

Finally, the voice of God sounded in the courtroom. "Slavery is a manmade institution. My laws were to regulate it, not sanction it. Humanity is free to discard their own institutions. The trial has been fair and just. The ruling stands."

The lights vanished. No one moved a muscle. It was like we were encased in solid glass. Who would be the one to shatter it?

Turns out it was Michael. He shot to his feet, pointed at Fulton, and bellowed, "*TAKE THAT, CHURCH BOY!*" Activity returned to normal.

Barachiel and the Tribunal exited their respective doors. Douglas raced out of the dock to thank me, not even looking at the defeated Churches sulking as they walked up the aisle to leave. Douglas went through the Petitioner's exit on the left side of the courtroom. I willed my wings away and turned behind me. Michael, as usual, was beaming with pride. Gallows simply smiled peacefully and left.

The sun was bright and the air was balmy. A typical summer day in Madrid, Spain. I was touring the Museo del Prado, looking over the amazing paintings. As I looked them over, I heard a voice say, in perfect English, "From the Spanish Royal Collection, right?"

I recognized Michael's voice right away. By speaking English, we wouldn't have to shift to our spiritual voices to keep from being overheard.

I smiled. "That was hairy back there, wasn't it?"

"Glad to see you aren't mad at me."

I reached out and squeezed his shoulder. "You know me better than that, big brother. The courts come first. You were counting on me to pull it off by myself. That's more important than socializing."

"I'm glad it's over with. Up for some lunch?"

"Always."

We wandered until we found a little restaurant. We sat down and placed our orders.

"You certainly pick wonderful places to visit, Hannah," Michael said. "Took me a couple of tries to find you."

"Where did you think I was?"

"Somewhere in Italy."

I made a face. The proximity to the Vatican gave me the creeps. "What's on your mind, Michael?"

"Why would something be on my mind?"

"I was just touring an art museum. And you didn't just wait for me to return. What's up?"

Michael looked to the side for a second. "How did you figure that out?"

"Figure what out?"

"About God's laws and human institutions."

"St. Thomas Aquinas gave me the idea."

"Did he tell you?"

"No." I recounted the discussion with him to Michael. Michael simply nodded.

It was silent for a while. Our food arrived and we started eating. I wasn't sure what was going on. It's not like Michael to be so quiet.

Finally, Michael spoke. "That was my defense."

I smiled. "Great minds think alike."

"Not just great minds. Fulton knew about God's laws and human institutions, too."

I dropped my spoon. "He did?"

"Why do you think he prevented me from getting involved? I was ready to lead the defense, and he backed me into a corner. It's also why he threw a scare into anyone that could help you."

"Because he knew, if anyone could figure it out against all the odds, it would be me."

"You're the best, Hannah."

"You're no slouch, Michael. He tied your hands, and you still found a way to protect Douglas."

"Just like you did. You're almost another me, you know."

I blushed. I could never figure out how to handle high praise from an archangel. "Nah, I'm not. Not really."

I silently prayed that Michael didn't hear the sadness in my voice when I said that.

TWIST OF FATE

It may come as a surprise, but there is a turnover rate for Advocates in the Celestial Courts. On both sides, of course. I know that I'm unusual for an Advocate -- there aren't many that have been arguing longer than I have. It's like that for Church Advocates, as well. Although, they're replaced at a far more frequent rate than Celestials.

There are a few different reasons to replace a posted Advocate. The post is rarely taken away. But if too many Petitioners request a new appointment, saying they'd rather have someone else representing them, you may be informed that Advocacy isn't for you and you should vacate. However, the most common reason for an Advocate to leave their post is burnout. The continual arguing, the close-mindedness, it takes its toll. If you don't incorporate some downtime into things, it can not only eat you up inside, it could cost you the Heavenly reward you've earned. I, for example, sometimes go to Earth and watch laser light shows. None of the others do that, and lots of humans think they're cheesy, but it works for me.

This does add another element of stress to some trials, as you will run across a newly minted Church Advocate who hasn't quite figured out how things are supposed to go. Determined to uphold Truth and Integrity, he will view it as his sacred duty to eternally damn people, regardless of how heartless and merciless that is. And they will often overlook life difficulties or atonements or other things that should render whatever charge they are pursuing moot.

St. Michael keeps a close eye on the trials. New Celestial Advocates get paired with very experienced Celestials so that they don't get overwhelmed. And he makes sure that only the experienced go into trials against new Church Advocates. Just trying to keep up with misunderstandings, mistranslations, or faulty logic works them over, so just imagine doing your first Advocacy and having to cope with that. I've been there. It's not fun.

Because I've sort of drifted into senior status (and believe me, no one is more shocked that I'm doing this or have been doing it for this long than I am), that means I get to square off with new Churches who turn the trials into a Crusade. For the most part, I can handle them easily. New Churches have a certain thought process. When you understand it, you can figure out what arguments and angles they will take. Exposure helps, too. You start to notice certain arguments and lines of logic will repeat, since they all think they are the first people to conclude whatever and haven't done their research to see why it will fall apart. But every once in a while, someone will come up with something no one considered before, and you find yourself facing the real possibility that some soul who has put their trust in you is going to get Cast Down if you don't think really really fast.

His name was Lewis Essington. He lived in a rural area. Good guy, family guy.

Wife, two kids, worked as a truck driver, did everything he could to honor God and lead a Christian life, from going to church every Sunday to leading Bible studies. Even among other Christians, this guy was squeaky clean.

Essington's daughter was the youngest of the kids, and he absolutely doted on her. He didn't spoil her, turning her into a self-centered princess. But he gave her everything he could and she was a daddy's girl. She was growing up and started showing in interest in boys. Essington tried to teach her about boys who look for women they can dominate instead of love. She did listen and tried to pick good ones, and Essington kept a close eye to make sure they wouldn't hurt her.

But one slipped through the cracks. She was fifteen when she finally decided to give her classmate, who had a crush on her since grade school, a chance. Everyone in her family was fine with it. After all, they'd known him most of his life. But when the dynamic between the kids changed from friends to lovers, he changed as well. He became possessive and mentally abusive. She tried to tough it out, trying to figure out where things went wrong and how to fix it. But she started crying one night. Essington came to see what was wrong, and before she knew it, she had spilled the entire story to him. He convinced her to cut him out – no boy was worth it if he made her that miserable. She dumped him cold. Two days later, in class, the boy leapt from his desk and punched her in the head. A scrum broke out as her classmates pulled him off of her. In that instant, a happy, sunny girl became a frightened little girl, hearing threats even in silence.

The boy tried stopping by her house a couple of times, but Essington wasn't about to let anyone hurt his little girl. The boy's visits became more frequent and more belligerent. His family tried to reign him in, but it was too little too late. One night, he showed up at Essington's house. Essington stood in the doorway, refusing to let him in. The boy then pulled a gun, and demanded to speak to his daughter. Essington refused, which says a lot for him – not many have what it takes to look down the barrel of a gun and not back down. The boy became more forceful in his demands and finally decided he was done playing around. He squeezed the trigger, sending a bullet into Essington's chest. Essington started to sink lower, still holding onto the doorjamb, whether for support or to continue to block the boy, who can say. The boy, suddenly realizing what he'd done, took off running, throwing the gun into some bushes along the way. EMT's arrived shortly afterwards, Essington blacked out, still clutching the doorjamb.

It was a lucky shot, the bullet getting to Essington's heart. He was pronounced dead on arrival at the hospital. The boy was found by neighbors, who subdued him before calling the police. He spent a few days in intensive care and longer in traction afterwards. He was tried as an adult and is spending a lot of years in prison. Essington's family is in shock and still trying to get together something resembling a life. They are carrying on, although they have sort of isolated themselves. They are part of the community and talk with their neighbors and that. But their hearts have slammed shut – it's doubtful any of them will take in anyone else as family, through friendship or marriage, ever.

Essington wound up in the Valley Of Death, where a Celestial Advocate found him. Essington knew he'd led a good life, so he wasn't afraid. It didn't take much to convince him to petition for entry into Heaven.

I finished reading the case file. I looked up over it. Michael was looking back at me, a quirky look on his face contrasting with the Bermuda shorts and T-shirt covered with happy faces he was wearing. We were standing next to the Heavenly Fountain in the courtyard of the Archives.

I rolled up the scroll. "Seems pretty open and shut to me," I said. "Am I missing something?"

"If you are, then so am I," Michael shrugged. "Most Churches don't even bother with these cases. They receive the petition, they say, 'No contest', and it's over. Petitioner gets the Express Train to Heaven. But this Church decided to contest the petition."

"Must be someone new."

"You're right. The Church is a guy called Jacob Palini. Even the other Churches are wondering what he's up to. Won't talk, just says he's got a whale of a case."

"What exactly is his problem with Essington? Did he know him or his family in life or something?"

"Not as far as we can see. They even share the same Christian denomination. Nothing tips his hand."

I rolled my eyes and put the scroll in my robes. "And that's why I'm getting this. I know enough Church tricks to keep him from Casting the poor guy."

"Well, there are a couple of other Advocates, but they operate from precident. If Palini really has some new angle, I'd rather have someone who thinks on their feet in there. To stop this before it gets used against anyone else."

"Nip it in the bud, huh?"

"You got it. Give him a real Celestial Court welcome."

Like all Petitioners, Lewis Essington was staying at the Interim. A hop, skip, and a jump away from the Archives, I decided to stop there first instead of the Office Of Records. I wanted to see what Palini was feeding off of.

Essington was standing, looking at the Eternal Sunrise by the far vistas when I approached from behind. I wanted to see just how friendly he was. I called his name, "Lewis Essington?"

He turned as soon as he heard me. I was hoping Essington gave off some sort of strange vibe or had an attitude or something that would explain why this guy who looked good on paper was being targeted. But there was nothing. Essington looked like a typical, ordinary man. Average height, meaning I'd have to tilt my head or I'd be looking at his nose instead of his green eyes. Brown hair with occasional grays, typical short cut with the part on his left. A bit overweight, but solid, not sloppy. And a smile that could warm the coldest climes.

I closed the distance between us with my hand extended. "I'm Hannah Singer. I'm your Celestial Advocate."

He took my hand from the side and bowed his head deeply. "It's a pleasure to meet you, ma'am." A gentleman. The smile on my face was natural. What exactly was Palini's problem with him?

He straightened and released my hand. He was clearly nervous, but he wasn't timid. "I just wanted to review your life."

His smile drooped a bit. "Did I do something wrong?"

I held up my hand. "Don't worry, it's just standard protocol before a trial," I said with an assurance I didn't exactly feel. "Just to be prepared."

He started shifting uncomfortably. "I thought I'd be in Heaven by now."

"You should be. And that's why I've been assigned to you. To try and speed this up a bit. Why don't we sit down?" Strictly speaking, souls don't get tired or experience physical fatigue, but life conditions you to respond in certain ways, and the habits carry over. I wanted him to be at ease, and embracing his life behaviors was the best starting point.

"Is here okay?" He motioned to the steps leading down towards the vistas. He'd still be facing the Eternal Sunrise. Fine with me, I like looking at it myself. I motioned with my hand, and we sat on one of the middle steps.

I pulled the scroll with his case file out of my robes and unrolled it, giving it another solid read through. Essington was silent, and when he spoke, it startled me. "Is that a sunrise or sunset?"

I looked at the eternal sunrise and thought about it. It never changed position, never got darker or lighter, the glow making the white and pale blue of my robes look slightly orange. "To tell you the truth, I suppose it could be whichever you want it to be."

He thought for a second. "I think it's a sunrise."

I nodded and went back to the case file. I got a couple of paragraphs further when he asked, "So which is it? Really?"

I smiled at him. "It's a sunrise."

"You wouldn't lie to me, would you?"

"Absolutely not."

"You're a terrible lawyer."

"That's why I'm an Advocate instead."

He laughed. It sounded wonderful, the slight tension I detected in him gone for that moment. "So, where do we start?"

"The beginning works for me," I said, returning to the top of the scroll. But by the time we got through it, I was even more confused. He was a model soul. There was no reason to contest his Petition. I thanked him for his time (he grabbed my hand from the side and bowed again) and I left the Interim. Going out the front, I made a sharp right and went straight for the Church's Residencies.

I asked nearly everyone there where Palini was. No one would talk.

Apparently, Palini was somewhere else, hiding out to keep his element of surprise. The only place I could really think he would be was the Valley Of Death. But searching for him would take a lot of time. Time I could put to better use preparing for trial. I stalked back to the Archives and the Office Of Records.

Russell was at his usual post at the Records window, and it was quiet behind him. "A little break in the action, Russell?"

Russell perked up. Few things make him happy as working. "For the moment, Hannah. So, how did the Essington trial go?"

"Hasn't happened yet. I haven't even requested the hearing yet."

"You have another Petitioner? I mean, you already have Essington's file."

"Nope, I need the file of someone connected to the trial. I need the file for Jacob Palini."

He arched his eyebrows at me, but immediately went into the back. Asking for the files of Advocates for either side is almost unheard of. But I needed to start somewhere. He reappeared carrying a rather small scroll. Whoever this guy was, he didn't have a lot of accomplishments while he was alive.

The scroll gave me a rough idea, but nothing concrete. Fundamentalist preacher, cut his teeth on the upper-middle class, insisting that their success was guaranteed to send them to Hell if they didn't praise God every chance they got. Reinstituted tithing instead of just general collections, and would pounce on any parishioner who got a new car or suit or anything that he could accuse them of not giving enough with. Died about twelve years prior (natural causes – heart attack). Has yet to petition himself. Almost as soon as he appeared in the Valley Of Death, he sought out the Church residencies.

I stared at the scroll without really reading it. He'd been with the Churches for almost twelve years, and was only now doing his first Advocacy. That was a long time to learn. On Earth, he was constantly organizing revivals, so I doubted he was just relaxing until he was ready. He was studying cases, and he seemed to have hit on something. It made me nervous. The possibility of an untested argument coming from someone with what we Celestials call a "bully pulpit" was bad news. In the entire history of the Celestial Courts, no one who deserved to get into Heaven had ever been denied. And here was someone aiming to be the first to make it happen.

A sickly feeling welled up inside me. I wanted to just throw up so it would go away. But I was a spirit now. I had no stomach. So I went to brainstorm and prepare, the sickly feeling with me the entire time.

The court opened and the Advocates started coming in. A few new Celestials took their places in the Gallery. They usually prefer watching trials with new Churches. It's a crash course in basic arguments they may face and can prepare for.

I got to my table and set my scrolls on it. You can tell how much I think I'll need them by where I put them on the table. The less critical I think they are, the more casual I am about their position. This time, I was lining all the scrolls up and stacking them within my immediate reach.

I had about half of them ready when a pair of Guardians brought in the Petitioner, Lewis Essington. The Guardians are always huge and imposing, but they were the acting as unimposing as they could. They even had the scabbards for their swords moved to the side, where a quick draw would have been impossible. Essington still looked like he was ready for them to lop off his head without warning.

The Guardians brought Essington to my table. He smiled weakly at me. I gave him my best smile back. "Relax. This should be quick. Palini would have to come up with something really unique to make this into a trial. Nothing to worry about."

One of the Guardians cast a quick look at the scrolls on the table, then looked at me. Thankfully, Essington had no clue. "Thank you, Miss Singer," he said. "What do I do?"

"Just sit here next to me, when you take the stand, just keep calm and let me do the talking. Keep your mouth shut and don't give the Churches anything they can use."

Essington sat in the Petitioner's chair. He noticed there were four chairs total. "Expecting any others?"

"Nah. Whatever Palini's reason for contesting the petition, I don't think it'll hold up. I've heard just about every argument there is."

Essington relaxed a little, and I silently prayed that I was right.

As I did a review, I noticed the noise from the gallery seemed a little louder than usual. I took a look, and saw it was actually filling up. That's unusual. Even stranger was that there were a good number of Church Advocates mixed in the with the Celestials. They don't usually sit in on trials they don't have a stake in.

Sitting front and center was my old nemesis, Jeff Fairchild. He was looking at me with something akin to worry. Usually, he looks at me with annoyance and fury. I took a quick walk over. "Hello, Fairchild. Expecting a show?"

It was really strange seeing him react humanly instead of judgmentally. "I don't know. I'm really sorry about this. We tried to get him to drop the challenge, but he's got something in mind."

"Would you give me hints if he had told you anything?"

"This time? Yes."

A familiar voice floated towards us. "Now, now, Fairchild. Quit tampering with council."

Michael stood there, smiling. Fairchild didn't seem surprised. I was, but shouldn't have been. With the turnout and mystery, it was only natural that my boss would show up.

I excused myself and went back to my table, letting them jaw with each other – not backing down, but not pushing, either. I sat down and inched the scrolls just a little closer.

I thought about the psychological profile of Palini I built in my head. The doors opened, the gallery got quiet, and I knew I was about to find out how accurate my conclusions were. Palini's footsteps told me I was off to a good start. Unlike most attendees in the Court, he was wearing sandals. Stiff ones that clacked. His stride was forceful, measured, and with a stomp. Great. Another Crusader, looking to make an example of my client.

I peeked from the corner of my eye as he came in and took his place at the table. He stood ramrod straight, steel grey eyes looking out from white eyebrows. They were the darkest part of his face, with light skin framed by buzzcut white hair and a clean shaven complexion. He was scrawny, but his posture made him appear strong. Had he stood like a regular person, you'd think a strong breeze could lift him off the ground. His white robes actually looked dimmer on him.

I stood up and walked over, hoping to establish a little contact. Before my hand rose up to offer a shake, he said without turning his gaze, "I hope you're ready for me."

It was surprising how deep that voice was for such a small man. So surprising, I forgot to be offended by what he did. "I believe so. Essington should be on his way to Heaven."

He looked at me for the first time, moving his eyes to the corners and turning his head until I was just in his field of vision. A smile snaked its way onto his face. "You really think that?"

I wasn't about to let him cow me before the trial started. "Ambush tactics are nothing new, and I've dealt with them all."

He turned his attention back to the bench. "You haven't dealt with this one."

"Ambush tactics are always a bad idea, and they don't work with me under the best circumstances. Your approach may be different, but everything else, including the end result, will be the same."

"How does God not despair at your twisting things to let undesirables in?"

I had heard enough. I went back to my table and began reviewing my scrolls. I didn't just want to defeat his arguments. I wanted to squash them like grapes. My fierce determination seemed to have a side effect – Essington seemed to be relaxing a little. He was starting to think he might have a fighting chance.

Before I knew it, the chimes sounded. I stood up, and Essington followed my lead. I deployed my wings. I stole a quick look at Palini. He wasn't an actual angel, so he had ceremonial wings like mine. Although, mine are pretty plain. Basic wing shape and flat. You'd think they were part of the background if they didn't move with me. Palini's were noticeably larger and had dimension. With the details for feathers, they almost looked like real wings. The only way to tell he wasn't a real angel was the wings still floated behind him instead of protruding from his back.

The Tribunal came in, twelve angels, wings already out. Once again, I was in awe of the collected feeling from them. Strong, wise, compassionate, and somehow, that made them more intimidating. I looked behind me at the Gallery. It had filled, and everyone, angels and Churches, had their wings out. It was a beautiful sight. And also scary. It's never this packed. Everyone was expecting a big surprise. And I was sitting at the impact point.

The presiding angel then appeared, wings already out. It was Barachiel. I silently breathed a sigh of relief. He was well known for keeping proceedings from spiraling out of control. Clearly, Michael and the others behind the Celestial Court weren't going to let an upstart like Palini make a mockery of things. I wondered if I really wasn't looking at some untested argument and was simply watching a show of force to send a message to Palini about his ego – your arm's too short to box with us.

Barachiel looked out and folded his hands. "Who is the Petitioner?"

Essington was off to a flying start. Most people like him will answer, "It's me," or raise their hand or something. But he didn't bat an eye, move, or make a noise. He was taking my instructions to heart. Smart move.

"The Petitioner is Lewis Edgar Essington," I declared.

"And who are his Advocates?"

"Hannah Singer, acting alone."

His gaze shifted towards Palini. "And who Advocates for the Church?"

"I do, sir," he said as soon as Barachiel had finished speaking. "Jacob Palini." He gave Barachiel a smile that seemed to say, "Buddy, have I got the used car for you!"

Barachiel opened a scroll and called over it, "Will the Petitioner please take the stand?" Essington moved carefully, as if stepping too hard would break the floor and send him hurtling to Hell. It's always scary for Petitioners, because the trial is still a gamble. Their minds fill with memories and doubts as they wonder if they could have done anything different to insure the best result. Still, he stood tall and proud on the stand. I couldn't help but admire his resolve.

"Advocate for the Petitioner goes first. Singer?"

Palini had a master plan, but I didn't trust him to stick to it. If he was presented with another avenue to deny the petition, he'd take it. I decided to keep my comments general and stick to what facts Barachiel and the Tribunal already knew. Basically, I was throwing my turn, but I had the luxury of being able to do that. There was nothing in the case file that had to be explained or justified. I wanted to force Palini to reveal the direction he was heading in if nothing else. I put on my most blasé voice and attitude. "Essington is a good family man. He never lived beyond his means, he always provided for his family, was faithful, loving, and devoted. He was firm without being cruel. He spread the teachings of God. He was good as a child, didn't even steal a piece of candy. Forthright, honest, and true. In conclusion, the petition should be granted because there is no reason it should not be granted." I twitched up the left corner of my mouth, like I couldn't accept the utter gravity of the situation.

I threw in the "In conclusion" because I was aware how short my opening statement was. I didn't want Barachiel to be waiting for me to say more, setting a casual pace. I wanted to rush Palini before he had a chance to read the mood of the court. Barachiel could have asked questions and made clarifications, but he knew what I was up to. Palini was actually shifting a little bit. He reminded me of runner, ready to do what he was made for. So Barachiel raised the starter pistol and fired. "Palini? Your argument to deny the petition?"

I sensed the attention in the Gallery ratchet up. This was what everyone was waiting for, this big surprise tactic that supposedly hadn't been tried before. My gaze turned towards Palini, as well. The only one not looking at him was Essington, staring straight ahead on the stand, like the Steadfast Tin Soldier.

"The petition should be denied and the Petitioner Cast Down due to circumstances of death. Essington committed suicide."

They say that hearing the angels laugh is the most beautiful sound. Not this time. The derision and disbelief was matched only by volume. Even the Churches were laughing while trying to hide behind the wings of the angels, trying not to be noticed and not succeeding. Barachiel wasn't laughing, and a little over half the Tribunal were serious. The rest weren't laughing, but they were having trouble keeping their faces straight.

Me? I wasn't laughing. I was too busy scrambling. Palini had promised an argument I'd never heard before. Well, he didn't lie.

Palini continued on as if the courtroom was quiet. "Suicides are treated differently from regular deaths. The Bible regards them differently. Churches regard them differently. Taking your own life is the ultimate betrayal of God. God creates us. Our bodies are His. It is wrong to for someone to stop another's life. But stopping your own? You are declaring you are the master of you body, not God. And for such blasphemy, those like Essington should be Cast Down."

I didn't like the direction this was going in.

Barachiel spoke first. "Have you reviewed the correct case file? Essington didn't commit suicide, it was accidental death."

Palini's smile grew bigger. He closed his eyes and tilted his head back a bit. "Suicide involves ignoring survival instinct and intentionally doing something that will lead to your demise. Essington had someone clearly dangerous pointing a gun at him. What other outcome did he think would happen? Instead of taking reasonable measures to preserve his life, he left himself in harm's way. He took his life in his own hands. There was just an intermediary handling the gun instead of Essington himself."

Barachiel looked at me. His expression was blank, but I knew what was going through his head. It was up to me to argue against this in way that the Tribunal could rule against it and it wouldn't be used again. Palini was aiming to create a precedent, and a dangerous one at that. It would undermine all sorts of previous rulings and could be easily abused in future rulings. It would put too much power over people's destinies in the hands of the Church. So, you know… no pressure.

I looked to the Gallery. Michael had arched his eyebrows at me.

Advocates have little signals they can send when they are in trouble with a case. They can also ask for a recess while they confer with their bosses. This way, arguments can be shaped or even entire teams replaced if an Advocate is suddenly in over their head.

Fortunately, Palini's statements gave me a general direction. He was clearly ready to twist and spin his points to get the results he wanted. I would start with the basic assumptions that he based his conclusions on. If I exposed those as faulty, the conclusions would be easy pickings. Just getting rid of the branches meant other branches could grow in their place. Attack the trunk of the tree, and the branches wither away.

First things first: I had to restrict his definition, box him in. It would not only make changing his story obvious, but if he did change it, he would be unable to use the one he was abandoning. "So, the responsibility for taking his life is not in the hands of the boy with the gun, but his own."

"The shooting was the direct result of his actions and choices."

"And you aren't willing to consider it accidental?"

"Do you consider it an accident if someone closes their garage and starts their car engine? No one would argue that is suicide, even though the car is killing them, they aren't killing themselves, right?"

Palini liked to run on. He wouldn't just say something and let it go. I kept at general points, hoping he would keep feeding me counterarguments. "Ah, but the boy wasn't a machine that could be controlled. There was no automatic action. The boy could have not killed him. He could have accidentally pulled the trigger."

"How could that be considered accidental? You have someone aiming a gun at you. They clearly intend to use it. What else could he expect?"

"The boy was conflicted. Therefore, he was thinking. So it wasn't an automatic assumption that he would kill, it was simply a possible outcome. The boy chose to pull the trigger, the fault is his. It isn't suicide."

Palini's expression didn't change, and he continued to face Barachiel. "When the encounter started, yes, that is true. But as the boy became more desperate, the likelihood that he wouldn't kill became less."

"So, the boy stopped being a thinking creature and became a machine. To what degree was the result guaranteed?"

"What else would have happened?"

"The boy was trying to be assertive. So he could have just been trying to act forceful and hope to convince Essington to let him by. It could have been a bluff, a reasonable assumption."

"Even as his anger rose?"

"People get angry and talk about how they'll kill somebody. Everyone knows it's metaphorical. If you put a gun in their hand, they wouldn't actually kill the person."

"And everyone knows that, when they are in a garage and the car is running, that they should take steps to prevent the situation from becoming lethal. You could say the toxic fumes were building, and Essington did nothing to alleviate them."

As long as Palini was stuck on the car metaphor, I wasn't going to win. I thought about his statements, and found something I thought I could use. "So, by simply giving in to the boy and allowing him to see his daughter, Essington would not be on trial for suicide, right?"

I saw it. A flash of doubt. Palini knew a leading question when he heard one, and looked like a rabbit in a field that hears a strange noise. "You are attempting to oversimplify the question. There are many factors to consider."

"You have proposed no other factors. The boy was a killing machine. And the only way Essington could preserve himself was to allow the boy entry to the house."

"You're putting words in my mouth."

I thought to myself, No, I'm putting your foot in there.

Barachiel decided it was time shore this up. "Answer the question, Palini. If Essington had stood aside, would you be charging him with suicide?"

Palini wasn't about to argue with an angel. "No, he would not be on trial for suicide."

I had a plan of attack. "So, when Essington finally died, he'd be on trial for murder."

I heard a sigh of frustration. Palini knew that, in order to deny the petition, he had to keep his train on track. Barachiel and I had just forced it off the rails. "No, he would not."

"The boy was a killing machine. He would have murdered his daughter."

"No, he wouldn't have. He loved her too much to kill her."

"Then he wouldn't have necessarily killed Essington. There was still choice being made on the boy's part, and Essington didn't commit suicide."

"He loved the girl too much to kill her, but he didn't love Essington enough."

Nice try, but not enough. "There are plenty of other people that he doesn't care enough about. They weren't in any danger. Why should Essington have been?"

"Because he was specifically denying the boy what he wanted."

"The boy's parents tried to deny him seeing Essington's daughter. They weren't targeted for death."

"Once again, he cared more for them than he did for Essington. Essington was more disposable than the parents."

"He was a friend of the family, wasn't he? Wasn't it safe to assume he cared enough about Essington to protect instead of hurt?"

"No, because he was denying him access to the girl."

"So were his parents."

"But he could get around his parents. He couldn't get around Essington, and that made him kill him."

"So, the daughter would have been killed, too."

"No, she wouldn't have been."

"She didn't want anything to do with him. So she would ultimately deny him access to her. If that was the most important thing, then loving her wouldn't matter, and he'd kill her. His love for her didn't stop him from attacking her in school, after all. So, by Essington taking the bullet, he actually saved his daughter's life. He sacrificed himself so she could live. That's a Noble Death, and is grounds to automatically grant petition." And just to tweak Palini, I added, "After all, atheists are automatically granted Petition under Noble Death. Why not a True Believer?"

"It is not guaranteed that he would have killed her!" I heard a rise in volume, and he clipped his short words.

"But you have said yourself that he was determined to kill. Cause and effect."

"He was mentally unstable. It's possible his love for her would have won out and prevented him from pulling the trigger."

I aimed a kick for the goal. "So he was still choosing what to do."

He went for the block. "No. At that moment, he was acting automatically. Seeing the girl would have snapped him out of it."

"He was in a trance?"

"In a matter of speaking, yes."

"And how would Essington have known that?"

"It's a reasonable assumption."

"There was no indication he was trancing and that the actions were guaranteed. He acted like someone that could still be reasoned with." I made a point for the benefit of the Tribunal. "After all, if the boy was truly that far gone, why is everyone so surprised that he pulled the trigger?"

Palini was really getting upset now. "You are attempting to use general rules on a specific situation. This wasn't something that could be done to just anyone. A specific combination, like mixing the right components to create an explosion."

A Mousetrap. An argument he couldn't possibly wiggle out of. For the first time, I smiled. This was going to be fun! "Do you want to Cast Essington right away, or wait until you can carpool together?"

I had caught Barachiel off guard. That almost never happens. "Wait... what?"

"When Palini finally petitions, he's going to be Cast Down."

For the first time, Palini turned to face me, his words becoming cold steel. "How dare you say that! I am righteous! I am God's Chosen!"

I wanted to keep him fired up. I kept my attention riveted on Barachiel. "By his own definition, he committed suicide."

As soon as I said it, the Guardians shifted their scabbards and put their hands on the hilts of their swords. I could tell from how they were glaring that Palini had made some move in my direction. Time to put this away while Palini was too distracted to do anything useful. I jerked my thumb in his direction. "This is roughly what Palini's body was like when he was alive. Kind of small, kind of skinny. Died of a heart attack. Fifty-two years old. He could have lived a lot longer if he had just taken better care of himself. He neglected his body. He killed himself."

Palini turned to address Barachial, and a pleading tone underscored his words. "She is twisting logic around! My heart attack could have happened to anyone!"

"Irrelevant. We are talking a specific combination of factors, unique to you. Maybe you could have toned down your preaching a little bit, reduced the hypertension." Here, I turned to look at him. He looked back at me. "By your own definition, you committed suicide."

Palini was livid. He was actually starting to shake. I could imagine how loud his heart would be beating had he been in a living body. He had only two choices – either stick to his arguments, in which case, his own arguments could be used against him and other Churches, or concede the point, and lose the trial. And I knew what he would choose.

Palini closed his eyes, turned to Barachiel, and clipped, "I withdraw my contest."

Barachiel didn't smile, but I could hear it in his voice. "As there is no objection from the Church, Petition is hereby granted." He slammed the gavel. The chimes sounded. Palini was stalking out of the courtroom before the chimes had faded. As the Tribunal slowly made their way out of the box, Barachiel kept his face straight until he got to the exit door. As he turned and headed out, I saw the smile.

Essington didn't come out of the dock until the Tribunal was gone, half the gallery was gone, and I motioned him that it was okay. He came down, face beaming. He grasped my hand in both of his and pumped rapidly. "I don't know how to thank you!"

"You don't have to thank me. It's my duty and my honor."

"So what happens to me now?"

"You'll be taken to God, and He'll tell you what comes next."

Essington actually paled. "He still hasn't judged me yet?"

"Relax. This was the trial. God might have something else for you to do before you go to Heaven. I'm not privileged to know what He might have in mind, but I understand your family might need some help healing and moving on. Living life so they can join you in Heaven."

His smile burst onto his face. "When do I start?"

I pointed to the Petitioner's exit on the side of the court. "Whenever you're ready."

He didn't even slow down when he reached the door. He shoved it open without missing a beat. Good thing no one was on the other side of it.

Michael was waiting for me outside the Courts at the bottom of the steps. He had taken off his angelic robes. He was wearing a baseball jersey and jams with flipflops. I smiled. THAT was more like it.

Michael took a bunch of the scrolls that I was balancing. We fell in step, heading back for the Archives in companionable silence. I was looking forward to returning all the scrolls to Russell. But before we got to the Office Of Records, a putto named Rosemary came flying up.

"You have someone who wants to see you. Jacob Palini," Rosemary said in that singsong voice the putti have.

Michael and I looked at each other. "Where is he?" I asked.

"By your personal quarters."

"Can you tell him I'll be there in a second?"

"Absolutely!" And Rosemary sped away.

Michael and I walked to my quarters. Palini gave off a pretty dangerous vibe. The rage he radiated was that strong. However, even if he tried getting physical, there wasn't much he could do to me.

Palini was waiting outside my quarters, not pacing so much as stomping back and forth. He saw me as soon as I rounded the corner. He looked like he was ready to spit flames.

I continued to walk up to him towards my door. "I hope you aren't planning on trying anything that can get you removed from your post as Advocate."

It was an almost imperceptible hesitation before he said, "Never crossed my mind."

I opened my door and walked into my quarters. Before he could move in, Michael had muscled his way past him to get inside. Palini just stood outside the doorway. Finally, he asked, "Can I speak to you in private?"

"You can talk in front of me," Michael smiled. "If you can't trust an angel, who can you trust?"

"It's okay," I told Michael. Then I called to Palini, "Sure. Come on in."

Palini came in. Michael walked out, making a point to bump into him on the way. "Sorry, her quarters are a bit on the small side." He stepped through the doorway and closed it.

I sat on the sofa, stretching my legs across it. Even if I was feeling hospitable enough to invite him to sit down, I wanted to make sure he knew I had boundaries. "What's on your mind?"

"You are corrupting Heaven!"

"How so?"

"Atheists getting into Heaven. Non-believers! People who haven't repented! How can you do this?"

"I am extending God's mercy. Let me remind you the Celestial Courts were set up before I was even born, let alone died."

"God's mercy is for the deserving!"

"Everyone deserves God's mercy, not just those the Church feels deserves it."

"The Bible states who is deserving and who isn't!"

"You think I don't know what you're doing?"

This caught him off guard. "What do you mean?"

"You aren't about to argue with God about what He should be doing, so you're going to focus on the Advocates. Because you know God isn't about to do as you order."

"God made a covenant. What we hold true on Earth, He would hold true here."

"And He is. But this isn't Earth. And let's face it...the Church has had a long history of being more concerned being the masters and turning God into their own personal attack dog."

"Blasphemer!" He took a step towards me and I saw his hands go up.

I smiled. A very evil smile.

He stopped cold, frozen like a statue.

"Oh, yes. Please try and assault me. I dare you."

He slowly lowered his hands, turned on his heel, and stalked out. He got out the door, looked to his right, and actually jumped a little before stalking off to the left.

Michael came around the door from where Palini had looked. He already had his sword out, the flames brighter than the sun. That's the great thing about Michael – he always has your back.

Michael looked at me. Before he could say anything, I told him. "You know, he couldn't have really hurt me. All he would have done was annoy me."

"No one assaults an officer of the court. No one assaults an agent of God. And no one assaults my friends."

"Three strikes, huh?" I pointed to the sword. "Aren't you supposed to not swing anything after that?"

He relaxed a little. The flames on his sword dissipated and it vanished. I swung my legs off my couch and simply held my hand out to it. Michael came in and sat down. On the stand next to my couch, I had my copy of "The Hitchhiker's Guide To The Galaxy." It's one of my favorites. God has all the books in the series, and, like the rest of us, He got them all signed by Douglas Adams just before he went to Heaven. I started thumbing through it when Michael finally spoke.

"You could have let him attack you. Then you could have had him removed as an Advocate."

"Are you kidding? And risk them putting someone competent in his post?"

Michael laughed a little. He started making little circles on my floor with his big toes. "They really don't get it, do they?"

I kept my eyes on the book. Michael needed to vent.

"Heaven was not set up for them to be in charge. God is not their servant or their genie. But they do everything they can to change that. And the kicker is, if everything truly followed Biblical rules, they'd never get into Heaven. Their intolerance alone would guarantee that."

I really had nothing to say, only my own complaints to add. "Well, that is the whole reason the courts were set up." A thought struck me, making me look at Michael. "You know, I've been doing this for almost seven centuries. And yet, it's the same arguments every time. You think you'd see things change over time, especially that much time."

"It's a sacred duty. And it's great. It's just a shame it has to be done."

I put my arm over his shoulder and hugged him. "Hey, I got an idea. My schedule is clear at the moment, and I need a little pick me up. You ever been to a laser light show?"

He thought it was lame.

BRING 'EM FAST, BRING 'EM YOUNG

There are two kinds of bad cases. The first is when you are looking at the very real possibility that some soul you are representing is going to be Cast Down. It really makes you focus and give it everything you've got. No one wants that on their conscience, the second guessing, the "what-if's", the guilt. The second is when you are facing two competing interpretations of one rule. I'm actually surprised this doesn't happen more often than it does.

It had started off a pretty regular session in the very early 21st Century. I was in St. Michael's chambers in the Celestial Courts. There was an uptick in the number of petitions for entry into Heaven being filed, and Michael wanted some extra help. There was no way I'd say no to my big brother.

So we were at his desk, going over petitions and reviewing them against the Petitioner's life scrolls. I was in my regular white robes and blue overrobe, Michael was dressed in pajamas and fuzzy slippers. We worked until I got to a scroll belonging to one Moshe Liebowitz. Well, sort of a scroll. There was no tie around it. Usually, that means that the person is still alive somehow. "Oh, great," I told Michael. "Another near death experience."

Michael looked at me and at the scroll. "We better fast track this one, then. If he stays separated from his body too long, he'll actually die. What are we looking at?"

I started skimming through the scroll. "Orthodox Jew. That's a relief. Those cases are relatively straightforward. If he wants Heaven, I'll have him in in a flash."

Michael smiled at me as he rolled up the life scroll he had been reading. "Nothing says you're getting this case, Hannah. One of our Jewish Celestials can handle this."

I got to the bottom of the scroll and stopped. "Uh, I'm not sure that's an option."

Michael had almost finished tying the scroll closed when I said that. He stopped and looked for a moment, then let the scroll drop, completely forgotten about. "What? What's going on?"

I showed Michael the bottom of the scroll. "According to this, Liebowitz died about ten years ago and he's been hanging out in the Valley Of Death since."

Michael snatched the scroll from my hands. He flipped it around so he could see the back and rolled through it. "So where's the tie?"

"That's what I was wondering." Life scrolls don't get a tie around them until the person dies and there is nothing more about their life to add. Things they do in the Afterlife can still be recorded on their scrolls, but the tie remains. The fact that the scroll said Liebowitz was dead but it didn't have a tie meant only one thing.

"This is a copy," Michael and I said in unison. Advocates can make duplicates of scrolls, we just don't do it very often. The copy will only have the information up to that point, it doesn't modify like the actual life scroll does. No Advocate worth their salt bases any decisions, from trial strategy to whether or not to contest, on a copy.

"I'm thinking I want to see Liebowitz's actual life scroll," I said absently.

"I'm thinking we should see it right now," Michael said. A flash of light replaced his casual wear with his robes. He put his hand on my shoulder, and with the speed of angels, we were at the Office Of Records.

Russell runs the Office Of Records and was just pulling away a mess of scrolls from the counter top window to return to storage when Michael and I appeared. Just popping up like that meant a problem. He immediately returned to the counter. "Rush job?"

"You got it, Russell," I said.

"Scroll for Moshe Liebowitz," Michael said. "You got it?"

"No. Was checked out for Jeff Fairchild," Russell responded.

Checked out for? That meant it was supposedly in Fairchild's possession, but he didn't pick it up. I don't usually question things like that, but when something looks this bad, I start asking. "Who picked it up for him?"

"Joseph Wright."

Michael slapped his hand to his forehead. "Oh, no. Don't tell me...."

I barely had time to register the name and remember that he was the Church who specialized in Mormon theology when Michael grabbed my shoulder again and we materialized outside of the senior Church's chambers on the Campus. Michael practically pounded at the door. "Fairchild?!?"

"Come in!" came Fairchild's response. The door opened, and Michael and I strode inside.

Fairchild looked completely flummoxed, like a kid that knows daddy's about to let him have it but he can't remember what exactly he did. Usually, he's defiant around Michael and I. I think he knew there was a bigger problem this time, because he was actually being cooperative. "Whatever you want to know, just ask."

Michael was in full blown Head Of The Celestial Court mode. He demanded, "Have you decided whether or not to contest Moshe Liebowitz's petition?"

"Yes. I filed, 'No contest.' Why? What's the problem?"

"Let me see his life scroll," Michael ordered.

Fairchild fumbled a little bit, retrieving the scroll from the pile of other scrolls, but his hands didn't shake as he handed it to Michael. Whatever was going on, Fairchild was completely clueless.

Michael didn't even take the scroll. He looked at it like it was a cursed artifact. "That's not the real life scroll," he clipped.

Fairchild looked at the scroll, and his eyes focused on where the tie was supposed to be. His eyes flew open in shock, and he unfurled the scroll, rolling through it to the bottom. When he got to the bottom, he looked up at Michael, his expression like his insides had turned to ice.

"Where's Wright?" Michael demanded, his temper starting to rise up into his voice.

Fairchild hunkered back in his chair like he was being given the third degree. "He's off duty. He should be in his quarters. Other than that, I don't know."

Michael vanished in a flash, leaving me with Fairchild. It was quiet for a moment, giving me time to process the situation. And when I finished my math, the resulting answer didn't look good. "They didn't try baptism by proxy again, did they?"

Fairchild leaned forward, resting his elbows on his desk and his head in his hands. "Looks like. Michael will probably have me reincarnated just so he can rip me a new one."

"He might be satisfied just doing to that to Wright."

"Hope springs eternal."

Baptism by proxy (or "vicarious baptism," as it is sometimes called) is a practice of the Mormon church, supposedly received by founder Joseph Smith in a vision. It enables people who are deceased to be baptized by using a living person as a stand-in. While this is uncommon, it's not unheard of. Several Native American tribes, some European Neo-Apostolics, and the Mandaeans of the Middle East practice it as well. However, there's a difference. Those others baptize people who want to be a part of those faiths. Mormons have been encouraged to perform the rite for as many non-Mormons as they can, dead or alive. They claim it's so people can have the chance to accept their faith in the Afterlife. But no one believes that. They do it to forcibly convert people into Mormonism. Which just shows Mormons have no better idea how things work on the Other Side than any other religion on Earth.

Whatever might be said about the libertarian dangers of baptism by proxy, doing it on the dead is, for the most part, a waste of effort. If the soul enters Heaven, the effects of the baptism won't reach them. Same if they get Cast Down. And if they are reincarnated or whatever, the ruling of the court or their new lives cannot be overridden by those on Earth, especially if their identity has changed and they are not the same person being baptized by proxy. But if the soul has not petitioned at the time, it causes problems. And it looked like Liebowitz was about to become Exhibit A.

Mormons have baptized people from all over the world, and even pulled this with some Catholics, so this isn't restricted to non-Christians. They had been really big on trying to vicariously baptize Russian Jews and German Jews who were killed in concentration camps. Understandably, this hacked off the Jews about the violation of their religious rights. In 1995, the Jews became the only group to have a "truce" of sorts with the Latter Day Saints church. The Mormons said they would not to do that anymore unless the person had a living relative who was Mormon, given the whole interconnectedness of family spirituality for them. (The Catholic church simply forbade sharing records with the LDS, as if genealogical records and the Internet didn't exist.) But within a couple of years, Mormons were updating their databases with new surprises and triggering fresh outrage every time.

Fairchild looked at me sadly. "How is this going to go?"

"Why are you asking me?"

"Because, whatever happens, Michael's going to make sure his best grey Celestial is leading the charge."

Well, he was right about that. "Let's first see if Michael finds Wright and gets Liebowitz's scroll back."

"You think Wright will give it up?"

"Mormons don't have it in them to lie to angels. To say nothing of a riled up archangel."

Fairchild just nodded. After a moment, he glared at me. I immediately glared back.

"Pain in the neck," he said.

"Pratt," I responded.

Fairchild reached into his desk, pulled out a Bible, and started reading. I simply went to one of the chairs and sat, waiting.

"Don't get too wrapped up, Fairchild," I said, pointing to the Bible. "Michael will be back before you know it."

No sooner had I finished than Michael appeared in the doorway, holding Wright off the ground by the back of his robes with his left hand and a scroll with a tie around it in his right. Clearly, Wright had substituted old copies of the scroll for Fairchild and Michael and was hoping no one would notice.

Wright was an older white man. Early sixties but surprisingly spry and energetic. His hair had gone grey but hadn't gone silver. Decent build with the usual weight people gain during their lives. Blue eyes that could be beautiful if you weren't concerned about what might be behind them.

"What's this all about?" Wright asked.

"You trying to queer the pitch," I answered.

"The Latter Day Saints do not condone homosexuality."

I forgot Wright was British-impaired. I said to Michael, "Request permission to box his ears."

Michael rolled his eyes. "Hannah, I have enough problems to deal with right now."

Michael opened his left hand and let Wright drop to the floor. He's about 5'8", barely taller than me, so he looked completely dwarfed next to Michael.

Fairchild's voice was a dangerous growl. "How dare you hijack someone's religious faith. Especially the Jews." He had put the Bible down and was glaring at Wright. I knew Fairchild was angry. It was the same look he constantly gave me in court.

"We are not hijacking their faith! We are saving them! Jews! Muslims! Atheists! Pagans! Heathens! 'Except a man be born of water and of the Spirit, he cannot enter into the kingdom of God!'"

I recognized that passage. It was a quote from Jesus found in John 3:5.

He was defending himself....

He was arguing....

The same way he would in court.

I stood up and said, "Well, Mikey, I guess we need to go back to your chambers and prepare for trial."

Everyone looked at me. Wright and Fairchild were in shock. Michael just nodded at me as if to say, "I know that look."

"What trial?" Wright asked. "He's done nothing wrong, you have no grounds to contest."

"I'm going for a recommended fate of being accepted into Heaven based on Jewish doctrine and law, not his absolution through Mormon baptism."

"Why? He's in either way."

"He's in through your choice, not his. I will defend his choice and get your vicarious baptism disallowed."

"You can't do that!" Wright screamed.

"Watch me!" I shot back.

"That will violate the covenant! God said what we hold true on Earth, He will hold true in Heaven! We have every right! You will not deny us practicing our religion as we see fit!"

I ignored the dripping irony of his last sentence for now. I wanted him to bring it up at trial so I could deal with it properly. "You really think you're hard enough for a go at me?"

"Not just me, Singer. I'll have Fairchild on my side."

Fairchild looked like he was just invited to go for a swim with a toaster. "Oh, no! This is an LDS problem, so the LDS Church will deal with it!"

"You are senior Church!" Wright shot back.

I looked at Fairchild and smirked. "Lead him."

Fairchild stared at me. "For cases that turn on points specific to a particular subset, it is bad form for Churches to pull rank over those who specialize in that particular faith!"

I just reiterated, "Lead him."

Fairchild clearly wanted no part of this. But he also faces me enough in court, he knows when I'm setting something up. At least this time, he'd be facilitating my plan instead of being the target. "Fine, I'll lead."

I smiled evilly at Wright. "You just messed up big. I'm going to establish a precedent at trial, and you and the rest of those burkes won't ever be able to pull a number like this again."

Wright looked at Fairchild. "Request a trial by God."

I looked at Fairchild. He was lost, this was now completely beyond his control. I looked back at Wright and said, "Yeah. Let me know how that works out for you. See you in court." I strode happily out of Fairchild's chambers with Michael following.

Once we got off the Campus grounds and back on Archives turf, Michael started talking. "You don't think God will grant a trial." It was a statement, not a question.

The confident spring never left my step. "I know He won't. He can't. If God decides this, He will nullify the covenant because He's saying what one side holds true is more valid. It will have to go to trial and it will establish a precedent, one way or another."

"And how are you going to stop the entire Mormon church?"

"Don't know yet. But I have to. So you can bet your wings I'll find a way."

I didn't see it, but I could feel Michael's smile beaming at me.

By now, dear reader, I can sense a myriad of questions filling your head about Judaism and what this has to do with an ostensibly Christian set-up in the Celestial Courts. So, I'm going to take a moment to explain the basics. Not everything, that's not allowed, but enough that you can follow what's happening.

Okay, it's said that Jews believe in Heaven, just not the Christian Heaven. This is actually the first error. There is only one Heaven. There is no Christian Heaven or Jewish Heaven or any other kind of separate Heaven based on individual faith. God wants all His children to live in Eternal Peace, not just one exclusive group of people based on religious affiliation. People need to get used to the idea that God created Heaven so EVERYONE could share in Paradise, it's not just for them.

That said, there are many different ways to get there. Religion is not a series of instructions. You cannot barter your way into Heaven. Unlike the devil, God doesn't make deals. Instead, religion is supposed to help you understand your nature, those around you, and what constitutes living a good life. When you develop a good and compassionate heart, that's when you are cleared for landing.

Judaism was God's instructions on how to return to Him after death. Just one problem - this left a lot of people in the world out in the cold, so to speak. After all, they didn't practice the Jewish rites. What would happen to them? Well, those that could get into Heaven did, but it took a lot of wrangling in the Celestial Courts to make it happen. When enough of humanity had organized into societies, moving beyond the immediate savagery survival required, God kicked off Phase 2 of His Master Plan.

God had always wanted everyone to have a chance at Heaven. Jesus' birth was to streamline the process. Jesus would be born a man and live among men and as a man. From that, God and Jesus could understand what mankind had truly developed into (God can poke around inside our thoughts, but He doesn't just do that without good reason, He respects our privacy). With that knowledge, they could start a new religion that could be truly inclusive, saving all.

It's important to note that, while this new religion initially referred to as "The Way" was a new set of rules, at no point did God say that it was to replace Judaism. It was another path for people to follow, another way out of the wilderness, not the only one they could take. In fact, in the early days, there was considerable debate about whether new converts had to do everything in accordance with Mosaic law (if you wince at the thought of babies being circumcised, imagine a full grown man going through it in an era before the discovery of anesthetic). It was eventually decided no, The Way was for anyone who sought it. Gentiles had a separate identity and should be allowed to keep it.

This is why Jews do not have to believe in Jesus or accept Him as their savior or any of the other stuff Christians do. If they want to convert to Christianity, that's their business, but it's hardly necessary. Jews already have their rules and precedents established. They may not be brothers of Christ, but they are still children of God.

As a result, God does not allow anyone to mess with the Jews. They have every right to live, to worship, TO EXIST that Christians do. But as Christianity grew, people lost sight of its Jewish origins. They started seeing themselves as separate from Jews, as different and better (and, of course, once that was established, the Christian subsets turned on each other), instead of being part of them, the other side of the coin of Faith.

Much of the blame goes to Paul the Apostle. While he was largely responsible for making The Way accelerate as quickly as it did, his methods did result in a lot of bad habits among Christians. And the most obvious example of this is the rift between Christians and Jews. But it's not solely his fault. Everyone has the choice, and everyone can embrace each other as brothers and sisters. Unfortunately, they don't see a reason to.

And so you have various Christian denominations thinking that the Jews, simply by being Jews, are doomed to spend eternity in The Fire That Burns But Does Not Consume. In fact, the exact opposite is true. God promised the Jews a place in Heaven. The only question is what size chunk do they get, and that is determined by their lives. Just becoming Jewish isn't enough, something quite a few people found out a little too late.

Cases that hinge on Judaism are handled pretty much the same as the regular Christian cases. It all hinges on how someone lived their life. The why of their actions, not the what. Usually, Judaism doesn't factor in that much. Only rarely do things turn on specific points of the religion. When that happens, there is several Celestials who specialize in Judaism. The most senior Jewish Celestial is Jacob Abramson. He's been doing this more than three hundred years longer than I have. When he calls me "kid," I have no choice but to put up with it.

I was sitting in the Water Gardens, going over Liebowitz's scroll and jotting notes. I was also reviewing the basics of Judaism. I was going to ask Abramson to consult with me, but he was in the middle of a trial. I left a message asking if he could help me when he was done and pulled some reference material. Might as well get a jump on things.

I was partway through my review when I heard the familiar voice of Clarence Jones, the first black Celestial, say, "Hello, Hannah. Up to anything interesting?"

I rolled my eyes. The only things that travel faster than angels are rumors. "Mind your own bee's wax."

Clarence moved up next to me and leaned his head conspiratorially to me. "Aw, come on. I hear it's going to be a reeeeeally big shoe."

"And where did you hear this from?" I couldn't imagine Michael blabbing about this.

"Fairchild and Wright," Clarence smiled.

I slapped my hand to my face. Advocates weren't granted omniscience. With Fairchild, that was a good thing. God only knows what secrets would get out with him. "And where was this discussion held?"

"Across the Campus," Clarence said. "Fairchild was storming after Wright, and Wright just kept on smiling. Has to do with a Jewish guy."

"What makes you say he's Jewish?"

"His name."

"Names are just labels. They don't mean anything."

"'Moshe Liebowitz?' What else could he be but Jewish?"

"Your name is 'Jones.' Does that make you Welsh?"

Clarence just gave me his "You're not fooling me" glare and said, "Hannah…"

"Fine. I'll concede your point in this one instance," I said with a sigh. I debated whether or not to bring Clarence into the loop. He wanted to be a grey, and hung on every detail and constantly begged to be selected as a junior for such trials. I could just tell him he couldn't junior and that would be the end of that. But if I kept quiet, he wouldn't stop bugging me.

I was about to explain what was happening when I heard fast approaching footsteps. I looked and saw Abramson closing fast. And boy, did he look angry. The way he was bouncing when he stomped, I'm surprised his kippah stayed on his head.

I was on my feet just before he got up to me. "What's this about you opposing a Jew getting into Heaven?"

"Mormons baptized him by proxy, recommended fate is being allowed into Heaven in accordance with Jewish law."

Abramson relaxed and stopped looking me in the eye. "Sorry. I should have known you better than that."

"Spilt milk," I told him with a wave of my hand. "That's also why I'm leading instead of you." It didn't matter that Abramson had so much experience on me. I was still senior Celestial, and I was also senior grey. The only one in the Celestial Courts who could force me to surrender the case was Michael, and he wasn't about to do that.

Abramson held up his hands. "No argument from me. This is a Christian problem, you are better suited to deal with it than me."

"I still want your council. And for you to junior for me."

"You got it, kid. What do you want to know first?"

Clarence bounced up between us. "She wants to know if I'll junior. I'm saying yes."

"And I'm saying no," I said without hesitation. "You want to see this? Sit in the Gallery."

160

"Aw, come on!" He was like a kid who wanted to go with mommy and daddy.

"No," I reiterated. "Just because I've got this in the bag doesn't mean I'm picking just anybody."

That caught both their interests. "You've got it already?" Abramson asked.

"Yes. But, I'm not just trying to help Liebowitz. I want a precedent that will blow the whole idea of baptism by proxy out of the water, pardon the expression. So I'm going to need your help, Abramson."

"Any questions, just ask," Abramson smiled.

"Pleeeeeeeeeease!" Clarence begged.

"No!" It was time to put my foot down. "I already know the other junior I want! I need someone focused! You aren't there yet!"

Clarence calmed down, but he clearly was despondent. He really wanted to join the greys. But his lack of discipline worried me. Some people just aren't cut out for being greys. It's why there are relatively few of us.

Clarence sulked away, but only after promising us he'd be in the Gallery. That left Abramson and I to locate my other choice, Harold "Smack" Kowalski. Smack had been a sportswriter before he died at seventy-five. He had a lightning quick mind that wasn't afraid to go in different directions or honk people off. He would be perfect.

Meeting with Liebowitz was uneventful. He reacted to seeing Abramson as if Superman has shown up. He had no idea what the problem was. That is, until Abramson explained it (I let him do the talking. It seemed he'd rather hear it from him).

Liebowitz just looked at me after Abramsom stopped talking. He was a little confused. Which was natural, given this whole set-up. "Can she really do that?"

"I think so," Abramson said. "She's not usually this confident this early."

Prep work was uneventful. Liebowitz was a model citizen. He did everything he was supposed to under Jewish law. If I could get the baptism thrown out, he was as good as in. Not that I expected that to come up. The entire trial was going to be about whether or not baptism by proxy was allowed. The life Liebowitz led was an afterthought.

As I had filed my request for trial with its recommended fate, all that was left was to stay sharp until a hearing was assigned. One came down in relatively short order. I strode to the appointed courtroom, several scrolls at my side. I was still a little nervous. I mean, what I was doing was tantamount to an act of war. And I had no guarantee that I could pull off either goal, of nullifying the baptism or establishing a precedent. But if I lost, no one would be able to say I didn't give it everything I had.

Entering the courtroom, it was crowded. The Gallery didn't have much room left. Clarence was already here, sitting in the third row from the front and towards the middle of the Celestial side. The first row aisle seat was open. It was likely being held for Michael. Usually, it's because he wants to have my back. But as I explained what I would be doing at trial, he suddenly became more interested in watching.

I got past the divider and header for the Celestial table on my right. Abramson was already here, saying a prayer. I simply sat, letting him finish. I wouldn't dare interrupt him.

I looked to my left at the Church table. Fairchild was sitting there in the lead spot, facing resolutely ahead. Liebowitz was already in the Petitioner's chair right next to Fairchild, looking very nervous. Not helping was the guy on Liebowitz's left, Wright, who kept giving him that bright as day smile. "Don't worry," he told Liebowitz. "I won't let her cause any problems. You'll be spending eternity with Jesus before you know it."

Oh my God! Liebowitz actually turned green for a moment!

Abramson had finished his prayer and turned to look at me. "Sorry. I hope I didn't seem rude."

"Not at all," I told him.

"Are you sure this will work?"

"No. And that makes it my job to make it work."

Abramson just nodded at me. "The infamous Hannah Singer determination."

"As sure as the sun rising."

A loud "ahem!" interrupted us. We turned our heads to the left and saw Wright glaring at us.

"You don't have to do this," Wright said.

"Yes, we do," I stated. "It's not right, and you know it."

Wright looked a little nervous. Strictly speaking, he was still a lesser Church and pretty new. Fairchild could only lead off, he didn't know Mormon theology very well. Which meant Wright was going to have to argue against the best grey Celestial ever. "What difference does it make why Liebowitz gets into Heaven, as long as he gets into Heaven?"

I looked at Abramson and deadpanned, "You smell somethin', Rabbi?"

He took a couple of audible sniffs and said, "Fear."

Wright went back to his stool, clearly feeling some heat. He went back to consulting with Fairchild. Fairchild didn't do much talking, just listening and nodding his head.

After a little bit, I heard the familiar footsteps of Smack coming down the aisle. He had a stern look on his face. He wasn't happy about the whole baptism-by-proxy thing, either. Smack had just gotten past the divider when Michael came into court. He was wearing proper robes and had a look of anticipation on his face. He was expecting this to be good.

Smack went to his seat, third in from the aisle. He sat down and reached to take off his fedora. This caught my eye, as he usually wears it up until the chimes sound to start the session. Smack removed his fedora, but I wasn't certain what he did with it. I was too focused on his head.

He had been wearing a kippah under his fedora.

Smack noticed me staring at him. "What?"

I could only state the patently obvious. "You have a kippah on your head."

Smack looked like he'd just found out the Earth was banana shaped. "I thought this was a yarmulke."

"Same thing. Kippah is Hebrew, yarmulke is Yiddish."

He smiled at me. "You were expecting maybe an Easter bonnet?"

"It'd make more sense. You're Catholic."

Smack put his pen in his mouth, it and his head at a defiant angle. "Just a show of solidarity." He then reached in his robes and pulled out another kippah. He held it out to me in front of Abramson. "You want one?"

I shook my head and held up my hand. "No. In Orthodox Judaism, women aren't allowed to wear kippot."

Smack looked mortified. He took the pen out of his mouth with his left hand and grabbed his kippah off his head with his right. He held the kippah over his heart as he turned to Abramson and said, "Sorry. No offense."

Abramson gave him a smile and a friendly wave. "You didn't know. Besides, it's not like you were trying to burn me at the stake."

Smack put the kippah back on and looked sheepish. He absently played with the pen on the tabletop in front of him. The sooner I wrapped this up, the less damage Smack's ego would take.

It wasn't long before the chimes sounded. Everyone in court stood, and we deployed our wings. I took a quick look at Abramson's wings. I always liked looking at them. Bold and strong, they reminded me of the wings of a bald eagle -- the only bird brave enough to fly into an oncoming storm.

I realized I'd never seen Wright's wings, so I took a look. They almost looked like they'd been made by hand with crafting supplies. A very good job, looked almost like regular wings, but still a little surprising.

The door on the right by the box opened and the Tribunal entered, wings already out. Stoic and wise, I gave in to the feelings from seeing them, reveling in their grace and beauty.

The back door opened and the presiding angel, wings already out, entered. Interesting. It was Jegudiel. Jegudiel is the patron of people in positions of authority. Kings, presidents, police officers, all those charged with protecting people and their world at large and doing right by them. That also meant Wright had an uphill battle. Jegudiel couldn't directly intervene in the trial, but he could lead it in certain directions by what he would and would not allow. If Wright wanted to prove his case, he had to prove baptism by proxy wasn't abuse of authority. And with Jegudiel, that wasn't likely to fly.

Jegudiel set a record scroll to the side, sat down at the bench, then banged the gavel. The Gallery and the Tribunal sat. Jegudiel looked at Fairchild with some distaste (not surprising, given the nature of the case), and called, "Who is the Petitioner?"

"The Petitioner is Moshe Liebowitz," came Fairchild's response.

"And who are his Advocates?"

"Joseph Wright and Jeff Fairchild, acting as lead."

Jegudiel looked at me. "And who Advocates for the Celestials?"

"Harold Kowalski, Jacob Abramson, and Hannah Singer, acting as lead," I responded.

"Will the Petitioner please take the stand?"

Liebowitz walked carefully out and climbed into the dock. He was overwhelmed, and had a lost look in his eyes. Two sides fighting over his fate, and there was nothing he could do.

"Advocate for the Petitioner goes first. Fairchild? Your opening statements, please."

Fairchild took a deep breath and started. "God wants His children to go to Heaven. It's really that simple. He gave all religions rules and laws to help guide their followers so they could be with their Creator in the Afterlife. Proof of this is in the form of my counterpart for the Celestials."

Oh, great. He was using me as an example. He continued, "Hannah Singer was an Atheist. And yet, she was allowed a trial and has been given a Heavenly reward. All that matters is that she has a way to get into Heaven. Her beliefs don't matter. Likewise, how she got her reward doesn't matter. She may have gotten it through a court ruling instead of by living in accordance with religious doctrine, but she got it.

"This same principal applies to this trial. Liebowitz was baptized by proxy. He's in. He has nothing to worry about. And yet, the Celestials are challenging his admission. Sort of. Their challenge is pretty weak. They are contesting Liebowitz getting into Heaven. And what is their recommended fate? Allowing him into Heaven. Arguing over which religious philosophy he should be admitted under is splitting hairs. The important thing is that he gets in. That's the only concern. This trial, with two fates that are the same, is a waste of time. It will open the door for more Advocates, Church and Celestial, to challenge petitions based on trivial differences. Stop this before it starts. Rule that Liebowitz should be allowed into Heaven as he is, not as the Celestials wish him to be. Thank you."

Jegudiel looked at me. "Miss Singer, your opening statements, please."

"God is merciful. God is kind. God is loving. He wants all His children to be with Him in the Afterlife. To do this, certain conditions must be met. His children must show love. They must show grace. They must show understanding and compassion.

"They must also show will. They have to WANT to spend Eternity with God. God does not just pluck everyone out and drag them into Heaven. There'd be no ghosts, because He'd take them home. There'd be no Celestial Courts, because He'd simply take them home. And there would be no religion. What would be the point? God could simply take you or guide you or whatever.

"It comes down to the person's choice. God won't turn anyone away, but He won't force them, either. They have to volunteer for a life in accordance with a specific religion. That is the debate we are having. It's not the what we are debating, it's the why. Liebowitz has been told all the study, all the sacrifices, all the devotion he practiced in life...none of it matters, because another group can hijack his soul and change the rules on him. This creates a dangerous precedent, one I will expound on as my case unfolds. This isn't about Liebowitz getting into Heaven, it's about him getting into Heaven in accordance with his choices, exercising the Free Will God granted him, not the Predestination forced on him by another church. Grant his petition on the grounds that he's a good person, not because some church doesn't believe how he believes. Thank you."

Opening remarks were over. Fairchild and I looked at each other. He had a resolute look in his eyes. He couldn't throw the case. Churches can present a token case, one that was easy to get tossed. They did it all the time for lesser sins, like swearing and that. They knew it wouldn't stand in court, but they had to try anyway. If Fairchild threw this or structured his arguments in a way easy for me to shoot down, he opened himself up to a mistrial or, worse, Collusion charges. And even then, he could be forced out as senior Church since this was such an important case and he handed it to the opposition in general (and me in particular) on a silver platter. He had to fight, and he was hoping I'd be sharp enough to get past everything he threw up.

I had to fight two fights. My first objective was to remove Fairchild from the equation. If I wanted that precedent, I had to take down Wright. And Fairchild was an insulating layer. If I shot him down, I could use my arguments on Wright. And I knew I could win against him. I just had to get to him.

I didn't wait to see if Fairchild would make the first move. I made it. "Your actions will condemn Liebowitz to Hell."

Fairchild looked taken aback. He wasn't expecting me to go straight for the heavy ordinance. "He's been baptized. All sins are forgiven. Washed away."

"He was not baptized to wash away his sins. He was baptized to be indoctrinated into the Mormon church."

"It washes away Original Sin."

"Original Sin wasn't part of baptism until the early Medieval times. It is indoctrination."

"Many Christian sects regard it as a cleansing and purification ritual."

I turned to face Jegudiel. "Move to disallow the baptism as purification."

"On what grounds?" Jegudiel asked.

"The mikveh," I responded. "A pool of water for purification that is a key tenet of Judaism. Orthodox Jews are required to do enter a mikveh before Yom Kippur, and some communities require it before all Jewish holidays. Liebowitz has faithfully observed Jewish traditions, and that includes entering a mikveh. As such, a Christian baptism for purification is redundant and unnecessary."

"Motion should be denied. That's a purification ritual, not forgiveness of sins," Fairchild said.

"Since when does 'purification' not mean 'forgiveness of sins?'"

Wright shot to his feet. "If he went before Yom Kippur, that means there is a gap between when he last entered a…what did you call it?"

Oy, gevalt. "A mikveh."

"…a mikveh and when he died. There could be other sins that he never got a chance to absolve! The Christian baptism is for his benefit!"

I quietly tapped the tabletop twice with the two middle fingers on my right hand to signal my juniors that I needed a rescue, and fast. Abramson rose to his feet and was cool as the fastest gun in the West. "Jews do confession everyday. The Vidui is also said before death. We ask to be forgiven for all our sins and to be healed. It absolves all sins, no if's, and's, or but's. Liebowitz has been absolved, and there is no sin for a Christian baptism to wash away."

Ooo, a nuke! Beautiful! Fairchild and Wright just stared in numb shock as any potential argument they could make got blown away. They didn't blink as Jegudiel tapped the gavel and said, "Struck."

I turned my eyes to Abramsom and whispered, "Thanks."

"Anytime, kid," he whispered back as he sat back down.

Wright had plopped back on his stool. It was back to Fairchild and I. "So, as I was saying," I said, "indoctrinating Liebowitz into the Mormon church will get him Cast Down."

"Neither of us are advocating that fate, Singer."

"Doesn't matter what we think, what matters is how the Tribunal will rule. They can and do disregard our recommended fates if they think what we say is inappropriate. Mormons forbid certain things that Jews allow. He is being judged by different standards, standards that demand he be Cast."

"Then it's too bad you got the purification of the baptism tossed," Fairchild responded.

"Thank you for proving the baptism was to indoctrinate."

That one hurt. Fairchild actually winced. From my right, I heard Abramson say to Smack, "She is GOOD."

"She's just getting warmed up," Smack responded.

I knew I'd plowed the road. Fairchild and Wright started whispering among themselves and gesticulating like crazy. Fairchild knew he was on a loser, he was completely out. That meant that I was going to be facing Wright next. Just want I wanted.

Then Fairchild did something I wasn't expecting. He looked at Jegudiel and said, "Move for substitution."

"What substitution do you seek?" Jegudiel asked.

"Wright to be made lead."

Uh oh. "Motion should be denied!" I yelled, the words rushing from my mouth. I knew what Fairchild was up to. "This is to establish a precedent for church doctrine. The most senior Church should lead."

"It concerns doctrine specific to the Mormon church," Fairchild countered. "He should be allowed to lead."

"He can still argue as a junior without being made lead."

"He needs the freedom to argue as he sees fit without interference. It will enable him to adapt on the fly. He should be made lead."

I looked at Jegudiel. He had to know what was happening. Juniors can't call for a mistrial, only leads can. And asking for a mistrial without a good reason cost the Advocate their post.

Jegudiel looked at me. I caught the hint of sadness and resignation to him. He simply said, "Substitution is allowed."

Fairchild's face took on a sinister smirk. All I could do was hope that I so overwhelmed Wright with my arguments, he'd be too stunned to call for a mistrial. No matter what he did, though, I had a duty to perform to protect other souls from his church's interference. I took a deep breath and hoped for the best.

I came out swinging. "Move to strike the baptism by proxy."

"On what grounds?" Jegudiel asked.

"Inconsistently applied."

"It is not inconsistently applied!" Wright was after me. "Joseph Smith instructed us to baptize all we can so that they can be with God and share in his glory!"

"It is not necessary to be baptized to be with God."

"Your precious mikveh is baptism. Liebowitz was even supposed to enter it before Yom Kippur. Baptism is a crucial part of the religious experience."

He was going over ground I had already been over with Fairchild. Time to put this on ice. "You are stealing these people's religious choices and forcing them to observe your own."

"We are doing it to save them! We will not just abandon our brothers and sisters!"

"The end justifies the means?"

"Yes! We are to find any Jews we know that are not baptized and save them!"

Look straight ahead and say, bye-bye! "So when are you going to baptize Jesus Christ?"

The courtroom erupted into hysterics. The only one not laughing was Wright, who just stared at me in shock. Fairchild had his head down on the table and his arms wrapped around it, shoulders heaving with laughter. Smack and Abramson were hanging on each other, each providing the support the other needed. The Gallery was nuts. Michael had fallen forward out of his seat, leaning on the divider and striking the top of it with his fist. Even the Tribunal and Jegudiel were laughing.

It took a while for order to be restored (curiously, Jegudiel didn't call for it). Aside from the odd snicker, it was finally quiet enough for Wright to attempt redress. "We would never dream of baptizing Jesus Christ."

"Why not? He's a Jew. Aren't you going to try saving him?"

He thought quickly. "He was already baptized."

Not good enough. "He was baptized by John The Baptist, yes, but not into Christianity. Christianity didn't exist then."

"Jesus was Christianity," he responded. "There was no need to indoctrinate him into what he was."

I started ticking names off with my hand. "St. Peter, the first pope? Jew. John? Jew. James? Jew. Simon? Jew. Your church has a lot of work ahead."

"They were already baptized! Jesus baptized by fire and the Spirit!"

"But they are still not part of the Mormon church."

"They don't have to be part of the Mormon church, just Christian!"

"They why are you baptizing Catholics? They're definitely Christian."

Wright's mouth moved, but no sound came out. I smiled at Jegudiel. "Move for closing arguments."

Jegudiel looked at Wright. "Do you object?"

Wright still couldn't speak. Jegudiel made the decision. He looked at me and said, "Proceed."

I quickly ran through my closing arguments in my head. I made adjustments. I had to. My goal had been achieved. Baptism by proxy would never be recognized as anything but a power grab ever again. I had a new objective. I had to keep Wright from calling for a mistrial, and my closing argments would be my only chance. I thought about how God would rule, what He would say. I had to make sure there was no debate about how this would go. If court adjourned and Wright didn't call, then he wouldn't be able to. All he could do was file for a retrial, and by then, Liebowitz would be safely installed in Heaven. But a retrail could be denied. It wouldn't cost Wright his wings like a mistrial would.

I organized my thoughts. I rewrote my words.

It's star time.

"The Mormon church is trying to save people that don't need to be saved.

"God says so.

"Jesus came to Earth to create a path to salvation for Gentiles, not Jews. At no point did God say Christianity was to replace Judaism. It was another option to be TAKEN BY THOSE THAT WANTED IT. It was, if you want salvation, you do this. It was not, you must do this, period.

"The Mormon church is attempting to expand itself beyond its proper borders. There is no one true church. There can't be. Everyone develops differently, everyone has different spiritual needs. The multitude of churches on Earth exist for people to learn from. That is the churches' obligation -- to teach the willing. Not try to take over the world through faith.

"Many churches are guilty of this expansion. This is not to minimize their crimes. However, that is only among the living, where the people they pursue still have the option. They still have the choice. The Mormon church is specifically going after people who have no recourse. They do not baptize the living. They do not baptize everyone. They target specific individuals who are separated from the world by death. All to boost the profile of their church. 'Look at what we did! Aren't we wonderful?'

"The answer is, no, they are not wonderful. God Himself does not support baptism by proxy. Jesus doesn't, either. If it was truly that necessary, it would have been in the laws He taught to His disciples as they spread the word.

"Hillel the Elder explained the entire Torah by saying, 'What is hateful to you, do not do to your fellow: this is the whole Torah; the rest is the explanation; go and learn.' This is so important, Jesus, a Jew, taught it to listeners during the Sermon On The Mount. Each person's shalom, or peace, is paramount. Baptism by proxy violates that peace because it is being forced on the person. It is not what they deal with, it is not what they want. But that's only half of the crime being committed here. The other half is changing people for their own good. We are to be allowed to do what we want. We are to be allowed to learn our own way. It is not a mistake for us to be what we are and what makes sense to us. There is nothing wrong with not being Christian, full stop. I'm proof. I was an Atheist. And not once has that been held against me. I was granted a place in Heaven, not because of what religion I followed, but because of what kind of person I am.

"Baptism by proxy is not part of Christianity. Jesus did not encourage it in the early days, when what He taught was called The Way. It was not part of the legacy left to the Apostles. Baptism by proxy is not part of Judaism. The first religion to acknowledge, love, and honor God! God doesn't endorse baptism by proxy. If He did, we'd know it! God gave 613 commandments. He gave laws. Very specific laws. Procedures. Traditions. Not ONE of them is baptism by proxy. People are to enter Judaism or Christianity by their free will, not because someone dragged them into it.

"And, in addition to, on top of that, baptism by proxy violates the covenant. God told His followers, whatever you hold true on earth will be held true in Heaven. Baptism by proxy, if recognized, will establish one church's will is superior to all others. Will other religions have to set up special task forces to undo a baptism by proxy that they may or may not know has happened? And what will happen if the Mormons rebaptize because they feel like it? Where will it end? All someone has to do is point to someone and say, 'You're a Presbyterian now?' Just thinking and willing people to be a religion makes it so? What about the traditions those religions espouse? If simply baptizing is good enough, what's the point of sacraments? Of learning? Of developing spiritually? The glory of God means nothing compared to the glory of how many people can be indoctrinated into a religion whether they want it or not!

"This cannot be allowed. Baptism by proxy is wrong. It is disrespectful -- even if we aren't brothers in Christ, we are still children of God. It is a sinister act. It must be stopped. And it can be stopped by establishing this precedent. Allow Liebowitz into Heaven, not as a Mormon, but as what he is and wants to be. Grant his petition as a Jew. Thank you."

I took a look at Wright. He just stood there, mouth open, the only sound the breathing through his nose. Jegudiel tried to focus him. "Mister Wright, your closing arguments, please."

No words were forthcoming.

Jegudiel turned to the Tribunal. "You have heard the Advocates for Moshe Liebowitz state their recommended fates. You may now make your decision. You wish to confer?"

The lead Tribunal stood up. "We are ready to rule." No one corrected him.

"And what is your decision?"

"The baptism by proxy is to be erased, and the Petitioner is to be granted immediate entry into Heaven as a Jew."

Jegudiel declared, "So be it!" and slammed the gavel.

I closed my eyes and started counting. One one thousand...two one thousand...three one thousand....

I heard nothing.

When I reached ten, I opened my eyes. Jegudiel had already left court and most of the Tribunal was gone. Wright was slowly padding up the aisle to exit court, wings put away. Fairchild was just glaring at me. The window was closed. Wright couldn't call for a mistrial now.

It was over.

Once the last angel left and the Tribunal door closed, Liebowitz bolted from the dock and started shaking my hand. It took me a minute to come back to reality. He also thanked Abramson and had a little love for Smack. He raced for the Petitioner's exit and vanished through.

Fairchild never stopped glaring at me. He was infuriated. And I'm not talking casual. He looked like he was actually going to shake with anger. His voice was barely audible as he said, "I hate how smart you are."

Michael leaned over the divider and pulled me to him, arm over my shoulder. Abramson came up on my other side and put his arm over my other shoulder. Michael said, "And we love how smart she is." I later found out Smack simply stood next to us and gave Fairchild a thumbs up.

I didn't have time to shake off my nerves. I still had a few cases coming up, and I jumped right into them. Won all cases, and I was feeling good again. Fairchild's fury was simply another instance that I soon forgot about.

Turns out, I should have kept it at the front of my mind....

FULL COURT PRESS

I had never seen Jeff Fairchild so angry.

Facing him in court, he looked like, if it weren't for being on duty, he'd physically attack me. Don't get me wrong, violence from Fairchild doesn't scare me. St. Michael is my sparring partner. I could take him with one hand tied behind my back, and that's not bravado. What scared me was the pure fury. The anger. The evil. When the motivations are that strong and the mind that creative, there's no telling what will happen when the torrent is unleashed. All you can hope is that you can find a way to survive it.

Fairchild had led a case against me dealing with a Mormon baptism by proxy, juniored by the most senior Mormon Church, Joseph Wright. Partway through, Fairchild had switched positions, making Wright the lead. Fairchild was hoping that Wright's indignation would do him in. Not as far as the trial goes, that was over as soon as I became lead for the Celestials. Mormons have a nasty tendency to be self-righteous. As such, the chances of them calling for a mistrial are exponentially higher than any other group. If you call for a mistrial because you felt you should have won instead of a serious concern about miscarriage of justice, you lose your post as an Advocate and don't get it back. We lose more Mormon Advocates that way.

Fairchild had been hoping Wright would call for a mistrial and lose his post. I reworked my closing arguments on the fly in hopes I could punch through Wright's fog and keep him from doing that. It worked. The trial ended with Wright just walking away and Fairchild seething with anger. He wanted Wright gone, and he wasn't. All thanks to me.

Dealing with Mormons takes a different touch. They have a different mentality. I didn't really have to deal with them in the early days. Around the middle of the 1950's, Michael came up to me with the Book Of Mormon and told me to read it. "Sooner or later, you're going to have cases with this."

I read it, and then went to Michael's chambers. Michael was just sitting there, watching me, as I stood in the doorway holding the book up, a look of disbelief even I could feel on my face. "Some people actually believe this?"

"Some people believe Liberace is straight," he shrugged.

For the most part, I was uninvolved in Latter Day Saint cases. Your average, everyday Mormon, the rank and file, if you will, are pretty much shoo-in's to get into Heaven. Church elders are a whole other matter, and those get handled by the Mormon Celestial, Thomas Rulin. Rulin is a great guy, but he kind of separates himself from the rest of us. We know everything about Christianity, including what is real and what isn't. He doesn't feel he fits in with the other, older branches of Christianity. He even avoids the angels. Please note, no one shuns him, we treat him with love and respect and try to include him, he just balks. Maybe it's because I used to be an Atheist, but he tends to gravitate towards me, and I'm constantly trying to get him involved in things up here.

Rulin and I would talk about his cases and everything he had to keep up with. I felt sorry for him. Some of his cases dealing with Mormon doctrine were so tricky, you'd think grey cases would be a vacation for him. He wasn't recruiting me, although maybe he should have. I know I could have helped. Our relationship was more like two kids, separated by a high fence, leaning over it and telling each other what life was like on our sides.

I was walking back to the Celestial Courts, ready to grab another batch of scrolls to review. I had just gotten to the steps that lead to the court buildings when Fairchild appeared over the top. He was heading out and he saw me. He adjusted his course, making a straight line for me. He had that look on his face, the one that said we'd be facing each other in court and it was going to get ugly.

I stopped to wait for him. He was maybe halfway down the steps when a putto, Solomon, flew up to me. "There you are, Miss Singer. Rulin is looking for you. Please wait here."

Before he could vanish, another childlike angel flew up, Jude. "There you are, Miss Singer. St. Michael is looking for you. Please wait here." By now, Solomon had vanished, and Jude did the same.

Fairchild had gotten up to me and was starting to open his mouth when I said, "There you are, Miss Singer. Jeff Fairchild is looking for you. Please wait here."

Fairchild just stared at me as if I was reciting Shakespeare in Swahili. He blinked in confusion and could only say, "What?"

That was all the time I needed. By now, Solomon must have located Michael and told him where I was. Michael didn't materialize next to us, but the speed of angels made it look like he did. I'm used to it, Fairchild isn't. He jumped defensively in a very amusing way. When he finally settled down, he noticed my smirk and glared at me. I said, "It's a real shame we can't capture these moments on film."

Michael wasted no time. "Hannah, you're leading the case of Donald Jaymes."

Fairchild actually got in Michael's face. "This is a Mormon case, Rulin should handle it."

Michael started to draw himself up to his full height, like an alley cat ready for a scrum. Amazingly, Fairchild didn't falter. "This is a grey case," Michael clipped. "Hannah gets it."

"She has no right to."

"I'll take it," I said.

"No, you won't," Fairchild said, trying to bore a hole through me with his eyes.

"I'm senior Celestial and senior grey. The only one who can stop me from taking a case is Michael, who is trying to give it to me."

Suddenly, Rulin came up at the bottom of the steps. He dashed up to me and said, "Can you please lead the case of Donald Jaymes?"

I smirked at Fairchild. "Rulin wants me to take it. Michael wants me to take it. And you don't want me to take it. That last one alone is enough to convince me to take it."

"It turns on Mormon doctrine," Fairchild snarled.

"Does it now?" I knew better.

Fairchild realized he'd been outgunned. The attention and his desperation telegraphed this wouldn't be an ordinary, open and shut case. In other words, it was my specialty. He stormed away, calling over his shoulder, "You better bring your best, Singer! I will not lose this one to you!"

"Burn!" I yelled to the departing figure. I returned my attention to Michael and Rulin. "What's going on?

"Fairchild is trying to have Mormonism declared a false church," Michael said.

My eyes popped. "That slime!"

"My thoughts exactly," Rulin said, handing me a scroll. "This is Jaymes' life scroll. Regular Mormon churchgoer, family man, did everything right."

I took the scroll and split my attention between it and the conversation. "Why go after him? If I was looking to decertify a religion, I'd pick someone with some dirt on them, like a church elder."

"That's what I was thinking," Michael said. "Fairchild is up to something and is using an innocent man as a pawn. No one deserves that, no matter how we feel about the church they belong to."

"Fairchild hasn't mentioned a strategy yet?" I asked.

"No," Rulin said. "He knows he doesn't have to tell us what he's doing. So we need someone who can look beneath the surface. Someone who thinks so fast, they can't be caught flatfooted."

"Someone who will defend the Celestial Courts to the bitter end," Michael said.

"In other words, you need me," I smiled at them.

"I'm clearing your other cases. I don't just want you to shut Fairchild down, I want you to establish a precedent. I don't want this happening again. I want all good souls to know they don't have to pay for the sins of their leaders and the stupidity of the Churches. Get Jaymes in, and drop the hammer on Fairchild."

I stood at attention and gave Michael a salute with the scroll. "It will be General Sherman meets Atlanta, sir."

"Good," Michael said with a sinister smile and a return salute. "Rulin is being made your assistant for the duration of this case. Keep me posted."

I extended the index finger on each of my hands and crossed them above my head. Five guardians appeared around us. "I need protective guard around Rulin and I."

"What kind of threat?" one of the guardians asked.

"Collusion charges," I answered. Fixing a case got you Cast Down, and everyone went out of their way to keep from being accused of it.

"Three of us should be fine for the most part," the Guardian said. I nodded and two of the guardians took off. Then the rest of us went our separate ways, Michael back to his chambers, and the rest of us for my quarters. I felt the need for some jasmine tea as I examined the case of Donald Jaymes and what Fairchild was hoping to accomplish with him.

The first kettle whistled happily, breaking my concentration. I had three of them going on my stove to make sure I had plenty of tea for my guests. In the middle of preparing the first cups of tea, the other two went off. Soon, my guests were sipping happily as I drank and buried myself in my work.

Donald Jaymes was a model Mormon. He was devoted to his family, working hard to provide for them. One wife, seven kids, good education, lived pretty comfortably. Attended church faithfully. Gave to charity. Volunteered.

I downed my cup of jasmine tea quickly, went and refilled it, then downed the second one quickly.

"Puzzled, Hannah?"

Rulin's question punched through the fog of my thoughts. The two Guardians in my quarters with me just stood resolute (the third was waiting outside. My orders. My quarters are small and I was getting frustrated tripping over all the wings).

"Yeah," I said. "Fairchild is trying to eliminate the Mormon church's standing. And he's doing it with a guy he wouldn't contest if he came up at trial under any other religion."

"Is it that important?"

"It has to be," I told him. "Fairchild isn't stupid. There are all kinds of ways he could handle this. Instead, he's picking this guy. Why? What can he gain from him?"

"What does he want to gain from him?" Rulin asked. He was clearly exasperated. "Ever since the Mormons were granted their own representative among the Churches, he hasn't said or done anything. Why does he have a problem now?"

Joseph Smith first published his Book Of Mormon in 1830. Fairchild died about the start of the 19th Century and was only junioring at the time He wouldn't become senior Church until Henry Gallows stepped down in the early 20th Century. So he wasn't in a position to complain when enough Petitioners were coming in with points specific to their faith that a specialized Church was established for Mormons. There was some grumbling, as there always is when such additions are made. Some of it comes from not seeing the need for additional branches of faith, what's wrong with the current ones? Some of it comes from resentment, that these people are now senior Churches. Doesn't matter that it's only A senior Church over a subset, not THE senior Church over all of them. Success breeds jealousy, a dangerous part of the human make-up that never goes away.

"That's the million pound question," I told Rulin. "Whatever the reason is is the key to beating Fairchild in court and keeping the Mormon church from being decertified."

It was silent for a little bit. Then Rulin asked, "Why?"

I didn't look up. "Why what?"

"Why are you doing this? I'd think you'd be glad that the Mormon church is going down."

I looked at Rulin. He seemed genuinely confused. Given how I fought tooth and nail to get vicarious baptism struck down by the court, I could see why he was confused. I answered him. "People are not their church."

"Huh?"

"There's a lot of people down there who are Mormons," I said. "They have spent their lives trying to be good people. How would someone react if they spent their life doing what they thought was right, only to find out all their beliefs are meaningless?"

He thought for a moment. "I'd panic."

"That's not all. You'd be enraged. You'd rebel. You'd think your whole life was a waste, that you were a lie. When Mormonism was a small little religion, that wouldn't have been a problem. But now, it is an institution, an entity unto itself, and a lot of people look to it to give their lives meaning, direction, and hope for what lays beyond."

He smiled at me. "You're doing it for the regular people."

"If it was only church elders, like the ones baptizing by proxy, I wouldn't care. But it isn't." I leaned towards him for emphasis. "No one's life is a waste."

"Even if we know the truth?" he asked.

I smiled at him. "Even then, it's not a waste. If you knew the truth while you were alive, would you have done anything different?"

He didn't even hesitate. "No."

"Then how can you feel you were a waste?"

"What about afterwards?"

"You are trying to help people get the Heavenly reward they strived so hard for. Again, how can you feel you're a waste?"

Rulin seemed to relax a bit. He just sipped his tea as I resumed working on the case.

Meeting with Jaymes didn't result in any surprises. He couldn't understand what the hold-up was. I didn't tell him that neither could I.

"Don't let it worry you," I told him. "We're going to fix this."

"Oh, I'm not worried," he said with a bright smile. "God won't let me down."

"You have a lot of faith," I told him with admiration.

"We are all tools for God's purpose. Whoever or whatever you are, you are who God needs to see this done. I'm not worried in the least."

I didn't say anything. I just left Jaymes in his own happy little world.

During this time, Joseph Wright attempted to come around. The Guardians kept him plenty distant. He tried to tell them he had information that would help the case. That made them draw their swords and chase him. Wright was so intent on stopping Fairchild, he didn't realize the risk he was taking trying to contact us. Eventually, another Guardian just followed Wright around and if he got too close or tried anything funny, took action.

Michael and I were sitting in his chambers, two of the Guardians with us. The third was with Rulin, keeping him safe from trouble. "I'm not getting this," I told Michael, rubbing my face in frustration.

"If I figured anything out, you know I'd tell you," Michael said glumly.

I had Jaymes' life scroll with me. I was absent-mindedly twirling it like a baton as thoughts marched through my head. "It has to have something to do with Jaymes. That has to be the key."

"I agree, but what? Unless Fairchild is trying to willfully misinterpret his life. Churches have tried that before."

I thought about Lewis Essington. "Don't I know it."

"I hate Fairchild making an example out of someone innocent."

"I know," I said. "Jaymes was the salt of the earth. If he was anything other than Mormon, Fairchild wouldn't dare contest."

As soon as I finished saying that sentence, my eyes popped. I looked at Michael. His eyes were wide, too. We slowly smiled at each other and started giggling.

"You think that's it?" Michael asked.

"Gotta be. Nothing else fits, and nothing else will work for his plan to decertify the Mormon church."

"Stay sharp just in case that isn't it."

"No problem, Michael." I stood up, and the two Guardians pulled themselves to full attention. "I'm going to go over some options just to be sure, but I think I'll be putting in my trial request soon."

"Sounds good, Hannah," Michael said as my escorts and I left.

It didn't take long for me to request trial. Rulin was keeping Jaymes company, telling him that this was just a minor delay. After all, he had the best Celestial on his side.

I chose Rulin as a junior, as he was more intimately familiar with Mormonism than I was. I also recruited Harold Kowalski, "Smack," and that was it. I actually made it to the courtroom first. I took my usual seat at the Celestial table. A quick look behind me showed that Michael's usual seat in the Gallery was open and being held for him. He wanted to see this.

As I sat, collecting my thoughts, others started coming in. Michael was first. He didn't bother saying anything, he just sat. I continued to turn things over in my mind as Burke Finley and Edward Fiedler, Fairchild's two favorite juniors, entered the court. They worked hard to be clones of their leader. Smack showed up and took the fourth seat at the Celestial table. Fairchild showed up, taking the lead Church seat. Rulin showed up, taking the third seat. Jaymes was brought in by the Guardians. He took the Petitioner's seat on the Celestial side. The Guardians went to stand in front of the bench. No one said a word, not even in the Gallery. I couldn't recall it being so quiet before.

The chimes shattered the silence, making some in the court jump. We deployed our wings as the door on the right by the Tribunal box opened. Twelve angels marched in. Usually, I get lost in the feelings of awe and wonder they inspire. But there was an irritated demeanor to them this time. They knew what was at stake, and they weren't happy about Fairchild trying to pull this.

Once the Tribunal was installed, the back door of the court opened. Sachiel came in. I detected the subtle hand of Michael as I breathed a sigh of relief. Sachiel just sort of sat back and only got involved if things got out of control. Metatron, for example, was a stickler for procedure. Camael didn't like me and would hinder my arguments. This wasn't a trial about doctrine and procedure, but Fairchild trying to force his judgment. I'd have to argue with him directly, and the most likely to let that happen was Sachiel.

Sachiel climbed up the stairs to the bench, carrying a record scroll close to his chest. That was unusual, he usually carried it at his side. He sat down, opened the scroll, and made sure everything was in its place. That was really unusual. Finally, he looked out over the court with a wry look, picked up the gavel, and lightly cracked it. The Tribunal and the Gallery sat down.

"Who is the Petitioner?" he asked casually.

"The Petitioner is Donald Michael Jaymes III," I called out.

"And who are his Advocates?"

"Harold Kowalski, Thomas Rulin, and Hannah Singer, acting as lead."

"And who advocates for the Church?"

"Burke Finley, Edward Fiedler, and Jeff Fairchild, acting as lead," came the voice on my left.

"Will the Petitioner please take the stand?"

Jaymes walked out to the dock, his smile never wavering, his demeanor pleasant. He walked by faith, not by sight. He climbed into the dock and just stood. The ending wasn't in doubt for him, so he was simply waiting. I prayed I wouldn't let him down.

"Miss Singer, your opening arguments, please," Sachiel said.

"Jaymes has lived life according to Christian beliefs, ideas, and disciplines. He has done nothing to warrant being denied Heaven. His petition should be approved immediately. Thank you."

I threw my turn. I wanted Fairchild to advance his ideas first. There was a chance that he had something else in mind, and I didn't want to waste my effort on arguments that would ultimately be moot.

Fairchild smirked at me. He knew what I was doing, but apparently decided to gamble. "Jaymes worshiped a false church. Mormonism is a recent construct that incorporates Christian theology but is not actually it. He should be Cast Down."

I started working my mind. I needed some way to get Fairchild to advance his ideas without giving him anything he could use. What could I say?

Turned out I didn't need to say anything. Gun up, and Sachiel fired the starter pistol. He asked, "Every denomination on Earth incorporates Christian theology to varying degrees. What makes Mormonism different?"

Fairchild and I blinked. Sachiel didn't usually inject himself directly into things like that. Not only that, but it showed the direction things were going in. Sachiel thought Fairchild's argument was bull. He wasn't just battling me, he also had to keep Sachiel from diverting the flow of the trial away from him. Pressure's on, I thought.

"Other denominations are based on interpretation of ideas. Martin Luther. John Calvin. They founded their beliefs based on what was established as Christian doctrine. Joseph Smith received a 'vision,'" and Fairchild made little quote marks with his fingers, "that told him these things. No, wait, he received TWO visions! His bluff was called, and he made up a new story! It's fictitious! It's no more real than the Sandman and the rest of the Endless! The Ten Commandments state, 'Thou shalt have no other gods before me!'"

Paydirt! Fairchild's momentum had carried him too far and gave me my first opening. Sachiel barely had time to look at me in anticipation when I spoke. "You are misapplying the Commandment."

Fairchild glared at me. He looked ready to tear me up. "Seems pretty straightforward to me. What, *pray*, am I getting wrong?"

"The Commandment explicitly states, 'No other gods before me,' not 'No other gods, period.'"

Fairchild looked furious. "Why would God find worshiping other gods acceptable?!?"

"Think about the era when the Commandments were handed down. The Israelites had no land of their own, they were part of other lands. Religious celebrations were public, and they had to participate in order to fit in and be left alone. God was allowing them to participate in such things, as long as they put Him first. No other gods *ahead* of Him."

"Meaning nothing," Fairchild countered hotly. "Those were recognized gods at the time, not manufactured gods by contemporaries."

"Do you ever get tired of being wrong?"

"Prove it!"

"'Gods' refers to anything revered as a deity, not just actual deities."

"Such as?"

"Money. People worship financial success. Anything that people can build up as bigger and more important than it is. Money. Beauty. Social standing. Intellect. Athleticism. *Themselves*." I leaned towards Fairchild as I said that last one, and was rewarded with him turning a violent shade of red.

"People shouldn't do that!" Fairchild thundered. "God is supreme!"

"And no one denies that," I countered. "Teenagers with posters of rock stars on their walls? They aren't saying they are mightier than God. They aren't offering burnt sacrifices to them. They just admire them. No matter how much of a rock god Ronnie James Dio is, everyone recognizes he's not God. He is not being placed ahead of God."

"Which proves my point!" Fairchild looked triumphant. "Those people are admired, but not worshiped! Joseph Smith's religion actually is worshiped! People are not acknowledging that it is false!"

"How do they know it's false?"

"Oh, come on! The golden spectacles?!? The great societies with streets paved with gold and chariots?!? No archaeological records?!? How could they possibly believe that?!?"

"How could you have believed what you did?"

That stopped him short. "What?"

"There is no archaeological evidence of Jesus existing on Earth."

"We know He's real. You talk to Him constantly yourself."

"That's here. Back on Earth, there is no record. No birth certificate, no death notice, nothing. No archaeological records. But you believed anyway."

"I was told He was real."

Nine ball, corner pocket. "And Jaymes was told Joseph Smith's visions were real." I decided to push, keep the momentum on my side going. "History is irrelevant to belief. Those details are irrelevant to their faith in God."

"If that is so, why does the Bible act as a historical record? A chronicle of the life and times of those in it's pages?"

Fairchild was calming down. His wits were returning. Time to shake him up again. "'The Ten Commandments.'"

"What about them?"

"I'm talking about the Charlton Heston movie. Thanks to the movie, lots of Christians believe the Hebrews were slave labor to build the pyramids. Not true, they were built by skilled laborers. They also believe Moses was assertive and commanding. We KNOW that isn't true, Moses is quiet and almost shy. The movie depicts Passover being held on a half-moon night. Passover is always mid-month. It should have been a full moon in the sky, since the new moon always marks the start of the month on the Hebrew calendar."

"People don't know that…" Fairchild started to say. Then he gasped and clapped his hand over his mouth.

Too late, the damage was done. "So, you will defend far more egregious and widespread 'errors' over these?"

Fairchild's eyes shifted. He knew he was in danger of losing. He didn't look at his juniors, though. He wanted to win this, he didn't want to be rescued. But that didn't stop Fiedler from jumping up from his seat and saying, "Mormonism is a false church because it is redundant! The values it teaches are taught by other churches, there is no reason for it to exist!"

Fairchild looked conflicted. He wanted to nail me at this trial, but he wanted to do it himself. But with no other options to achieve his goal of decertifying the Mormon church, he had to take it. His eyes took on a steely glint as he said, "Fielder's right. That, as far as faith goes, the Mormon church establishes nothing new. It is redundant. It is false.'

I went right for Fairchild's rawest nerve. "Then you are guilty of worshiping a false church, too, Fairchild."

Bingo. "I am a Protestant. Heathen."

"The first sect to identify as Christian was the Coptic Church founded by St. Mark in 42 AD. That means everyone, from the Montanists on through time, by creating their own sects, created false churches."

Finley shot to his feet. "The Catholic Church is the one true church!"

"Formally recognized in 313," I shrugged.

"It was founded by Jesus Christ Himself when the Holy Spirit came upon the Apostles!" Finley was leaning around Fairchild to see me.

"What Jesus taught was called, 'The Way.' Search Acts, you'll see it referred to as such. Adherents were loosely organized. Therefore, any organization of Christianity is counter to the first church and is false. Coptic, Catholicism, Protestantism…." I leaned over to see Fiedler. He was hunched down in his seat, trying not to be noticed. "…and Lutheranism." Fiedler sagged a little lower when I said that.

Fairchild does not like having his authority questioned. "Those were not false churches!" he yelled. "They were founded because the Catholic church was teaching incorrect doctrine about the nature of God!"

"Catholicism at the time was very lenient and open. What did Calvinist sects offer? Predestination. And that God is cruel. He can't wait to punish those who disappoint him. Now THAT sounds like a false church to me."

"Not everyone is ready for that. Souls go to Earth. They find a church that provides the instruction they need. Some people needed the discipline and sacrifice of Calvinism."

"And what makes you think there aren't people that need what Mormonism provides?"

"Other churches offer the same thing. Community. God's love."

"They don't offer it the way the Mormon church does."

"Not our problem. Churches don't just do all the work to help people, they have to make an effort as well. They could advance far more in a church like mine than they could with Mormonism."

"Then why do we choose our own churches? Why do we choose our own beliefs? Why doesn't God sort us into what church we need when we are born?"

"God does not live for us. It is up to us to find the truth, not Him to force it on us."

"And what is wrong with the truth the Mormons seek, teach, and learn?"

"It's redundant. It exists elsewhere."

"Like your current arguments?"

"It's not my fault you're being thick."

"Being forceful. Being insulting. Being condescending. Being intolerant. What a good Protestant you are. I can't understand why Mormons would prefer their own congregation over yours."

I had this in the bag.

Fairchild blinked. I took advantage of his shock. "The Mormons have their own church because other denominations like yours chased them away."

Fairchild's fury came to the fore again. "We welcome all brothers and sisters in Christ!"

"I'm your sister in Christ now. I became your sister long before you were born. And you still treat me like a leper. You treat others in your own congregation that you disagree with poorly. And you expect people seeking love and acceptance and community to trust you enough to treat them well? When the differences between them and you are greater than the difference between your own congregation and you?"

"The church leaders are wrong, therefore what the church believes is wrong. Therefore, what the followers are taught is wrong. Therefore, the followers are wrong."

I turned to Sachiel. "Move to strike Fairchild's last argument."

"On what grounds?" Fairchild asked in exasperation.

"Inconsistently applied."

"Prove it!" he bellowed.

"Sergius III was pope from 904 to 911. He became so by murdering his two predecessors. Paul II from 1464 to 1471 was involved in racketeering, forcing Jews to pay for Roman carnivals. He also tortured and had a wild sex life. There has never been a challenge in the Celestial Courts to Petitioner's souls on grounds that who they looked to for guidance was in a state of sin at the time."

"We have to start somewhere," Fairchild responded.

"People accept council from friends and family. ALL people sin, and some never get around to repenting. Are you going to contest petitions if they were influenced by such people then, too?"

Fairchild knew his argument had been reduced to absurdity. He simply sighed, looked at Sachiel, and said, "Concur with the motion to strike."

Sachiel tapped the gavel with satisfaction. "Struck."

Fairchild closed his eyes and breathed deeply. "Move for closing arguments."

That was fast. He had some other plan and it involved his closing arguments. I had a suspicion what it was. There was one argument that he could advance but hadn't yet. And it offered a chance to cost me standing in the eyes of the Tribunal and undermine my arguments. I had to risk it, though. There was nothing more to be mined by arguing directly with him. I had momentum on my side. The only way to see what he was up to was to let his idea poke its head out of its burrow. Only then would I be able to grab it and crush it. "I concur."

Fairchild faced the Tribunal, giving them a sinister smile. "This trial is really very amusing. At the heart of it is the question of whether or not the Mormon church is a false church. Singer has put up great arguments to try and validate its existence."

"Doing so, however, highlights her own hypocrisy."

Paydirt! Knew it was coming. I kept my smile down, I just faced resolutely ahead, letting him read what he wanted from me. Fairchild continued, "Singer recently led a trial that struck down the Mormon practice of baptism by proxy. She herself believes the Mormon church has no right to operate as it does. She did not just nullify the baptism by proxy at the heart of the trial, she established a precedent that prevents vicarious baptism from ever being recognized as legitimate. She made no secret she was out to establish a precedent.

"If the Mormon church were truly legitimate in her eyes, if their beliefs and practices were truly valid, she would have simply nullified the baptism in that one particular case. Or she would have just left it alone, asking the Petitioner be allowed in Heaven as a Jew instead of having the baptism disregarded. The greatest grey Celestial ever believes the Mormon church's doctrine and practices are wrong. Therefore, the faith itself is wrong. For her to try and defend it after trying to tear it down is disingenuous at best.

"Singer knows the truth, just as we all do. The Mormon church is simply a social club. Like minded individuals gravitate towards each other. They could easily find a home at other denominations, ones with the wisdom and experience to handle their questions and crises of faith. Is there a single church anywhere that would not welcome these people with their love and devotion to God and family with open arms? To treat them as their own? To help them and protect them? No! By creating a false church, they not only do themselves harm, removing them from the more advanced knowledge and study they need, but they harm those churches whose presence they would enhance. They are a false church. Their existence is defiance to God Himself. He should be Cast Down. Thank you."

Fairchild looked at me, clearly hoping he'd done enough damage that I wouldn't be able to undo it. He also knew that I'd handled far greater messes.

Jaymes had waited for his Heavenly reward long enough. Time to get this show on the road. "People have been misrepresenting churches and people all through time. The Reformation was hardly the first. All of them hinge on one detail – what the church thinks is unimportant, what we think outweighs that. To this end, there are two avenues. There is philosophical difference, and there is misrepresentation.

"Misrepresentation is the easiest and most common. For example, my motivations in this case and the one where I nullified vicarious baptism. Fairchild believes that my actions constitute hypocrisy because I was decrying the doctrine of the Mormon church one day and affirming it the next.

"This is a gross oversimplification.

"That case was about specific doctrine. This case has nothing to do with doctrine. That case did not hinge on whether or not vicarious baptism was wrong, but whether it was wrong in that instance. After all, I didn't move for other vicarious baptisms to be nullified, just those done counter to people's will. It is about allowing people to do as they see fit and not as someone says they should.

"This is also why I oppose Fairchild in this case. He is guilty of the same thing the Mormon church leaders are with baptism by proxy." I heard Fairchild gasp, but I ignored it and soldiered on. "He is attempting to rewrite people's faith in accordance with his own ideas of what constitutes living in faith. In doing so, his actions will condemn some people to Hell. Because they are living by rules they are not aware they aren't supposed to. This is a dangerous precedent. It is a miscarriage of justice. It should not be allowed.

"Jaymes did not participate in any of the ceremonies or sacraments at issue. In fact, if you strip away the fact that he was Mormon and what the church does, you are left with a good Christian man who honored God, obeyed the Commandments, and everything else good Christians do. There is no reason to oppose his petition. Could he have followed another religion? Sure. Just like everyone else. But everyone follows their own path. Everyone seeks their own truth. And no one is ever told, just because the path you took was not traditional, you can't have a Heavenly reward. This former Atheist before you is absolute proof! Do not punish Jaymes for belonging to an unusual church. Do not punish those coming behind him, who look to that church for guidance of how to live a good life and do as they should. Do not make them suffer. Approve his petition. Thank you."

Sachiel looked at the Tribunal. "You have heard the Advocates for Donald Michael Jaymes III state their recommended fates. You may now make your decision. You wish to confer?"

The lead Tribunal stood. "We are ready to rule." No one corrected him.

"And what is your decision?"

"Petition for entry to Heaven is granted."

Whew! That was a relief! Sachiel declared, "So be it!" and slammed the gavel. Session was now officially over. Sachiel gingerly rolled up the record scroll. He knew I wouldn't call for a mistrial. After all, I had won. What did I have to complain about?

Jaymes casually stepped out of the dock and walked up to me. My juniors rose and he shook their hands. As he shook mine, he smiled and said, "You see? God always provides for the faithful."

"Oh, go on!" I said, mock severely. He laughed good naturedly and went to the Petitioner's Exit on the left side of the court, not even glancing at the Church table.

Once he went through, I turned to fully face Fairchild. I knew he was still there, I didn't hear his footsteps going up the aisle. He just glared at me, his posture looking like some invisible hand was on top of his head and compressing him.

I asked innocently, "Aren't you going to apologize for the 'heathen' comment?"

"You know Mormonism is false," he said through clenched teeth. "Even Rulin knows it. And you continue to validate it."

"I validate the people, not the church," I answered, my voice getting terse. "No one deserves to pay for the actions of church officials. Those they follow, or those that oppose them."

"So you want people to continue to make a mockery of Christianity."

"They do not mock Christianity," I told him. "They believe it. They uphold it. They defend it. Take away the Mormon specifics, and they are every bit the Christians you and your juniors are, expressing their faith the best way they know how. How dare you attack them for not knowing what you do."

"If they would just think or examine, they would learn the truth."

"By that logic, anyone who hasn't taken holy orders will be condemned to Hell."

"It might be an improvement," he snarled. "Then people would really understand the teachings of God and Jesus."

I thought about it. "You know, that might be a good idea after all."

That caught him off guard. "Well, thank you for acknowledging my point, Singer."

"After all, if people truly understand the teachings of God and Jesus, they won't need people like you anymore."

"Burn!" he screamed, and stormed out of the courtroom. His juniors meekly left, although I noticed Fiedler did look a little odd. Clearly, this was one area he wasn't sure he agreed with his leader on. Although good luck getting him to strike away from it.

With the trial over, there was one last order of business to handle, and that was meeting with Wright. There wouldn't be any basis for Collusion now.

I didn't seek him out, I knew he would find me eventually. He did. I had another batch of life scrolls to go over and was heading for my usual spot in the Water Gardens. When I got around the corner, he was there. He was sitting on the side of a pond wall and holding a copy of a scroll at his side. Most likely, from the record scroll of Jaymes' trial.

I didn't break my stride. After all, I wasn't surprised. I simply kept walking until I got under one of the shade trees that extended over a water trough. I sat down on the ground, leaning against the wall. It put me across from Wright. I untied one scroll and started reading. After a moment, I looked over the top of it at Wright.

"Nice work," he said, holding the scroll up for me to see and confirming my belief of what it was.

"Thank you," I said simply, and went back to reading.

It was quiet for a long beat. When he spoke, he said, "I'm so sorry."

I tilted my head up. "For what?"

Wright leaned forward. "I'm...I'm just sorry."

Uh oh. Crisis of faith. I'm not very good at dealing with these things. You don't ask a rabbi for pork chop recipes, and you don't ask an Atheist how to validate someone's faith. I calmed myself down. Just do what you always do, Hannah. Treat it like a court case. Let him advance his ideas, find out what he wants to figure out, and go from there.

"Why do they hate us?" Wright finally asked.

I just kept looking at him. "By 'us,' what do you mean? The Mormons in general? Mormon Advocates? Mormon leaders?"

Wright arched his eyebrows. He was thinking it over. "I guess all of that. I mean, we're fellow Christians. And yet, the one who cares the most for us is you."

"The enemy," I smiled.

He was silent for a moment. "No. I didn't mean it as in you're the enemy. You were an Atheist. You are the last one I expected to affirm any church to exist, let alone the Mormons. And yet you did. You didn't try to decertify us over the baptism by proxy. You objected to our doctrine, but not us. And you just defended us in the Celestial Courts." He sighed heavily. "The one that I would expect to hate us the most loves us the most."

I was taken aback. I hadn't thought of anything I did as an act of love. "Are you sure that was love?" I asked.

"Absolutely," he said. "Love for your fellow man. I mean, you demand atonement, you demand penance. But you also demand mercy. You exhibit it yourself, refusing to let anyone have less than your very best. And you make sure others can have it."

The silence stretched between us. He looked ready to despair.

I couldn't take it anymore. I set my scroll down, got up, and crossed over to him. I stood before him, the wall he was sitting on bringing him almost even with me.

I did the only thing I could think to do.

I hugged him.

My actions said what my words could not.

Wright hugged me back. Tightly. He was clutching to me, his safety in a roiling sea of doubt. His actions said what his words couldn't. I heard him starting to cry. No one likes feeling they are worthless. It's even worse when those you think would be on your side feel you are worthless, too.

When he finally recovered, he simply pulled back from my grasp. He was looking at me strange. It took me a minute to figure out what the look was. It was the same one I saw on people's faces, and that I felt on my face, when an angel was in our presence.

Wright scooted off to the side and dropped off the wall. He started walking away. There was certainty and purpose in his step. This wasn't good. My voice boomed, "Stop!"

People heed that volume when I use it. Wright came to a dead halt and turned to look at me. He looked afraid. Good. I could skip that part.

I stalked up to him. "Do NOT even think about it."

"Think about what?"

"You're going to try to shut the Churches down, aren't you?"

"No. I mean, how would I do that?" He was playing stupid. Mormons are horrible liars.

"By trying to challenge the validity of the covenant."

Wright blanched. I hit the nail right on the head.

"What, you think you're the first one to think of that? Not only can I guarantee you other Churches have already considered this, but I've already considered it. I held a bunch of brainstorming sessions, mock trials, and everything. I wasn't part of them, I led them. I came up with the angles, I came up with the defenses, it's all my work."

I was right up to him, close enough he could see nothing but my eyes and the fury they contained. "Don't even think of trying it. You try the nuclear option, you will lose. I've defended the Celestial Courts more times than anyone else. The courts were always there for me! I will always be there for them! No one tampers with it on my watch! Not you! Not Fairchild! Nobody! Not only will the courts be standing when I'm done, but I'll reconvene your trial!"

He was shaking in fear. I continued. "You will be putting yourself ahead of God and trying to force His hand. I will not stand for it. I will go for Casting Down, and you know I'll get it. I'm too good, I'm too determined, and Michael and St. Thomas Aquinas won't be able to save you. You know I don't bluff."

I grabbed him by the front of his robes, his hair actually moving from my breath as I bellowed, "You got that?!?"

He gulped and simply nodded his head.

I shoved him away as if touching him would infect me. I stalked back to where I was, taking my scrolls and storming off.

ABOUT THE AUTHOR...

Peter G is a card-carrying Renaissance man. When he's not working his office job, he is either making his own computer games or creating stories. A comic book fan since the black and white boom, Peter G's first officially puclished credit came in the Morbid Myths 2007 Halloween Special. Since then, his comic output has included dark superheroes (The Supremacy), an online comic strip about the office environment (Stress Puppy), an existential fantasy series (Head Above Water), his first all-ages comic about a little girl who becomes friends with a mermaid (Sound Waves), and, of course, his first collection of Hannah Singer, Celestial Advocate stories in the imaginatively titled "Hannah Singer, Celestial Advocate". He lives in Illinois where he spends most of his time complaining about politics and watching movies.

Made in the USA
Charleston, SC
02 July 2013